Act of Remembrance

Lynette Rees

Prologue

Two surprising things happened following Cassandra's marriage to Harry Hewitt. The first being that Harry was called in to attend the inquest for the Marshfield Pit Explosion and the other, that he'd been contacted afterwards by the pit owner Josiah Wilkinson's eldest son, James.

The findings were that Josiah arrived at the colliery at one p.m. two weeks before the disaster and went down the pit with the manager, foreman and other officials. A strange odour was then detected by some of the colliers which Mr Wilkinson dismissed as he had said, 'No canary has dropped off its perch!' which was found to be true at the time but did not ease the men's minds.

Two more inspections were made during the following week when Mr Wilkinson was accompanied by officials and several colliers were present.

In his report the Inspector commented:

From the evidence, *No men should have been allowed to work the lower side of the middle level until the gas had been cleared away which should have been detected not dismissed. In my opinion, there was a build-up of gas which was ignited and was the cause of the sad explosion, but as locked safety lamps are employed at the pit, I am unable to ascertain whether a naked light, defective lamp or improper use of one, fired the gas, hence causing the explosion. The pit owner, Josiah Samuel Wilkinson, had been alerted by the men via the foreman, Tom Langstone and manager, William Hewitt, two weeks previously of their suspicions of underground gas which alas was ignored by the owner of the pit.*

As a result of the evidence given, a verdict of manslaughter against the pit owner, Josiah Samuel Wilkinson, was awarded. After hearing all the evidence, the judge said there was no case against either the foreman or the manager who were both found not guilty of negligence.

As two members of the party mentioned were already deceased, the third, Tom Langstone, at being cleared of manslaughter, did not jump for joy. He'd already been left a life sentence to contend with even though folk were treating him as a hero as he'd returned to the pit to try to find the young lad. He'd lost the best manager the pit had ever had and that particular day, he'd also lost his peace of mind.

Chapter One

Wakeford November 1877

It had been a year or so since Tobias Beckett left Wakeford for America. There were some who missed him and some who most definitely, did not. One person who felt regret for the man's absence, for all his previous passion and his persistence in making things happen for the good was, Cassandra Hewitt, though deep down she was thankful that in the end she hadn't chosen to go with him and had remained in Wakeford with her husband, Harry, and their three children. Though at times it was natural for her mind to wander and to ponder, what if? Those times, though, these days, were far and few between.

Someone who did not miss the man was Clyde Clement as he might have taken the love of his life, Rose, away from him, forever.

It was astounding how one man and his actions could have affected a small village like Wakeford so much. It wasn't all bad because Tobias had done a lot of good for people especially child workers in the coal pit and at the mills but by and large, there were mixed feelings towards the man.

One person who missed him dreadfully though was his mother, Cynthia Beckett. Cassie had taken it upon herself to call on the woman regularly since her son's departure to see how she was doing and to keep abreast of what was going on. Whenever the woman read out his letters to her or on occasion, she often handed her one to read, it sounded as if he was doing very well for himself as he'd been offered the chance to buy into one of the coal pits in Pennsylvania, an opportunity that probably wouldn't have been afforded him if he'd remained in Wakeford.

Today, though, when Mrs Beckett handed the correspondence from her son to Cassie, she had a tear in her eyes. 'He's wed!' she sobbed, thrusting the letter into Cassie's hands. 'I never thought he'd do it, but he's gone and married some American lass and I wasn't even there to see my eldest son wed!' Cynthia's bottom lip trembled.

Cassie gulped. Surely her ears must be deceiving her? Tobias had always said he wasn't the marrying kind. But no, what Cynthia was telling her, appeared to be the truth.

'W...when did that happen?' Cassie asked, mouth agape.

'Last month. And me, his own mother, didn't know a thing about it until afterwards.' She shook her head sadly. Cassie stood and laid a comforting hand on the woman's shoulder. 'Me, who reads the tea leaves and tells folk their own future couldn't predict my own son's wedding.' She appeared almost as though she might cry for a moment as her eyes welled up but then she paused to swallow her sadness down.

'It can't be helped though, with him being so far away, Mrs Beckett. Here, let me make you a cup of tea,' Cassie said in a soft, reassuring tone of voice.

'That's very kind of you, dear,' Cynthia said taking her hand and holding it to her cold cheek.

'What is it that's really concerning you?' Cassie said pre-empting the woman. She seated herself at the table and gazed into the woman's eyes.

'I just worry,' she took a long shuddering breath of composure, 'that I'll never get to see him again.'

'Oh, don't talk silly,' Cassie scolded good-naturedly. 'It sounds as if Tobias is earning plenty of money to afford a trip back to Wakeford, or even to send you the money for a ticket to sail to see him at some time.'

Cynthia sucked in a deep breath and let it go. 'It's true. I have a feeling that I don't have long for this world.' She held the palm of her hand to her chest. 'Just lately, I've been feeling quite breathless. Me, who's hardly had a sickness in my life and borne all those kids.'

Cassie smiled. 'Then we must get you to a doctor, Mrs Beckett. Although all those herbs you've used for yourself and others over the years have done the trick, this might be one occasion when you need to see someone in the medical profession.'

She nodded. 'Aye, happen you're right and all.' She sighed deeply.

'Is it money you're concerned about?' Cassie arched a sympathetic eyebrow as she glanced around the small living room, which some might have described as shabby as most of Mrs Beckett's things hadn't been replaced for many a year. She'd had to make do and mend, that much was evident.

She shook her head vigorously. 'Our Tobias has been sending money back home for me and the kids since he left here. It's not that...' she paused.

'Then what on earth is it?' Cassie's eyes widened as if she feared what the woman might say next.

'It's just I'm worried that if it's bad news, how I'll cope with it all. I should have seen this in my own tea leaves or something, but sometimes it can be hard to predict your own future no matter how good you are at telling the fortune of others.'

Cassie nodded. 'Now, I'll tell you what. I'll make an appointment for you with our family doctor, Doctor Bryant. And I shall accompany you to his surgery.'

The woman nodded gratefully. 'Thank you, lass. I shall face whatever I have to with you by my side now our Tobias is no longer here.'

It was funny, Cassie thought later as she left the woman's house. Although Tobias was still far away his spirit seemed to be still alive in certain parts of the village. She bit her bottom lip. What would Rose think when she heard the latest news? She wondered. She was going to have to tell her he had married and not that long after he'd had a dalliance with both of them. Rose, though she felt most pity for other than herself, she'd been left high and dry with Tobias's baby to care for and the little girl who she and Clyde had named, Sophia, would always be a reminder of her father. She even had his raven coloured hair and complexion and oh, those ebony eyes. She'd turn out to be a heartbreaker, for sure.

**

'Married? Tobias Beckett?' Polly parroted the words back at Cassie through pursed lips when she called into the tea room the following day.

'Yes. No one was surprised more than I was.'

There were no customers around and Doris was out in the backroom tidying up so Cassie felt free to say what was on her mind.

'Surprise for you? I'd say shock more likely,' Polly laid a hand of reassurance on her shoulder. 'There but for the grace of God go I...as the saying goes. That might have been you, gal, if you'd have had the mind to go off with him.'

Cassie chewed her bottom lip. 'Oh, I know I made the right decision. It's Rose I feel sorry for as he kept claiming he wasn't the marrying kind and he left her high, dry and pregnant!'

Polly smiled. 'Ah, but Rose seems happy enough with Clyde and Baby Sophia these days. Don't you go worrying about her.'

'I'm thinking though, Pol, that maybe I ought to forewarn her of this?'

'But why on earth?' She shook her head.

'Because it's quite possible that now Tobias is a man of means, he now owns his own coal pit, that he'll likely bring his new bride to visit his mother and his brothers and sisters.'

'Aye, well that maybe so, but it's not really your problem now is it? Not unless you allow it to be.'

Polly's words were true enough but why was it so hard to put her acquaintance with the man behind her? It was Harry she loved for sure, but then a little voice in her head warned her that Tobias was not an easy man to forget.

***

On the approach to Christmas that year, garlands of holly and Ivy had been strung along the eaves of the shops across the streets of Drisdale where Cassie was taking her teacher training at a local school. How she enjoyed the training as well as working "hands on" at the school there. Harry was now supporting her lifelong dream.

As she crossed the busy street, narrowly side stepping a coach and horses that careered past her, she turned left to head off in the direction of the toy shop to see what she could purchase for Gilbert and Ernest for Christmas. They were now bonny little boys who were into everything. If they weren't waddling off in one direction then they were headed in another. She, and anyone else who took care of the rambunctious duo needed their wits about them. The twins were also beginning to speak more and more every day, but one thing she'd noticed was when they were together they even seemed to have their own kind of babble and understanding with one another, chattering away almost as if they'd invented some kind of new language that only they could interpret. Although, now Ernest had caught up in size with his older sibling in height, he was still smaller than his brother in weight. Though, Gilbert did appear a little chubby at times compared with other children of his age, but Doctor Bryant had reassured her that as he grew, he'd lose his "puppy fat".

As she approached, the sign suspended from outside, swung back and forth in the light breeze and she shivered as it was becoming bitterly cold of late. "Grimsdike's Toy Shop" was painted on a black background with fancy gold lettering. She peered inside the bay window to see all manner of toys within. The centrepiece was a carousel like the sort she'd seen at the fairground, with white horses with flowing manes. She guessed it was probably musical as a large gold key stuck out of the side. To the right of that was a colourful wooden sailing boat, a cricket bat and a train and to the left were the girl's toys, the usual china dolls with piercing blue eyes and soft silky hair in gorgeous gowns, not unlike those she'd once worn herself when she'd lived at Marshfield Manor House. Why were the boy's toys more interesting than the girls? It was almost as though their creators, and those that sold the items, valued the boys more. Weren't girls allowed to get themselves dirty then or have some fun?

If there was one thing she prided herself on it was treating all three children equally. If Emily wanted a boat or a cricket bat, she'd be happy to purchase those items for her, but sadly, she'd asked for yet another doll for Christmas. Maybe it was the way of the world expecting women to conform? But then again, she hadn't exactly conformed herself to what society expected of her. How many women in Wakeford had their own businesses? None, apart from Lizzie Butterworth who ran her own guest house. At least Cassie could say she'd started her tea room business from scratch and made a success of it. It hadn't been easy as she'd met with opposition from some in the village, but it had gladdened her heart as in the end, she'd won them over.

She was just about to enter the shop when she heard someone call her name, turning to glance across the street, she noticed Rose who was heading in her direction. These days, she was Mrs Rose Clement after marrying Clyde.

Cassie swallowed hard. Oh no! She had intended visiting the woman at some point to mention to her the fact that Tobias had wed since he'd left for America. But now? Was it the right time to drop that information on her? She had no intention of ruining her Christmas but what if it somehow got out and Rose's father or brothers got to hear of it at The Ploughman's Arms? That would surely hurt her more. She remembered the time Rose's brothers had laid into him in the alleyway and Tobias had not been a pretty sight after that.

Cassie smiled tentatively as the young woman set foot on the pavement beside her. 'How lovely to see you, Rose,' she leant forward to kiss the woman's cheek. 'My, my, you do look well. Married life obviously agrees with you.' She noticed Rose had a sparkle in her eyes that had been missing for a long time. Being involved with Tobias had taken it out of her. He'd toyed with her emotions, she could recognise that now and he'd also toyed with her own. Really! What sort of a man was he?

'I'm glad I bumped into you, Cassie,' Rose said excitedly. 'Sophia is being baptised next week and I'd like to ask you a favour...'

Cassie smiled, pre-empting what she was about to say. 'I'll tell you what, let's go and have a coffee in that tavern over there.' She pointed down the street. Coffee taverns were becoming popular in the villages surrounding Wakeford as

9

they were seen as a way to conquer the evils of the demon drink.

Rose nodded enthusiastically. Cassie would give the girl time to ask her a favour and then she'd tell her the news about Tobias.

After settling themselves at The Castle Coffee Tavern and enjoying it's warm atmosphere with its cosy crackling fire and friendly welcome from the staff, Rose had taken it upon herself to ask Cassie if she and Harry would be Godparents for Sophia along with Jem and Doris. Cassie had been thrilled to accept on behalf of her and her husband but then she bit her bottom lip.

'What's the matter?' Rose frowned. 'Is it a problem for you?'

'No,' she shook her head. 'I'm really happy to accept. It's just I have some news for you, I had been hoping to wait until Christmas was out of the way before telling you but I guess now is a good time as any before you hear any gossip.'

Rose's eyes widened. 'Gossip?'

'I've been around to see Mrs Beckett again and she handed me the latest letter from Tobias to read...'

'Oh?' Rose's breath hitched in her throat.

'There's no easy way to say this...'

'It's all right,' Rose said smiling, 'I know all about how he's taken over the mine, Jem told me as he'd heard at the pub.'

Cassie shook her head. 'No, it's not about that...Tobias has taken himself a wife!'

Rose took a sharp intake of breath and let it out again, for a moment Cassie worried she might have some sort of anxiety attack. 'Are you all right, Rose?'

Rose nodded slowly as the colour drained from her face. 'I think so. He's a fast mover, it wasn't so long ago he was asking us both to go to America with him. He can't have cared for either of us...'

Cassie detected a crack in Rose's voice which told her this was upsetting news for the young woman. 'Well, anyway, at least we both know.'

Rose looked startled for a moment. 'Oh no!' she said suddenly. 'What if he comes back to take Sophia with him?'

'He can't do that,' said Cassie. 'You and Clyde have been bringing her up and making an excellent job of it. Not only that, but Clyde is wealthy too.'

'Don't you see though,' said Rose, 'I'll always be tied to that man as my daughter is a part of him.' She turned away for a moment not for Cassie to notice the tears in her eyes, but she'd already guessed how upset Rose was.

Chapter Two

Wakeford September 1914

There had been rumours in Wakeford since the previous Christmas time that Britain was heading towards a war with Germany, but following the assassination of Franz Ferdinand of Austria at the end of June, things began to surge forward at an alarming pace as the war progressed and folk in the village began to fret about it, the women in the area in particular, realising that soon they might lose their sons, fathers, brothers and husbands to some senseless war that would be fought in a distant land far from home.

All of this didn't appear real to twenty-year-old Alice Hewitt until she noticed a large, bold poster in her grandfather's book shop window which read: "Your Country Needs You". Above the bold words was Lord Kitchener's pointing finger as though he were pointing directly at the person viewing the poster. Britain had declared war on Germany back in early August and Field-Marshal, Lord Kitchener, who was already a national war hero, became Secretary of State for

War. He realised Britain needed a bigger army so an appeal was made as posters were displayed all around the area, letters were sent out, meetings held and speeches given by military spokesmen. Men were urged to enlist in the army to earn their King's Shilling. It was said that by the first weekend of the war, a hundred men an hour had enlisted up and down the land.

Further acts of aggression drew in countries including America, Australia, India and most African colonies. As a result, the men of Wakeford and the surrounding villages were looked upon to co-operate at any time.

Alice's father was Gilbert Hewitt who was one of a twin. It was all rather confusing really as her grandmother, Cassandra Hewitt, explained that really Gilbert and his twin, Ernest, were Bellingham's as their father had been Lord Bellingham who had once upon a time owned Marshfield Manor House and had been her previous husband. Following his sudden death, her grandmother who did not even realise she was pregnant back then, needed to vacate the stately home as his lordship had mired himself in severe debt and so she ended up on the day of her husband's funeral, a widow in Wakeford with her five-year-old daughter, Emily. Emily was Alice's aunt. Cassandra had been fortunate at that particular time to have taken Emily's nursemaid, Polly, and her Aunt Bertha with her to the small cottage she'd been bequeathed, and along with not much else, she'd had the task of beginning all over again.

What had begun as a nightmare for her grandmother when most of the villagers had turned against her for some reason unknown to Alice, turned into a fairy tale when she met Harry Hewitt, Alice's grandfather. Although not her grandfather by blood, she realised, he treated her very much as though she were his real granddaughter and having no other grandmother or grandfather to speak of, Alice's grandparents were special to her. Indeed she had a real bond with them, particularly her grandmother. Sometimes she felt closer to her than her own mother, Marissa. Marissa had often been described over the years as a flibbertigibbet sort, quite frivolous and talkative as though she had little going on in that pretty little head of hers. But Alice realised that this was quite untrue. Her mother, although appearing a precocious sort who often shocked people with her upfront and forthright manner, was quite intelligent but prone to fits of melancholia from time to time that just could not be explained away by the medical profession.

Her aunt, Emily, had gone to Oxford University where she'd met her future husband, Benjamin Smallbrook, who became an eminent lawyer. Although being highly educated herself, Alice felt her mother had not lived up to her full potential as although trained as a doctor, these days, she only worked part-time at the hospital at Hocklea.

Gilbert, her father, was incredibly involved in Marshfield Coal Pit running it along with his twin, Ernest. Her grandfather had long since retired and these days concentrated on his book store, it was enough for him. Gilbert and Ernest, although identical twins, their personalities seemed to be the opposite to her. Her own father was quite out going, a robust man, whereas Uncle Ernie as she called him, was a quieter sort and seemed a slighter version of her father in his physique. Grandma had once explained to Alice that her father had been the first born twin and it was touch and go whether Ernest, the second twin would survive, but he'd turned out to be a fighter, nevertheless. She liked Uncle Ernie enormously and spent a lot of time talking to him. He'd never married and she often wondered why.

Her grandmother though had done a superb job over the years. She had trained as a school teacher and eventually had become headmistress at The Grange School in Wakeford, and it was hoped that as Alice now worked there, newly qualified, that she would eventually take it over herself, walking in Grandma's pioneering footsteps.

Aunt Bertha had sadly passed away before Alice was born, but she loved to hear all the stories about her grandmother's beloved aunt.

Polly, though, was still around running the tea room which eventually, she'd taken over from Cassie. These days she was elderly, but she still had bags of energy. Her assistant was a woman called, Doris, who apparently had been at the tea room since she was a young girl.

Alice was pleased that she knew so much of her family's history which was intertwined in the very bones of Wakeford and the surrounding areas, but now she felt herself being called in a different direction. Maybe she couldn't help the war effort as much as she'd like as a teacher but maybe she could as a nurse.

***

Cassandra and Harry were aghast as both their sons stood in front of them.

'So, you see,' said Gilbert with regret, as he stared out of the large French window and down onto the village below, 'we're both off tomorrow.'

Cassandra felt speechless for a moment. There was a lump in her throat that was causing her to feel choked momentarily. Finally, she found her voice. 'Do you know where you're off to?'

'We've no idea,' said Ernest. 'Rumours are it will be somewhere in France or maybe even Belgium.'

Their father nodded but said nothing. Cassie realised that this was difficult for him to digest too.

'But you could have got out of it, I suppose? I mean as you are both involved in running the coal pit. Coal mining, after all, is a reserved occupation?'

Both sons nodded. Then Gilbert spoke. 'We've already discussed that. But both of us wouldn't forgive ourselves if we let our country down. We were hoping, Father, that maybe you could take over the running of the pit once again, and maybe Tobias and James would step back in too?'

Harry rubbed his chin as if in contemplation. 'I had thought at my age I deserved an easier time of it and to be truthful, the book store is enough for me, but if returning to running the pit is going to help our country by allowing you both to fight for it, then I shall gladly return.'

Cassandra touched her husband's forearm and he turned to face her. 'I mean if that's all right with you, dearest?'

She nodded through glazed eyes. How she hated the thought of Britain fighting some senseless war overseas, but what was the alternative? If her sons, who were grown men, after all, had made up their own minds about it, who was she to refuse? She looked Gilbert in the eyes. 'How do Marissa and Alice feel about it?'

Gilbert raised his brow. 'Neither one is ecstatic about it as you can imagine, but Marissa says that she'd never be able to face the villagers if I became a conscientious objector and was thrown into prison. She said she saw two women badgering a young man to sign up the other day. He didn't want to go to war on religious grounds

LYNETTE REES

and one of them handed him a white feather and called him a coward! To be honest with you, maybe he's the brave one facing people like those women back home!'

'You may well have a point there,' said their father. 'Look, you're both in your late thirties so it's not as if either of you is that young. You're not old either, granted, but old enough to have some foresight into this and I respect that.'

Their mother chewed her lower lip. 'How do you feel about leaving Marissa and Alice?' She glanced at Gilbert, whose head was lowered.

He lifted his chin to meet with her gaze. 'Not too good to be honest, I think parting will be the absolute worst thing.' He turned to face his twin. 'At least you don't have that problem, Ernie?'

Ernie shook his head. 'Believe me, although I've never married, I'll hate to leave my family and this village behind but I accept it's got to be done.'

'We were lucky,' interrupted Gilbert, 'the line for the recruitment at the town hall in Hocklea was so long that some men were dismissed and told to return the following day. You should have seen the look of disappointment on those men's faces!'

Their mother bit her lower lip and then said, 'But think of the disappointment their women folk will feel when they leave the British Isles to fight in a land far away...possibly never to return home again,' she gulped. There was no getting

18

away from it there would be casualties, lots and lots of deaths and injuries.

'Aye, the police were there and all,' added Ernie. 'They had to bring the crowd under control as some were jumping the queue.'

Ernest approached his mother and wrapped a comforting arm around her shoulders. 'Don't fret, Mother. We're both robust sorts. We'll be back before you know it and I've heard they'll even send us back home on leave.'

Their father nodded. 'Yes, yes, of course. I've heard that James Wilkinson's sons are going to Ypres as commanding officers.'

Gilbert nodded.

'What happens next then?' their father asked.

'We'll be sent to a training camp before we go overseas...maybe in Tidworth, then when we've trained, apparently, we'll sail from Southampton,' said Ernie stoically.

'Those training camps?' their mother asked, 'Will you get a bed in a room in some sort of barracks maybe?'

Gilbert chuckled. 'More like we'll be in some sort of makeshift tents. It's the officers like James's sons who will get better treatment than us and them being wet behind the ears and all. Just because they went to Oxford or was it Cambridge University, they'll be giving the likes of us orders and yet, we know more about life than those lily livered squirts!'

'Now then,' said Harry sternly, 'please don't

speak about Dominic and Gerald like that. You've both seen more life, granted, but they'll also be risking their lives overseas.'

Gilbert's face reddened. 'Sorry, Father. It's just I get so angry at the sort who will be lording it up over us, especially those who have experienced very little of real life like we have.'

Harry sniffed loudly. 'That's understandable, I suppose. But what you two have got to understand is that you're all in this together, a team. You've got to learn how to take orders.'

Cassandra realised that any authority for Gilbert wasn't easy for him. As the eldest of the twins, he'd always assumed the role of being in control. She guessed that Ernie wouldn't mind as much, he was far more placid in personality, but she did worry about her eldest son.

'Anyhow,' said their father, 'as you will both be leaving us soon, I think this calls for a glass or two from my finest bottle of whisky.'

Cassandra grimaced. 'You men can drink that if you like, I'll stick to the sherry and toast you with that!'

Although all three of the men in her life were smiling and putting on brave faces, behind their eyes she could detect something that could be summed up in one word, fear.

***

After Gilbert and Ernest had undertaken training at Tidworth, the troops were sent to Southampton Docks for their passage overseas.

Southampton was used primarily for its deep water docks for the handling of large numbers of ships. It was also far enough away from the main body of the Channel to lessen the threat from German war vessels.

The trains went straight to the dockside sheds alongside the berth at which the troopships were waiting to take the men. High security measures were enforced to preserve the secrecy of this military movement. Soldiers from the territorial army guarded bridges and tunnels, passengers were faced with revised timetables and told to stay away from platforms until a few minutes before their train was due.

Though in Southampton itself, security measures were lighter as crowds of local people gathered to cheer the troops on at level crossings and all the while, a press ban was enforce throughout the deployment of troops.

As Ernie watched a military horse being hoisted high above the men's heads to be placed on the ship, his stomach flipped over. *This was really happening.* He glanced at Gilbert who was smoking a cigarette and chatting to a couple of other soldiers he'd recently palled up with. Making friends wasn't really for Ernie. Who knew in a few days, weeks or months, those men his brother was to become so friendly with might be killed, or even his brother himself. It didn't pay to get too close to someone, he thought. That's why he'd never married, if truth be told.

There were some yells as the horse was still in suspension as someone bellowed, 'Easy now! Be careful man, we don't want to lose our best horse before we even get to France!'

An officer, who Ernie hadn't noticed approaching him, said, 'Loading the horses is more dangerous than loading our men!' He smiled a smile that immediately put Ernie at his ease.

'Gerald Wilkinson,' he introduced.

Realisation dawned. 'You're one of James Wilkinson's sons!' Ernie said in astonishment.

'Eh? What of it?' Gerald cocked his head to one side in amusement, causing his flat peaked hat to go momentarily skewwhiff on his head. He straightened his pose and replaced it properly on his head. 'You know me, old boy?'

'Rather! I should say I do. Our fathers worked together for years at Marshfield Coal Pit and are now as we speak back working again.'

Gerald smiled broadly. 'Well, what do you know? So, you're either Gilbert or Ernest? One of the twins, are you?'

Ernie nodded eagerly. 'Yes, I'm Ernest, Ernie for short. But I haven't seen you for years. I have a vague recollection of us visiting your home when I was a young boy.'

'Oh yes, you won't have seen either myself or Dominic around Wakeford for many a year. We both went to Oxford University while you were still young and then we moved to London to work.'

Ernie quirked a brow. 'What line of work were you both in?'

'Dominic is the clever one, he was high up at the Bank of England. I was a lawyer. '

'Oh?' Ernie was well impressed.

'And you and your brother have both been running the pit since our fathers retired, I hear?'

'Yes, we have.'

'Well done you!' Gerald tapped him on the shoulder. 'I say, old bean, it appears that it will be a while until we can get on board this thing as they finish loading up the horses, fancy a snifter?'

Ernie noticed Gerald removing a small silver flask from the inside pocket of his jacket and he nodded eagerly. 'It's brandy. It will give us both a bit of Dutch Courage before we board that thing. I was never the best of sailors. I get dreadfully seasick, so I'm hoping after drinking this I might sleep some of the way.'

Seasickness wasn't something that bothered Ernie nor his brother, they had both sailed several times during their lives. It wasn't anything aboard the ship that bothered him, it was what was facing them at the other end of his journey that he cared most about.

Chapter Three

Wakeford December 1877

As Christmas approached that year, Cassie was determined to put all thoughts of Tobias well and truly behind her, it wouldn't be so easy for poor Rose of course as Sophia with that dark curly hair and those enchanting ebony eyes was the moral of her father. She hoped she hadn't instilled too much fear in the young woman that maybe Tobias would turn up in Wakeford soon, and in any case, even if he did, things had now changed—he was a married man so his new wife whoever she was, would be his number one priority these days not a dalliance with another man's wife or a romantic fling with a young woman like Rose. She hoped and she prayed that Rose could put all that behind her now.

Still, there was plenty to keep Cassie's mind occupied with the planning of the season, not just the food and presents at home but she also had the duty of organising a Christmas party at the school, so there was plenty on her mind without being concerned that Tobias Beckett might pop up in Wakeford in the near future, yet, in some ways she hoped he would as his mother missed him so very dearly.

Gilbert and Ernest were growing fast and Harry had suggested that they move out of the cottage in the New Year. There was a house he fancied near his childhood home where these days, Clyde and Rose, resided. Cassie had been surprised he should want to move back to that part of Wakeford after having been forced to move from that house, but he'd kissed her softly on the forehead and said it would be good to make a new start as the house was different, not as grand as Hewitt Hall was. It was a lot smaller but the view on the village down below was quite similar and it would be a step back up the ladder for them after living at Rose Cottage. No matter how cosy the cottage had been, it wasn't really suitable for a growing family of five.

She made her way over to the church school to collect Emily. Her daughter was also growing fast and had an enquiring mind, for a brief moment she recollected that time when she'd been about to take Emily to the new pie shop and when she'd rounded the corner they'd both bumped into Tobias. Her cheeks burned with embarrassment now at the thought of it. To think she could have been swept along like that and allowed the young man to accompany them both to the pie shop when she realised deep down what he had on his mind. Oh, not that he was about to ask her to run off with him to

America there and then, but the mere fact they had been growing close to one another. She bit her lip. It hadn't really been anyone's fault, it was chance and circumstance, she reminded herself. Harry back then hadn't had much time for her and she'd felt so low following the twins' birth. Tobias had appeared at a time when she'd been at a low ebb and had brightened her world. It seemed as if a lamp had been lit or even a flame ignited. Thankfully, she had quelled the heat that burned inside her before it was too late. If she had given herself body and soul to the man would she have felt remorse afterwards? Now though, it was obvious he was igniting someone else's flame.

As she approached the school, which was at the end of a lane flanked either side by two rows of smart terraced houses with bay windows, she spotted someone she'd not seen in a long time. Not since she'd been married to her first husband. *It was her!* That floozy he'd gone off with, she who had worked at The Crown and Feathers at Drisdale. After roughing her up the night of their wedding, Albert hadn't gone near her ever again in that fashion and soon, she'd discovered why as that little madam had been plying her wares. At the time, she'd felt like slapping the young woman's face until both cheeks stung like the Devil himself, but now, on reflection, all these years on, she recognised that she'd done her a favour. But what was she doing standing outside the Church School?

It soon became clear as Emily emerged through the school gates holding hands with another little girl of around the same age. 'And who's this?' asked Cassie.

'This is my new friend, Milly!' Declared Emily proudly, 'She started in my class today.'

Cassie glanced at the woman who was now approaching them at a brisk pace, her vibrant auburn air blowing in the breeze. Her daughter had boldly marched past her mother without a care in the world.

Oh no, don't say this is your daughter?

The young woman stopped abruptly and she stared at Cassie, her large emerald eyes shining brightly and then she narrowed them slightly as if recognition had dawned. Both women stood staring at the other for a moment, their impasse broken as Emily tugged on the sleeve of her mother's jacket to ask, 'Please Mama, may Milly come and play at our house?'

Cassie glanced at her daughter briefly before saying, 'Not today, poppet.'

Emily pouted but then began whispering in her new friend's ear, who giggled in response.

Cassie's mouth felt dry and she wondered if she ought to just take her daughter's hand and walk in the opposite direction without saying something but then she guessed Emily would protest and that might make a bigger scene than if she confronted the young woman in the first place. So instead, she opened her mouth to speak. 'Hello!'

The woman nodded at her but didn't say anything.

'I just said hello to you,' said Cassie now feeling that rush of anger coursing through her veins, the woman could at least acknowledge her publicly, after all, she had taken her first husband from her.

Finally, the woman let out a long breath as if realising Cassie wasn't going to walk away without saying anything.

'Hello,' she responded. 'I'm sorry for what happened,' she said quietly.

'What about stealing my husband or him dying the way he did?'

She shook her head as tears filled her eyes. 'Both,' she said.

Cassie swallowed hard. What was the matter with her? She now had a happy life living with a man she loved and that young woman had done her a favour in the end. 'It's all right,' she huffed out a breath. 'He wasn't any good for me anyhow, I'm married to a much nicer man these days.'

The woman nodded and made as if about to take her daughter away as she held out her hand to the child.

'Wait!' said Cassie suddenly, 'there's no need for either of us to fall out over that man. I tell you what, next time we run in to one another at the school gates, bring Milly with you back to our house for her tea…'

The young woman stared at her for a moment and then nodded. 'That's most hospitable of you all things considered. I'm so…so very sorry what happened.'

'We'll mention it no more,' said Cassie kindly.

'But you don't know, do you?' The woman said as though realisation had just hit her, smack between the eyes.

'Don't know what?' Cassie frowned.

'Milly, my daughter…'

Cassie turned her head to look at the little girl who was playing some sort of catch game with Emily. Milly's dark hair tumbled in waves on her shoulders, those dark eyes. She swallowed and turned her head back in the direction of the woman. 'You mean?' She gulped, 'You mean Milly was *his* child?'

The woman nodded slowly. 'I'm sorry, I always assumed you knew?'

'I had no idea,' Cassie shook her head blankly. The simple truth was, she had been so caught up in everything from her first husband's death to meeting Lord Bellingham and the affair they had conducted and then her marriage to the man. Why had no one told her of this?

'I'm so sorry.'

Cassie stepped forward and took the woman's hand. 'Please, do not reproach yourself. My husband was a difficult man to live with, he beat me, I was well rid.' Something occurred to her,

'Did he beat you too?'

She lowered her head and then lifted it to make eye contact. 'Yes, yes, he did. It wasn't until after his death I discovered I was pregnant. It wasn't common knowledge that he was the father as I took up with someone else soon after who has been more of a father to Milly than that man could ever have been.'

Cassie laid a gentle hand on the woman's shoulder. 'I understand,' she said. 'We have that much in common at least and of course, our daughters are half-sisters.' Cassie smiled through glazed eyes.

***

When Cassie told Polly about her discovery the following day at the tea room, the woman pursed her lips, 'Well, it ain't right if you ask me! That Jezebel having the cheek to send her love child to the same school as yours!'

Cassie smiled. 'Oh, to be fair, she had no idea Emily was a pupil there and the two girls seemed to have bonded with one another, after all, they are half-sisters.'

'Half-sisters or not, that must have been difficult for you running into that one yesterday?' Cassie nodded. 'What's the floozy's name anyhow?' Polly folded her arms.

'Jessica or Jess for short.'

'And you say she worked at The Crown and Feathers at Drisdale? Is she still a barmaid there?'

Cassie nodded. 'Apparently so.'

Polly sniffed loudly. 'Them lot what works in those sort of establishments are renowned for chatting up the menfolk and stealing them from their poor wives and girlfriends.'

'That may be so, Pol, but honestly, she did me a favour. At least when she was luring Albert, he left me well alone.'

Polly narrowed her gaze. 'What do you mean?'

'I never told you this before but once we were married he took me by force on our wedding night, it was awful. Thankfully, he left me alone when he met Jess. But...' She bit her lip as she stared out of the tea room window, 'he started beating her and all after a period of time. He never got to discover she was having his child and she met someone else soon there afterwards, who has helped to bring Milly up as if she were his very own.'

'Well,' tutted Polly as she wagged a finger in Cassie's face, 'yer a better woman than me, I can tell you!' She sniffed once again, loudly this time. 'I could'na be talking to the woman what poached my man from me. Never, not ever.'

Cassie smiled. 'Aye, maybe not but this was unusual circumstances, Jess didn't have a clue who I was and she told me yesterday that she didn't find out for some time afterwards that Albert was a married man.'

'She would say that though!' Polly's eyes widened profusely.

Cassie was having no more of it and said

31

lightly, 'Perhaps you'll change your mind when you meet her as I want you there for tea with us tomorrow along with Edna and Aunt Bertha.'

'Me?' She pointed to herself with her right thumb as if astonished by the invitation.

'Yes, you. It will be nice for all of us to get to know Emily's half-sister. Emily adores the little girl.'

Polly's features softened. 'Well, maybe for Emily's sake then.' She let out a long sigh and then said as her beady eyes narrowed, 'Does the child know that Milly is her sister?'

Cassie shook her head. 'I'm not sure whether to tell her or not as yet.'

'I can understand your thinking, but maybe it's best the girls know as there are a dreadful lot of gossips around Wakeford and the surrounding areas,' Polly said sagely.

Cassie guessed the woman was right, the thing was, where and when should she tell Emily and Milly they were related? And was tomorrow too soon?

***

Clyde paced back and forth in the drawing room. Something had been bothering Rose of late and he wasn't quite sure what that thing was. She had been in rude health since the birth of Baby Sophia, so he didn't think it was any kind of melancholia that some women were prone to after a birth, he thought it was something else that was niggling her. Was it something he'd done? He wondered. But if it was, he couldn't for the life of him think what it could possibly be. With Christmas on the horizon, he didn't want whatever it was to overshadow that so he bided his time that evening until Sophia had been put down to sleep in her cot before approaching his wife.

He watched from the landing as through the partially open nursery door, he could see Rose was busying herself picking up some of Sophia's toys and then she neatly folded a cot blanket, before departing the room, leaving the door slightly ajar.

'Rose,' he whispered, 'c...can you come downstairs please? I need to speak to you.'

She nodded and followed him down the stairs into the drawing room where two glasses of sherry had been poured beside a large crystal decanter. He handed a schooner of sherry to her, which she took. 'I shouldn't really...' she chastised herself.

'Look, it's nearly Christmas,' he smiled

'Are we celebrating early then?' She arched a curious eyebrow. This past year or so Rose had matured as a woman, she was no longer that young, headstrong girl with a flurry of emotions running through her body, now these days, she was far more composed so it seemed out of character to Clyde for her to be acting so strangely and unsure of herself.

'It's not r...really a c...celebration,' he said. 'I

just wanted to ask you why you're acting so anxious lately?'

She let out a slow breath. 'To be honest, I was waiting until after Christmas to tell you...'

'You're not leaving me, Rose, are you?' He asked as his forehead creased with alarm.

She smiled. 'No, I'm not leaving you but I've had word that Tobias Beckett may be returning to Wakeford and I wondered how you'd feel about that?'

Clyde frowned. He'd never liked the fellow, particularly the way he'd treated his beloved Rose, stealing her away from him like that and then getting her pregnant and dumping her. He was no gentleman in his book. 'Well, I w... wouldn't like to s...see him back here, but w... what c...can we do about it?'

Rose noticed her husband's stammer had got worse since she mentioned the man's name to him. So she reached out and lightly touched his forearm. 'Tobias is no threat to us as a couple now,' she said gently. 'But...I fear someday he might come and claim Sophia from us now he is married and might wish to take her back to America with him and his new wife.'

'Oh, please don't even think that, R...Rose,' Clyde said taking her into his arms. 'That happening at all would have to be over my dead body. I th...think it's best if I can manage to somehow legally adopt her.'

Rose looked up at him through blurred lenses

and let out a shuddering sigh. 'You'd do that for me, for us?'

'Of course I would, I'd lay my life down on the line for both of you, my sweet.' He held her firmly in the circle of his embrace so she felt thoroughly safe and protected by him, something she'd not felt ever with Tobias. 'Promise me one thing, Rose,' Clyde said.

'Yes? Anything?'

'You will not keep anything like that from me ever again, I was so worried about you.'

'I promise,' she said nodding and she meant it too.

***

The following day Cassandra and Emily brought Jessica and Milly back with them to Rose Cottage. Polly had made a couple of special cakes for the occasion, a sponge cake with lashings of whipped cream and jam and a slab of fruit cake. Edna and Aunt Bertha had prepared ham and cheese sandwiches and Doris had been around earlier to take the twins out in their perambulator for the afternoon so there'd be more room for Cassie to entertain in her cosy but small cottage.

The women had all got along well and no one, not even Polly now, was judging Jess for the situation she'd found herself in. It could have happened to anyone, Cassie thought. *This is the woman who in a way stopped Albert from being so brutal with me as he was consumed with her.*

It was lovely to see the two girls playing with some of Emily's dolls on the rug in front of the fire while the adults sipped their tea, the girls had their miniature cakes beside them on a china plate each which they were pretending was a tea party for the dolls while they took the odd mouthful of food themselves.

'This sponge cake is really good,' said Jess nervously.

'Polly baked it,' said Cassie. 'She bakes a lot for my tea room.'

Jess's eyes widened. 'You own the tea room in the village?' she said with some surprise.

Cassie nodded. 'Well, yes, but I don't have so much to do there these days as I'm training to be a teacher...' A sudden thought occurred to her. 'We're looking for a new member of staff as one of the waitresses left to marry last year and although Doris works there sometimes it's too much for her and Polly if one of them falls ill. If you ever fancy leaving The Crown and Feathers?' she asked hopefully then she cast a glance at Polly who rolled her eyes at her. No doubt, Polly thought she was entirely foolish to offer the woman who had taken her husband, a job too. This tea party had been quite enough for Polly never mind having the woman working in the shop as well, but it was too late, the offer had been made and now all eyes were on Jess as she mulled over the question.

Chapter Four

Le Havre October 1914

It seemed a long crossing on the ship to Le Havre in France, the men had been packed in like sardines in a tin can with their kitbags and rifles. The journey had been a rough one too as high waves lashed against the ship, rocking it back and forth, and many of the soldiers looked green, some actually running to vomit overboard. Thankfully, for Gil and Ernie, they had strong stomachs. There were many who didn't feel like eating any food but for those who did, there was tinned corn beef and hunks of bread available on board. Someone had told them on the journey over that talk was the war would be over by Christmas and not for them to worry too much as they'd be back with their loved ones by then. Gilbert had smiled and nodded at the soldier extremely grateful to believe it, as they smoked a cigarette together on the dock, but somehow though, Ernie doubted that.

Buildings far in the distance silhouetted against the sky and Ernie shielded his eyes from the early evening setting of the sun. So this was France. He'd travelled over the years but

France was one country he'd not visited as yet, even though it was comparatively near to Great Britain compared to some countries, yet they were separated by a stretch of sea called The English Channel. The men became excited as many emerged from below deck to stand against the ship's railings and they shouted and cheered as the ship sailed even closer into dock. There was a frantic time as they all disembarked and then they had to hang around for the unloading of the horses.

The British Expeditionary Force had landed on French soil. Gil turned to Ernie and said, 'Look, there are some French men over there, let's practice what we learnt at university!' Studying the French language had been part of their studies but neither had really spoken French since graduating many years since.

'Go on then,' urged Ernie, nudging him with his elbow.

'Bonsoir messieurs. Parlez-vous Anglais?' Gilbert smiled at the men.

Both men chuckled and one called out to them, 'What's the matter, you pair of buggers? We're English like you are!'

Gil and Ernie laughed uproariously at that with the men and they all had a cigarette together as they were instructed to wait as the horses were still being transported from the ship as they made all manner of whinnying and snorting noises. There was plenty of time to kill.

It turned out the small group of men were on some sort of leave and dressed in civilian gear for a couple of days. Gilbert wasn't going to live that one down.

Finally, the soldiers all assembled and marched along two abreast singing, *It's a Long Way to Tipperary* as they went along. It was a popular music hall song that had been first sang a couple of years previously. The French people seemed excited as they waved at them with handkerchiefs and scarves or whatever they had to hand, calling out to them. Some even rushed up to the soldiers and handed them a flower or a little keepsake. Children marched behind the soldiers trying to keep in step, amused by the scene before them. One dark-haired lady, with flowing hair and jade-green beautiful eyes, rushed over to Ernie and kissed him on his cheek, saying, 'Thank you, for all you do for the French people!' He blushed and smiled at her but had to carry on marching before he fell behind or out of step. He hadn't been expecting such a welcome.

But after extreme excitement, the novelty soon wore off as the cheering crowds fell further behind them and the sounds became more muffled and distant until all that could be heard was the soldiers marching boots as they carried full pack four or five mile up hill, it was hard going Ernie thought and he glanced at his brother beside him who didn't appear to be coping as well as himself being a few pounds weightier than he was and not as physically fit.

Finally, as night fell, they arrived at the campsite and Gilbert groaned loudly when he saw the rows and rows of bell shaped tents and the muddy ground surrounding them.

'What did you expect, men!' said their commanding officer, Booth. 'The bleedin' Ritz Hotel? You'll see far worse than this on the Front Line! This is sheer luxury compared to that hell hole!'

Over the next few days, Ernie and Gilbert felt like they'd already been sent to the outskirts of Hell and maybe they had, as it did nothing but rain, inside the tents it was freezing cold and rain seeped in as the tent tops bulged, and all the men could do was play cards or tell stories to keep up morale or sing songs when they felt like, which wasn't often. Outside the tent, if they went to the large tent which was the canteen, they had to wade knee high through slippery mud and then the food when they got it was like slops. It became so bad for some of the men that they were clamouring to be drafted to The Front, begging to get out of there.

Ernie, though, was not one of those sorts, he felt the longer they remained where they were, the safer they'd be but he did realise that someday soon, the inevitable would happen.

***

Cassandra's granddaughter, Alice, had signed up to join the VAD. County branches of the Red

Cross had their own groups of volunteers called Voluntary Aid Detachments. Members referred to themselves as "VADs". Both men and women joined up undertaking a range of voluntary positions which included nursing, transport tasks, and other much needed duties. Approved medical practitioners instructed the women on basic first aid, home nursing and hygiene so they were able to help treat the sick and injured. Men were trained up in first aid for in the field and stretcher bearing. Initially, Alice, after undertaking the required training, found herself working in a converted hospital where soldiers were recuperating ready to recover enough to be sent overseas. The building was an old manor house that had been temporarily taken over and kitted out into a hospital for that very purpose. Alice realised in her heart that the time might come one day when she'd have to offer her services to go overseas herself, following both her father and uncle to who knew where.

Her grandmother and grandfather were most proud of her as she rolled up her sleeves and got on with caring for the sick. Very smart she looked in her uniform too of a light blue dress, long white apron with a red cross on the front and starched white headdress. Having been brought up in quite a refined household, Alice hadn't known any poverty or hardship so far in her young life, so she was showing her mettle now by getting on with things. One of her first duties at the Farrington Hall Auxiliary Hospital was to bed bath a young soldier. Before this, she'd hardly ever glimpsed a male body, so with some shyness, she and another young trainee nurse, began to sponge the man down as they had been taught to do on a dummy during their training. She didn't know who was the most embarrassed, Jonathan Campbell, the young man concerned, or herself. She soon became accustomed to it, no longer batting an eyelid at such matters. Essential duties had to be attended to and to her, the most important thing was getting these men fit and well again so they could fight for their King and Country.

Jonathan, she discovered, had been due to go overseas to fight when he'd had an accident as a civilian after signing up. He'd suffered a bad fall down a stone flight of stairs and the doctor had told him, he was extremely lucky that his injuries were healing so well. He'd only broken a couple of fingers on one hand where he'd tried to save himself but had been in a lot of pain from the fall, his body was covered in severe cuts and bruises and he also had a couple of bad sprains, but all in all he'd been fortunate, the fall could have killed him. With time, it was thought he'd be well enough to finally fight for his country but for time being he was in her dutiful care.

Over the following weeks, Alice found herself growing to enjoy Jonathan's company, as the nurses were encouraged to walk in the grounds with the patients to build up their strength, following long walks in the healthy fresh air, sleep was promoted. It was on such a walk around the lake that Jonathan turned to her and said, 'Nurse, you know they'll send for me soon?' He was a handsome, tall, young man, with dark blonde hair and blue eyes and he had a very gentlemanly manner about him.

'Yes, Jon,' she affirmed. She always shortened his name when matron wasn't around, she was such a tartar that she insisted her nursing staff referred to the men in a formal manner such as Mr Campbell. Alice felt a deep pang within at the thought of him leaving her care as she had grown very fond of him. 'Are you fearful then?'

He shook his head and chuckled. 'No, it's not that. That's what I was trained for. It's more that I'm going to miss...'

'This place?' She arched a quizzical brow.

'No,' he paused for a moment and gazed into her eyes. 'No, not this place, it's you I'll miss.'

'Oh?' She hadn't expected such a frank admission from him. She realised he liked her of course but then he was affable and chatty with all the other nurses too. She just didn't realise that he regarded her as anything special. Her cheeks flamed for a moment.

'I was just wondering....when I leave here...' He paused for a moment as if the words wouldn't come to him, but then he took a deep breath, exhaled, and carried on, 'I've been told I'll have a few days to say goodbye to family and friends and I was wondering if you'd meet up with me before I go?'

Alice's heart skipped a beat, her mouth now dry. She swallowed hard. 'Yes, I'd like that, Jon,' she smiled, nodding.

Jon beamed. 'You don't know how much that means to me, Nurse.'

'Call me Alice, but only when we're alone,' she assured.

'Well, Alice, if you're the last person I see before I set off for overseas, I shall be a very happy man.'

It was a small thing for her to do to spend some time in his company and if she were being totally honest with herself, she felt more than a little attracted to the handsome young man. When he'd first shown up at the hospital his face had been covered in cuts and bruising from his fall and it had looked so swollen that she hadn't realised quite how attractive he looked beneath his battered veneer, but even if he hadn't she knew deep inside she had fallen for the very heart of the man, he was a gentle and kind soul to be around and she enjoyed his company very much indeed.

***

The talk amongst the men at the camp was that some of them would be despatched to Ypres in Belgium soon. Gil and Ernie had no idea whether they'd be separated or not as some of the men were to remain in camp. Ernie couldn't understand why most of the men were so keen to get going and go to war. It was all very senseless to him. Oh, he couldn't be one of those conscientious objectors, it wasn't that he actively didn't want to go and fight for his country because if it came to it he would, he hoped deep down that it would be all over soon but realised it wouldn't. Wars seldom ended overnight, they often dragged on even when there were peace talks in progress. No, as far as he was concerned this was going to be a long and costly war. He wished sometimes he had his brother's optimism. Gil seemed to believe that soldier who told him it would all be over by Christmas and had even spoken about returning in time for the festive celebrations. Ernie had just turned away and stared into the distance when he'd heard his brother saying that to a group of soldiers just last night. Gil slept soundly at the camp whereas he did not. He found himself waking up at all sorts of hours with terror in his heart. Last night he'd seen lights through the tent canvas, had heard vehicles and voices and thought they were being summoned to go to The Front in the middle of the night, but in the event that hadn't happened. Apparently, he'd heard when he was stood in line for his breakfast at the canteen tent that some high up officials had turned up without warning to discuss military plans with their commanding officers.

One thing he was sure of, it wouldn't be much longer now, he could sense it.

Chapter Five

Wakeford December 1877

There had been no sign so far of Tobias and his new wife turning up in Wakeford and Mrs Beckett hadn't heard any more from her son since his last letter so Cassandra found herself relaxing. If it was a relief for her then she imagined just how much of a relief it would be for Rose who seemed to believe the man would return to claim their child. When she'd mentioned this to Harry, he seemed unconcerned, but she had noticed a guarded look in his eyes.

'What's the matter?' She asked as they were seated at the dining table that night as the children had been earlier settled down to sleep.

'It's not him returning to claim his own offspring that I fear,' he said, then he cleared his throat to carry on speaking. 'I fear that he'll come back and try to claim you!'

Cassandra laughed nervously. She had no idea that her husband still felt that way. 'Don't be so silly, Harry. He's married now and if he returns, I'm sure he'll have his new wife on his arm.'

'Don't be so sure,' said Harry shaking his head.

'To think of the chances I gave that young man and all the while he was pursuing my wife!'

Cassandra's cheeks blazed red with embarrassment. 'Please Harry,' she implored, 'I explained it all to you what happened.'

He smiled and patted her hand across the table. 'It's not you I'm angry with, my dear, it's him!'

Cassandra shook her head as she fought to hold back the tears. How could a man who now lived so far away and was not even in the village, still cause so much upset and concern? It was beyond her way of thinking but then again, Tobias had never been an ordinary sort of man in the first place. Polly had been correct when she'd described him as a "rabble rouser" as what was that really? Someone who spoke with the intention of inflaming the emotions of others! Well, she'd think no more of it.

Calmly, she looked at her husband. 'Look what he's doing to us from a place so far away?'

He furrowed his brow. 'How'd you mean?'

'He's getting us both worked up and he's not even present in the village! He might never return here. In fact, his mother isn't well and he hasn't returned home. I've arranged for her to see the doctor tomorrow.'

Harry steepled his fingers as if deep in thought. 'To the house?'

'No, I'm taking her to the surgery at Marshfield.'

'But how will you get there?'

Cassandra frowned. 'Apparently one of her neighbours will give us a lift on his horse and cart.'

Harry shook his head vigorously. 'No, no. You can take the coach.'

'But you need it for work?'

'I can manage without it for an hour or two.'

Cassie smiled and nodded. She couldn't believe how kind Harry was being considering this was Tobias's mother she was trying to help, some men might have refused to get involved, but not him. That was the kind of man he was though.

***

The following day, both Jess and Milly arrived at the cottage unexpectedly. Initially, Cassandra was full of dread when she saw them on the doorstep.

'I...I decided to come around because...I'd like to take you up on your offer of working at the tea room,' Jess said with a nervous smile on her face.

'That's wonderful news,' said Cassie as she embraced the woman. 'Come inside and we can discuss this. Emily is playing on the rug in front of the fire with her brothers, go through Milly.' Then she whispered in a conspiratorial way to Jess, 'Then you and I can enjoy a nice cup of tea together with a slice of Polly's seed cake!'

Jess immediately brightened up as Milly ran past Cassie into the house in search of her half-sister. The girls were too young to understand what it all meant for time being, but hopefully, as they grew up they'd understand the close family bond as well as the friendship.

Cassie took the woman's cape and bonnet and hung them on a peg on the back of the kitchen door, then she proceeded to boil the kettle on the cast iron range. She arranged some homemade biscuits and cups of milk for the children and took them through to the living room warning Emily to keep an eye on the boys. Emily nodded sombrely and then she giggled at Milly and offered her a biscuit as the twins looked on longingly. Eventually, she gave them a biscuit each and there wasn't a pip out of either until they'd devoured every morsel.

Back in the kitchen, Cassie poured the steaming pot of tea into two pretty floral cups with matching saucers and handed one to Jess along with a plate of seed cake. Then she took a seat opposite the woman at the pine table. 'So, you've given up your job at The Crown and Feathers to take this one, then?'

The woman's cheeks reddened. 'Er, not exactly...' she paused for a moment. 'I've decided to work there just one Saturday night a week to help the landlord out as it's his busiest night of the week and I was hoping I could work during the day at the tea room.'

'That sounds perfect,' Cassie smiled. 'How are you managing for child care?'

'Well at the moment my Ma can step in if

Milly's not at school like she's been doing when I work at the pub. So how many days would I be needed?'

'Two and a half days, if that's possible?'

Jess nodded. 'Thank you, Cassie,' she said smiling shyly, 'it's more than I deserve after all I've done to you.'

'Think nothing of it and please, don't keep punishing yourself over and over. That man is just not worth a second thought any more...'

Jess nodded in agreement. 'You are right of course you are after he treated us both so shabbily but at least he left us with two beautiful daughters that no one can take away from us.'

Cassie smiled. It was true, both girls were proper little sweethearts especially when they were together.

Chapter Six

Ypres November 1914

Upheaval from the military camp didn't happen during the night as Ernie had feared, it was a few days later when the men were summoned together to tell them they were off to Belgium to a place called Ypres in western Flanders. Fighting had been going on there since mid-October. Flank attacks had been attempted by both the Allies and the Germans which failed to achieve significant breakthroughs thus far, and so both sides ended up settling into trench warfare.

The irony of it was that whilst Ernie was the one who'd have preferred to remain at camp, it was he who was despatched to Ypres and not Gilbert who was kept behind with the others. Yet, Gilbert was the one who was terribly disappointed at having to stay behind with the men. When asked why men had to remain at the encampment, one of the soldiers reckoned it was to replace any of them who got killed or injured at The Western Front, this point failed to cheer the already dismal Ernest. They were just cannon fodder to the authorities, replaceable, as far as he was concerned. They just wanted fresh sets of boots kept back at the camp in reserve. Ernie did wonder though if the fittest men like himself were being despatched first.

He'd written a letter back home in case he failed to return telling his parents how much he loved them and not to worry about him too much as it had been his own choice to sign up to fight in the first place. He took the opportunity to wish them all a Merry Christmas and a peaceful New Year and to send his loving regards to his niece, Alice, who he was so proud of as she was now working as a nurse. When he'd finished writing it, he passed the letter on to his brother telling him to ensure it was mailed back home. The truth was he really did fear he'd never see any of them ever again and was most choked up when he said goodbye to Gilbert. They'd shared their mother's womb together so felt even closer than brothers, although they occasionally fell out over trivial things, in the main they just got on fine even though they were like chalk and cheese in personality.

***

If Ernie could sum things up in just a few words in the trenches of Ypres it would be: blood, mud and bloody rain! If the men had thought things bad back at the camp, they were nothing compared to here. A couple of the men had even come down with something called "trench foot" as a lot of the time their boots and socks were soaked in muddy conditions. One poor young man had even lost a couple of his toes because of it. It was horrendous. The mud was bad enough but apart from that there were the rats to contend with which could be as big as cats. Ernie kept himself going by making little cartoon drawings of his time there and writing little ditties to go along with them. He preferred mainly to keep himself to himself but he'd been fortunate in running into Gerald Wilkinson who was one of the commanding officers there. So they were both able to chat about family and friends and have a chuckle between themselves about the folk and goings on at Wakeford. It was almost as though they had become surrogate brothers as the days wore on.

Then on November the 22nd the battle came to a halt as the wintery weather brought it all to a standstill, there'd been heavy losses on both sides. During that brief time, Ernie had seen many of his compadres die in combat, some were only young lads and he felt for them and their families, so in some ways he was glad he hadn't got too close to any of them.

During the month of heavy combat Ernie wondered what the hell he and all the other men had just been through, the sounds of the heavy shells and guns still ringing in his ears, particularly as he tried to sleep at night time.

***

Jonathan had been discharged from

Farrington Hall Auxiliary Hospital and had four days leave before being transported to Southampton with the other soldiers to sail for Le Havre. During that time, he'd decided to spend as much time as possible with Alice. She was able to apply for one day's full leave and Matron allowed her to work three shorter days in lieu of her making up the time the following week. Alice decided not to tell the woman the truth about what was going on in case she forbade her for going to meet one of their former patients, so instead, she told the woman an untruth that she would be spending time with a close cousin who was due to leave to fight for his country. She hated telling lies but figured it might be for the best in this particular case. Not only was she working at the hospital, some of the staff, including herself had been asked to live in most of the time so they were available if required even at strange hours. This, she didn't mind too much as they were allowed adequate leave on Matron's discretion.

So Alice found herself the following afternoon standing outside a tea room in Hocklea. She'd chosen to go there as it was near to Jonathan's home and there'd be less chance of any of her family seeing her as she wasn't quite ready to explain her relationship with him as yet. Her mother probably wouldn't understand why she'd want to meet up with someone she'd once nursed and her grandmother might ask too many questions. The dress she wore was a pretty flowered one Polly had sewn for her after purchasing the material from a market stall in Drisdale. The woman could turn her hand to anything and she often told her about Aunt Bertha who used to be a seamstress, apparently, she'd acquired a lot of skills from her but sadly, she'd passed away many years since, so Alice had not got to know the woman. All she'd known was that she'd been her grandmother's favourite aunt.

There was a mild breeze whipping up so she adjusted her hat and assured her hat pin was secured firmly, she'd hate to chase after it down the road. The town hall clock chimed ten o'clock. It had been decided that they'd meet earlier so they could spend the whole day together to make the most of Alice's free day. A sinking feeling gnawed in the pit of her stomach. Where was Jonathan? She was so looking forward to this meeting. People were beginning to glance at her as they passed by. It might have been her imagination but she assumed they could tell that she might have been stood up. Should she go inside and wait instead and watch from the window? It was now a quarter past ten and she was just about to turn and go inside when a woman's voice called out. 'Miss Alice Hewitt?'

Alice turned suddenly to see a very pretty young lady on the pavement before her. A sweeping assessment told her she was a couple of years younger than herself. Very smartly kitted out in a long dark grey dress with a matching short jacket and fur stole and a black hat with a flower in it, placed on in a jaunty fashion. Her vivid violet eyes sparkled with light and vitality from what Alice could tell.

She smiled at the young woman. 'Yes, that's me!'

'I'm sorry to have to tell you,' the woman chewed her bottom lip, 'but my brother was due to meet you this morning and...'

Alice's heart sank. Her gloved hands flew to her face. 'Has something happened to him?'

'No, it's nothing like that,' the young woman assured, 'he's perfectly fine but he's apologised and told me to tell you that he's been immediately drafted and as we speak is on a ship headed for France!'

'Oh, my goodness,' said Alice, 'he said he had a few days leave.'

The young woman nodded. 'That's what we all hoped for but instructions were changed last minute and they came for him in the middle of the night, he just had time to tell me and write a quick letter to you.' She dipped her hand in her jacket pocket and handed an envelope to Alice.

Trembling, she took the envelope from the young woman's outstretched hand. 'Th...thank you. I don't even know your name?'

'It's Elizabeth but most people call me, Eliza,' she said brightly.

There was a brief moment as if neither knew what to say to the other, then grounding herself in reality, Alice said, 'Where are my manners? You've come here especially to meet me and we're stood outside a tea room. Won't you come inside and take a pot of morning tea with me?'

Elizabeth nodded eagerly.

***

Once inside and settled at a table, both were more at ease with one another.

'I didn't even know our Jonathan had a young lady!' Eliza said, her bright eyes widening.

Alice giggled. 'I wouldn't exactly say that. You see I nursed him recently at the Red Cross hospital and he asked me to meet up with him before he left.'

'Oh, I see. I thought your face looked vaguely familiar, I must have seen you when I visited him there. I only went there twice though.'

'You might well have done. Sorry if I didn't notice you but things have been so busy of late. We're rushed off our feet.'

'I can quite imagine,' said Eliza, taking a sip of tea from her china cup.

'To be truthful, I don't know an awful lot about your brother. I mean we chatted when I took him for walks around the ground and that sort of thing but I know little about your family or where you live?'

Eliza smiled. 'He's not the boastful sort my brother, but we come from quite a wealthy family. My father is a landowner and our house, Huntingdon Hall, has been in the family for centuries. We have another older brother called, Spencer, who has already gone to The Western Front as a commanding officer. At the moment,' she chewed on her bottom lip, 'all is well as far as we know as we have been receiving regular communication from him.' She paused for a moment, 'Aren't you going to open the letter from Jonathan?'

Alice would have preferred to do so in the privacy of her home where she would be able to savour every word to herself. She could tell by the girl's expression she was keen to know what her brother had written and Alice hoped Jonathan would not have said anything too personal to her within the letter but she and Eliza were united by Jonathan so she made the decision to read it.

Carefully, she slit the envelope open with a spare knife that was on the table and unfolding the letter, began to read to herself, just in case.

My dearest Alice,

By now when you read this you will have learned that I had no choice but to leave with the other soldiers from my unit within the early hours of this morning and maybe by now I am already boarding that ship bound for Le Havre.

I just want to say that I regret that this has happened this way as I was so looking forward to spending time with you. Please pass your address on

LYNETTE REES

to Eliza so I might correspond with you. I shan't ask you to wait for my return as we both know, I may never return home again. But if I do, God willing, then you are the first person I shall seek.

Sending my love to you always.

Jonathan.

Alice's eyes began to water and she stifled a sob and then took a sip of her now lukewarm cup of tea. She passed the letter over to Eliza for her perusal, she read it and nodded, then gulped as both girls reached for the other's hand across the table. Although strangers, they both had something in common, they both loved Jonathan.

Eliza and Alice vowed to keep in touch with one another and relate any news that came to them of Jonathan. Alice was feeling she had found a kindred spirit in the young woman. Later that evening, as she lay on her bed back at the hospital quarters, she stared out of the window. It was a clear night where all the stars were visible and as she gazed at the large luminous moon, she wondered if Jonathan was seeing the same moon even though he had been taken so far away from her.

Chapter Seven

Wakeford December 1877

Cassie turned the key in the lock and walked away from the school building towards the main high street. Her feet were aching as she'd been on them all day as it had been a busy one. She'd arranged a school party for the children which had been such a joyous occasion. A large fir tree had been brought into the hall especially for it and tables and chairs arranged in long lines decorated with red table cloths. Special gifts donated by the more affluent in the area had been attractively packaged and labelled and placed beneath the tree: wooden spinning tops and boats for the boys and rag dolls and books for the girls. Mr Ivers, the headmaster, had taken to the stage to welcome one and all and, Mrs Peters, one of the other teachers, had played Christmas carols on the old upright piano in the corner of the room. Some of the more reliable mothers had remained behind and donned their pinafores to help dish out the food. There had been neat little sandwiches of cream cheese and ham too, sausage rolls, a couple of blancmanges: a white one was set in a copper mould of a snowman and the other, a pink one, was in a rabbit mould which had nothing whatsoever to do with Christmas but the children had gasped when they'd seen Cook enter with a large silver salver containing both. She'd placed it down in the centre of the serving table and someone else brought in two crystal glass bowls of red jelly to go with them. Oh, the children were pleased and all. They even got to drink homemade lemonade or ginger beer if they preferred. The mothers had a glass of sherry each and cups of tea too for all their hard work and as much of the children's party left-overs as they desired.

All in all, it had been such a good day. As Cassie placed the school keys in her reticule, she looked up to see the last of the stragglers leaving with their mothers who were carrying their Christmas presents for them.

It was almost dark now and in the distance as she walked away from the school gates she thought she glimpsed a recognisable figure perusing the jewellery shop window. No, it couldn't be, could it? Not Tobias as soon as this? Had he returned for Christmas? But then the man turned from the window he'd been gazing in and glanced in her direction. No, definitely not him. The man was much older and had a square jaw line. She'd been so sure too from the back. Or had you desperately wanted to see him? A little voice inside her asked.

Shivering, she wrapped her cape tightly

around her shoulders and headed off home with her head down as a cold north westerly wind blew a hard icy blast in her direction, heralding the promise of snow to come.

Tomorrow, she'd made a vow to herself that she'd get Cynthia Beckett to see a doctor.

***

Doctor Bryant, the Hewitt family doctor, now held a twice weekly drop-in surgery at Marshfield. Normally, he saw the more well-to-do sorts, but for the less well-off of Wakeford and the surrounding areas he held a surgery which was on a first come basis.

Determined that Cynthia should not have to wait too long to be seen by the physician, Cassie set out exceedingly early the next morning to collect Cynthia from her small house in Market Place. The woman was waiting on the doorstep, well wrapped up with two shawls around her shoulders and a bonnet on her head. Her skin pallor had paled significantly since Cassie's last visit and her lips appeared blue and it was obvious that she was more than a little breathless. However, it was a bitterly cold morning, and thankfully it hadn't snowed much overnight just a light dusting on the roofs and pavements so Cassie realised the woman needed to be seen now as soon as possible in case they became snowed in.

Cynthia lifted her head to stare at the coach and the look behind her grey rheumy eyes told her how worried the woman was. At that moment, Cassie made the decision to ask Cynthia for Tobias's address. He needed to know that his mother wasn't a well woman. No doubt, she never told him of her concerns in her own letters to him, and even if she did they might take weeks to arrive.

Cassie was about to disembark from the coach to help Cynthia on board, when she noticed the coach driver clambering down, opening the door and gently helping the woman on board who gasped and wheezed as Cassie helped settle her down in the seat opposite her. Cynthia closed her eyes and laid her head back against the leather squabs.

'I…I…' she began.

'Sssh now, Mrs Beckett,' Cassie soothed. 'Wait until your breath returns before speaking.'

Cynthia nodded and the coach began to move as the horses set off at a fair trot in the direction of Marshfield. Finally, after a couple of minutes, Cynthia held her hand to her chest and said, 'It's not getting…any better.' She shook her head sadly as tears filled her eyes.

Then Cassie moved from her own seat to sit beside the frail woman and taking her crepe-like hand said, 'I'm going to get Tobias's address from you later to send him a letter.'

The woman shook her head, 'No, please don't do that,' she said breathlessly.

In fact, Cassie had it in her mind to send Tobias

a telegram. She'd never used the service before but had been told by Harry she'd have to use as few words as possible due to the fact they were expensive to send. He'd had to send one himself once when James Wilkinson was in France and needed to return urgently to Marshfield Coal Pit.

'Very well,' sighed Cassie, realising she couldn't go against Cynthia's wishes, maybe first they'd have to see what the doctor said about her condition.

***

Doctor Bryant's kindly eyes looked full of concern as he examined Cynthia's chest with his stethoscope. 'Breathe in please, Mrs Beckett,' he instructed.

Cynthia took a ragged breath.

'Good, and now breathe out again,' he carried on listening through his instrument as he instructed her to do this several times.

Cassie could see what a struggle it was for the woman as she became short of breath.

Finally, he asked Mrs Beckett to adjust her clothing and take a seat beside Cassie. His face was giving nothing away and he sent the young nurse who had been assisting him to fetch something from outside the room.

'Can you tell me how long you have been having these bouts of breathlessness for, Mrs Beckett?' He took a seat behind his large oak desk and steepled his fingers as he waited for the answer.

'I would say a few weeks now, Doctor,' she said shaking her head.

Doctor Bryant raised his brow. 'Any other symptoms?'

Cynthia nodded. 'I sometimes get headaches and feel so tired a lot of the time.'

'And your diet? Do you eat well?'

Cynthia's eyes brimmed with tears. 'No, not really, Doctor. Since my eldest lad went overseas I haven't been looking after myself as well as I should. He sends me money but it's not the same. My appetite is poor most of the time.'

'I think you're missing Tobias badly,' Cassie interjected.

The doctor nodded. 'So I take it you're not getting to eat much meat or green leafy vegetables?'

'No, Doctor. I make nutritious meals for the children but live off bland food like potatoes, porridge and sometimes rice pudding.'

The doctor nodded. 'Let me examine your eyes.'

He rose from his chair and gently with his thumbs, lowered Cynthia's bottom lids and peered in her eyes. 'As I thought.' He seated himself at his desk. 'I think you have iron deficiency anaemia which is good news as that can be corrected but to do so you have to start looking after yourself. You need to eat red meat, beef and liver, that sort of thing, beans, spinach, kidney beans, fish and egg yolks. That's why you've been breathless. Now I want you to improve your diet over the next couple of weeks and the problem might well rectify itself. Do you think you can do that?'

'I'll help you.' Cassie looked at the woman.

Cynthia nodded and after turning away from Cassie, looked at the doctor. 'Yes, Doctor. I can do that. I just feared…'

'I know,' said the doctor, 'you feared it was something far more serious, didn't you?'

'Yes. Particularly as my son is so far away, I thought I might die without ever seeing him again.'

Cassie swallowed a lump that had arisen in her throat. Whatever she thought of Tobias and his new life, she felt she must still contact him. He needed to come home and see his mother as she was obviously missing him dreadfully. This was a symptom of grief, of that there was no doubt.

***

'Well, that sounds hopeful,' said Harry later when Cassie had arrived home after dropping Cynthia back at her house.

'It is, but you should have seen her, she was most distraught as I'm sure she thought she had something far more serious. The poor woman is grieving badly for her son.'

'But what can we do? We can't force him to return home to Wakeford. It's not like taking a boat trip across the river, he needs to cross an entire ocean. More even, as I expect he has a fair journey on land before he even gets in sight of a ship.'

Cassie shrugged. 'You are correct of course. I just wish there was some way we could help.'

'I know you do,' said Harry gently. 'It's in your nature to want to help others but you can't solve the world's problems. By all means write a letter to the man but don't expect him to come running back here. He has a new life now with good prospects and a new wife to care for.'

Cassie nodded with tears in her eyes knowing that what her husband said was perfectly true.

Chapter Eight

Wakeford April 1915

Alice had received several letters from Jonathan. It seemed he was waiting in some encampment somewhere while plans were put into place to send the troops into Ypres. This was to be the second battle there, he was to explain. Although it was obvious to her that he was keeping the tone of his correspondence light, she guessed he was doing his best not to worry her or Eliza.

There had been no news from her father or Uncle Ernie for a few weeks. The last she'd heard was that her uncle had arrived back at camp safely but her father was due to go to Ypres himself soon.

She couldn't help feeling she was helping soldiers recuperate at the hospital so they could get themselves maimed, injured or killed in a foreign land. It all seemed senseless to her. Yet, if that wasn't happening then she would never have met Jonathan and for that she was grateful, though she did understand there was a possibility he may never return home again, or if he did, then he might be badly injured. She shuddered at the thought of him losing a limb or limbs. She'd heard of several soldiers that had happened to and shortly she was due to move to another Red Cross hospital that dealt with the injuries of war. How mentally prepared she'd be for that, she wasn't sure.

At the end of April, there was an article in a newspaper which read:

GERMANS LAUNCH THEIR FIRST OFFENSIVE OF THE YEAR

On April 22nd, the Germans launched an attack in what is now being referred to as The Second Battle of Ypres.

Alice went on to read that there had initially been artillery bombardment and when the shelling had subsided, as the allied defenders had waited for the first wave of attack troops to descend on them, instead they'd been thrown into a blind panic when chlorine gas had wafted across No Man's Land and into the trenches. A total of four miles of The Western Front had been targeted with the poisonous gas that was blown by the wind, devastating French and Algerian troops but the Allies managed to hold on to most of their positions.

The first thought that went through Alice's mind was if her father, uncle and even Jonathan were somehow involved in any of this, and if so, had any of them been injured? Her second thought was that she wanted to be in the reassuring comfort of her grandparents' presence, so when she finished her shift at the hospital that afternoon, she made her way to their home.

***

By May of that year, Ernie found himself in a makeshift tented hospital in Ypres, Belgium, where occasional gunfire and the noise of bomb blasts, shook the ground beneath his camp bed. He'd been wounded, thankfully, not too seriously from the shrapnel but the surgeon needed to remove it from his legs. From his bed, his eyes searched the casualty clearing station to see if there was any sign of Gilbert, but there was none. A nurse in a long white apron bearing the Red Cross over a long blue dress, came walking towards him carrying a silver kidney shaped tray. She smiled at him and he forced a smile back at her as he noticed she had kindly cornflower blue eyes and a reassuring smile. Nervously, he glanced at the glass syringe in the tray with a needle attached to it. Oh no, he hated injections.

'I didn't realise I'd have to have one of those...' he gasped. 'I have a terrible fear of such things.'

'Now then, Private Hewitt,' the nurse said softly. 'It won't be as bad as you think. In fact, I bet that shrapnel you have in your legs will have hurt far more than this needle ever will. And besides, this is to sedate you for the surgeon to remove all those bits and pieces.'

'W...what's in it though?' Ernie furrowed his

brow.

'Morphine Sulphate. Afterwards, we'll mark a cross on your forehead so it doesn't get administered twice as it's strong stuff. Now please don't worry, you've already suffered the hard part. A little needle and a nice drowse will do you good as the procedure is known as debridement to remove the shrapnel and cut back any dead tissue to promote healing.'

He let out a long breath and tried to relax. 'I suppose that makes sense. But please, Nurse, tell me your name?'

'It's Moira...'

Ernie gazed into her deep blue eyes and saw only kindness there. 'Thank you, Moira.'

'Now once I've given you this injection, I promise I will hold your hand as the doctor removes all those bits and pieces.'

'Thank you. I'm sure I will be able to survive anything with you holding my hand.' But then he added, 'I'm sorry, I expect lots of the soldiers are saying things like that to you, you must be so fed up of it?'

'Not at all, Ernest.'

'How do you know my name?'

She chuckled as she went to the foot of his bed where his chart was clipped to it. She lifted it and showed him. 'It says here that you are Private Ernest Hewitt!'

'Of course, how silly of me.'

The nurse glanced behind her. 'The doctor's

coming,' she said brusquely, just refer to me as Nurse or Nurse Watkins, please. I shouldn't have given you my Christian name.'

He nodded, then tapping the side of his nose with his index finger said, 'Your secret is safe with me.'

After the doctor introduced himself, Moira held Ernest's hand as the injection was administered and he felt like he was being supported by nice soft comfy pillows and then he was floating on air. When he awoke it appeared to be dark outside the tent and inside was dimly lit by several lamps. All was quiet apart from the occasional groan from a soldier. Noticing he was conscious, Moira came over to him and smiled, then she whispered. 'Now don't worry, all went well. The shrapnel was only superficial. Your wounds have been cleaned and fresh bandages applied. Are you hungry?'

He nodded, his mouth feeling parched. 'I wouldn't mind a drink of water first though, Nurse, please.'

'I'll fetch you a mug of water now and then I'll see what the canteen has to offer. You'll have to take pot luck I'm afraid as they stopped serving over an hour ago when you were out like a light.'

'Thank you, Moira,' he whispered as he took her hand and held it against his tear stained cheek—he was crying and he didn't know why.

***

The following day, Ernie was transported to

a hospital in Northern France which was a converted chateau. Before he left he asked Moira if there was any news of his twin brother's whereabouts but sadly, she shook her head. Fearing he was dead, Ernie decided he had to firmly put him out of his mind if he were to make any sort of recovery. It was a double-edged sword really as the more recovery he made, the more likely it was he'd be sent to The Front to fight again. Some soldiers had purposely made their injuries worse because of this. One young man had rubbed soil into his leg wound to make it infected, which Ernie thought foolish as now the doctors were fighting to save his leg. Had it really come to this that the men were so frightened that they'd lose a limb? But was it far better to lose a leg than lose a life? Anyhow, for time being he'd been told he'd need at least several weeks of recuperation at the chateau. But one thing he wanted to do was keep in touch with Moira.

'Nurse Moira…' he said before he left.

She was folding blankets and putting them away in some sort of tent that contained supplies. She laid down the blankets on a trolley and turned to face him. 'Oh, you look a lot better today,' she smiled.

'Yes, the doctor has told me I'm to be sent to that chateau hospital in France.'

She nodded. 'For recuperation?'

'Yes,' he smiled. 'It's on the border between France and Belgium.'

'I'm familiar with it,' she said with a knowing look in her eyes.

'I was wondering if I might write to you?' She was silent for a moment so he carried on, 'I know you probably have a lot of soldiers who'd love to make you their sweetheart but I feel a sort of a connection with you, Moira.'

'I really don't know what to say. No, actually, I don't get that many showing an interest in me, for the most part they're in a lot of pain, but with you, it was different as your injuries are not as serious.'

Feeling awful as he realised how much trauma and suffering she must have seen of late, he said, 'I'm sorry. I should not have bothered you. You have a difficult and demanding job.' He turned to leave and she touched his shoulder.

'No, please.' Ernie turned back to face her. 'I should like that. It gets very lonely back here for me when I'm not working. It would be nice to keep in touch as letters from home can take some time to arrive, if at all.'

He nodded. 'Thank you. I don't know the address of the chateau but I'm sure if you ask the doctor, he'll know.'

'I will,' she smiled. She stepped closer, closing the space between them and to his surprise, she kissed him softly on the cheek. 'And if I hear news of your brother, I'll let you know. What's his name?'

'Gilbert Hewitt. We look a little alike but he's

bigger built than me. We're twins.'

'I see,' she said, her eyes widening as if somewhat surprised. 'Well, I'll be sure to let you know if he passes this way.' She lifted the folded blankets and carrying them in her arms said, 'Good luck, Ernest. I'm sorry now I really do have to go to make up some of the camp beds, there are more wounded expected shortly.'

He nodded and smiled wistfully as he watched her walk away and he hoped that he'd get to meet her again someday.

***

The road was bumpy and dusty Ernie noticed as he gazed out of the back of the army lorry. He was packed in tightly with the other men. "Walking wounded" they called most of them apart from one poor fella who they had to keep propping up. Ernie reckoned he shouldn't have been with them at all but the doctor had insisted he go with them. He'd explained he'd also had shrapnel removed but it wasn't superficial like Ernie's had been. The man's leg had got a little infected and the debriding process to clean away the dying tissue had been deep. It was hoped that leaving the busy casualty clearing station to go to a place of rest and recuperation would do the man good but the other soldiers envied him really as they reckoned he was going there to get fit and well for the journey back to England. No way would someone as injured as that fellow expect to fight any time soon if at all ever again.

Maybe he was one of the lucky ones.

The men began to sing as the lorry rattled along the country roads. Ernie wasn't in much of a mood for singing himself, maybe he would have been if he knew where his brother was right now. Before leaving he'd tried to find Gerald Wilkinson to ask him if he'd try to find out where Gilbert was but it appeared that Gerald himself was missing in action. Another commanding officer had explained this to him. He hadn't returned as yet from earlier manoeuvres but the officer reassured him that word would be dispatched if his brother showed up or even if he was found dead. For time being all Ernie had was the consolation that no news was good news.

**

The chateau itself was in a very remote area bordering a large forest. The windows were tall and some of the towers were high like those he'd one seen in a book of fairy tales as a child—indeed it was magnificent to behold. An impressive building which reminded Ernie of one of those big stately manor houses back home like Marshfield Manor only even more stylish. The hospital had been taken over by approval of the Anglo-French Hospital Committee of The British Red Cross. It had one hundred and fifty beds and was under the military command of the French Army. The hospital's first military casualties had arrived there at the end of January from the battlefront which was sixty miles away.

The staff to tend to the wounded and sick soldiers were comprised of female trained nurses, a small contingent of surgeons and medical students and auxiliary hospital staff provided by the British Red Cross volunteers.

Ernie noticed that the hospital appeared to be divided in two. One wing held the walking wounded, people like himself who were expected to make a good recovery and return to The Front, the other wing housed the more serious injuries which might require surgery even. The soldier who had been propped up in the lorry was admitted to the other section but the rest went with Ernie.

Whatever happened, the chateau hospital had to be a better place than the casualty clearing station. It was peaceful here, so far he hadn't heard any exploding shells or gunfire, just the sound of the birds in the trees when they'd arrived and the soldiers boots on the gravelled path as they'd marched into the hospital.

The grounds were quite spectacular. At the front of the property was a stone fountain centrepiece and either side were large flower beds. There was a lawned area where several wooden benches were scattered around and most breath-taking of all, at the rear of the property before the forest, was a small lake. He could see why soldiers were sent here for rest and recovery.

***

Ernie settled in well at the chateau and became quite popular with the men and staff for all his little cartoon drawings that he'd compiled, both in the trenches and later there at the chateau. He'd even drawn some on the latest letter he'd comprised to his mother and father. He wasn't sure if any correspondence they now sent him would get to him here, so he'd written his new address in his latest letter explaining what had gone on recently regarding his shrapnel injuries and how lucky he was that things weren't far worse than they already were. What he hadn't told them, however, was the men he'd heard crying out in pain in the trenches either injured themselves or at the shock of the men stood beside them being mortally injured. And he most definitely did not tell them that both Gilbert and Gerald appeared to be missing in action. There was no point in worrying anyone back home at this early stage, not unless needs be.

During the night, he'd heard hushed voices as several soldiers were brought in and put in beds against the far wall, he had no idea what had happened to those poor souls but he would find out during the day. Nothing stayed a secret within these walls, in fact, the men were encouraged by one of the doctors to talk about their experiences. Something which Ernie found strange as not many men he knew discussed their feelings, since they were little boys, most men had been encouraged to show their mettle and told things like, 'Don't cry, there's a good boy.' 'Be a big brave lad now, you'll be all right.'

Afternoon sessions were held as the men gathered to sit in chairs which had been placed in a circular fashion and the doctor spoke to them. They were encouraged to speak freely and even cry if they wanted to. Crying in front of the other men wasn't something Ernie intended doing so it came as a surprise to himself one day when he told them all about how he'd seen one man rocking back and forth in the trenches, clamping his hands over his ears and then finally getting out of the same trench against the orders of the commanding officer and trying to run away from it all. That same man was shot by a couple of his own men. They were supposed to be on the same side but the officer had ordered two soldiers to shoot him. It was thought that if someone got into enemy hands then they might pose a security risk as they might be tortured for information to reveal their battle plans.

'How did you feel when you knew that man had been executed?' Asked Doctor Granger.

Ernie paused for a moment. 'I was horrified!' yelled Ernie as his eyes widened as if reliving the horror of it all. 'Absolutely horrified. I hadn't realised that kind of thing could happen. He was a family man who didn't want to fight but people in his town would have turned against him if he hadn't signed up for it.' Tears trickled down Ernie's cheeks as he slumped forward in his chair and held his head, and as he dropped his hands from his face and looked up, he could see some of the other soldiers crying silently too, they could all identify as none of them now really wanted to be in this war. At first, it had seemed an adventure, a game even, but no longer. They were beginning to realise they were dispensable, they were being used as fodder against the enemy. Each soldier was replaceable by another just like himself eager to do his duty for King and country but now, soldiers were getting wiser to the tactics employed and were beginning to wonder if it was all worth the risk.

'Stay with that thought for a moment, all of you,' said Doctor Granger. 'I'd like to ask each one of you in turn your thoughts on this?'

As each man answered, one at a time, as they went around the circle of men, it was evident that each one felt exactly the same as Ernie did, indeed two of the men knew the executed man really well and all agreed, it was a travesty. They used words like "Feeling helpless", "Unjust", "Unfair". Not one man said he agreed with the commanding officer's actions, nor those of the soldiers who had shot him, but all agreed the three had been carrying out orders from high above them and to disobey, might mean death or imprisonment for either one of them.

Finally, Doctor Granger said, 'Good work, men. Sessions like this can be exhausting, but overall, getting out your feelings will help you. Now I think we'll take a tea break and resume again in twenty minutes or so.'

As Ernie slowly stood to walk unsteadily towards the tea trolley where the two volunteer female nurses stood ready to dish out cups of tea and plates of biscuits, he caught the eye of a middle-aged man who had been admitted during the night. 'Angus,' the man introduced himself. 'I'm from Aberdeen.'

Ernie nodded, 'I'm Ernest or Ernie.'

'I found that quite powerful what you said there.'

Ernie nodded gratefully. 'Why were you brought here?'

Angus chuckled. 'I didn't get caught by the enemy, if that's what you were thinking. I got caught in some bleedin' barbed wire. A wee trip over in the dark caused it as we charged over the top. I was all right as I managed to get away from it but it's caused one of the wounds in my arms to go a little bit septic. I feel well enough to fight but the doctor at the casualty clearing station thought it best I spend a couple of weeks here and has put me on rest and antibiotic therapy.'

Ernest nodded as one of the nurses handed him a cup of tea. 'Sugar?' she asked.

'Just the one,' he replied. 'Thank you.' He waved away her offer of a biscuit with the palm of his hand.

He waited while Angus took his cup of tea and a plate containing two biscuits and both men walked over to one of the tables and sat opposite one another.

'Ye know Ernie, this war is a mad thing. We're bloody lions led by a bunch of donkeys! So much for it supposedly being over by last Christmas!'

'Yes, you're right there.' Ernie took a sip of his tea. Then a thought occurred to him. 'I don't suppose you ran into someone called Gilbert Hewitt on your travels? He's my twin brother but he's larger framed than me.'

Angus narrowed his gaze as though deep in thought. 'You know what, I have heard that name but I *cannae* think where. Give me a few minutes and it might come to me.'

'Or Gerald Wilkinson, he's a commanding officer.'

Angus's face went ashen. 'Oh, I do know what happened to him. He was badly gassed. Last I heard he was carted off to a specialist unit somewhere with a bunch of other soldiers.'

'Gilbert or Gerald?'

'Wilkinson, the C.O. I still can't place your brother but if it comes to me, I'll let you know. I don't think he's dead or anything like that though. At least his name's not been mentioned...'

Ernie didn't know whether to feel relieved or not as a lot of the information forthcoming was a little vague. 'Thank you, I appreciate that.'

Angus put down his tea cup and whistled to one of the men who had been admitted with him during the night. 'Here, Bert!' He waved his hand at a young soldier, who limped towards them with his cup of tea. He placed it down on the table beside theirs and sat with them.

'Yes?' He only looked around eighteen years old, Ernie thought. Couldn't have seen much life so far.

'Have you heard of the whereabouts of Gilbert Hewitt?' Then he glanced at Ernie. 'He's a private?'

'Yes,' Ernie said.

The young soldier thought for a moment. 'Gil, you mean? Quite a large framed chap?'

'Yes, that's the one,' said Ernie eagerly.

'He's all right as far as I know. He survived the last lot of fighting and got back to the trench, but I didn't see him after that as I went over the top and got shot in the leg, that's how I ended up here.'

Ernie nodded. 'Thank you for that information. I hope your leg heals soon.'

The soldier smiled . 'Thank you.'

'Did Gil seem all right the last time you saw him?'

'Oh, yes, he was making us all laugh, trying to keep our spirits up like,' said Bert. Then he took a sip of tea.

Ernie decided not to question him any further.

He'd heard all he needed to know for time being. For the following five minutes they all sipped their tea in companionable silence.

Chapter Nine

Wakeford April 1878

Christmas had come and gone and now it was early spring in Wakeford. Cassandra had received no word from Tobias when she'd decided to send him a letter instead of a telegram regarding his mother. She'd chosen a letter, because in the end, the woman's condition hadn't been as serious as first thought. By eating more nutritious food and no longer neglecting herself, beneath Cassie's careful watch, the woman's health improved. Now she had gained a little weight and was no longer out of breath from everyday simple tasks. What concerned Cassie though was that the woman had received no further word from her son since his marriage and she didn't want Cynthia to fret any further.

As she gazed at her young sons as they played outside the cottage, she smiled. They were now almost two years old and already she could see their personalities developing. Gilbert, the elder of the two, was full of himself. He was bigger framed than Ernest and seemed to take over whatever game they happened to be playing. Not in a bad way though, it was more as if he were the leader and instructing or showing Ernest what to do. Ernest though had his own way of doing things and she discovered that in some ways, he had more courage than his elder sibling. Maybe that was because he'd almost died at birth, she thought. He was a fighter for sure.

As she waited for her husband to return from work she smiled and went to call the boys in for their tea. She normally bathed and changed them for bed afterwards so Harry could play or read to them for a short while and then settled them down for the night so she and Harry could have time to themselves eating their own tea. But this evening, by the time she'd got both ready there was no sign of Harry's coach. She had learned this past couple of years not to get alarmed as sometimes there were things going on at Marshfield Coal Pit that occurred suddenly, out of the blue. Sometimes the men held meetings and wanted certain demands met, though none of them were as forthright as Tobias had been, well according to Harry. Other times, James Wilkinson expected her husband to stay behind in the office for a drink and a chat, though that didn't happen all that much these days as Harry was definitely a family man. Whatever it was that was keeping him, she'd find out soon enough. Sighing, she decided to put the twins to bed herself. 'Well, boys,' she said smiling, 'Papa isn't home yet, so I'll put you both to bed and read you a story.'

Gilbert stuck out his lower lip into a pout but Ernest smiled, he didn't seem to mind which one of his parents attended to his needs but Gilbert was definitely Papa's Boy.

It was almost two hours later when she heard Harry's coach pull up outside and she dashed to the front door to meet him. Her husband's eyes were wide and glistening as he removed his bowler hat and stooped to kiss her on the cheek at the threshold of the back door.

'But where have you been all this time?' she asked.

'Let me come in and unwind and I'll tell you.'

She couldn't make out whether he was in a good mood or not, but something had definitely gone on the way his eyes were shining like that.

He removed his long coat and she took it from him to hang on the hall stand. Then he took a seat in the armchair by the hearth in the living room, and following suit she sat in the chair opposite. 'Well?'

Harry let out a slow breath. 'You'll never guess who arrived to see me just as I was heading home today...'

She shook her head then furrowed her brow. She honestly could not think who that might be.

'Only Tobias Beckett!'

She gulped. 'Tobias? But I thought he was still in Pennsylvania?'

'No. He's back over here now.'

'But what did he want?'

'Apparently, he's made quite a bit of money in America and he had the audacity to ask me if James and I will sell Marshfield Coal Pit to him!'

Cassandra felt a breath hitch in her throat. 'B... but you didn't agree, did you?'

'No, I most certainly did not!' yelled Harry. 'Sell to the man who tried to take my wife from me?'

She felt her cheeks flame as embarrassment coursed around her body. 'So, you sent him away with a flea in his ear?'

'Er, not exactly.'

'What do you mean by "not exactly"?'

'Just that. Instead, James and I have offered him the chance to partner with us in a three-way deal so we're all owners of the pit.'

Cassandra couldn't believe what she was hearing. 'But why? How?'

'Because we both accept that he's good for Marshfield Pit. He has good sense and he knows what makes the men tick. Plus, he now has plenty of money to invest as he's sold his share from that pit in Pennsylvania and made a fortune! He's also learned a trick or two from working out there. So, he'd be a definite asset.'

Cassandra's hands flew to her face. 'I hope he's been to see his poor mother!' she exclaimed.

Harry smiled. 'Yes, I understand he's been to see her and introduced his new bride to her.'

'D...did you get to meet her?'

'I most certainly did,' smiled Harry, 'and very

attractive she is too.'

'How old is she?'

'Only a little younger than you, my dear. He definitely has a type!' Harry chuckled.

Cassandra gritted her teeth. It was almost as though Harry were taking great delight in taunting her about Tobias's new wife. Taking a calming breath, she asked, 'So where is he living now?'

'He's been staying in a hotel in Hocklea for time being but he is seeking a property to purchase.'

Cassandra gulped. She didn't feel comfortable at all knowing the young man figured on sticking around and she guessed that Clyde and Rose wouldn't be too happy about it either.

Harry approached and draping a reassuring arm around his wife's shoulder, said, 'Look, Tobias is no longer a threat to us. I realise now how much I neglected you early on in our marriage and I'm making amends for it to you, aren't I?' He lifted a curious eyebrow.

She nodded, realising what he said was absolutely true. He had gone above and beyond lately to spend as much time as he could with her, particularly now she had her teacher training at the school.

'But what about Rose and Clyde? Rose has a personal history with him and she shares a young daughter. Has he mentioned Sophia to you at all?'

Harry shook his head. 'Not so far, no.'

'I don't even know if Cynthia told him the child had been born or even if he's enquired about her. She does know about her as Rose and I took her there for a visit once, but it seemed evident to me that the woman is in a difficult position as the child's grandmother. I think she fears growing close to her as Tobias as yet as had no involvement with his own offspring. It's an awkward situation to say the least.'

Harry nodded and then rubbed his chin as if in contemplation. 'Maybe we ought to then invite Tobias and his new wife, Prudence, here one evening for a meal. It would go some way to breaking the ice, what do you think, dear?'

Oh goodness! That was the last thing she needed right now to be faced with the man who had once pledged undying love for her and had wanted to take her to America with him. Not only that, how would she feel seated at the table opposite his wife who probably didn't have a clue how her husband had been passionately in love with another woman a year since, even if it was before he even met her. And did Prudence even know about Tobias's love child? There were more questions than answers it seemed to her but she found herself nodding and saying, 'Very well. Go and ask them both but please, do me one favour?'

'Anything, my sweet?'

'Give me plenty of warning of when they are due to arrive, I don't want to be caught out or anything. I need time to prepare a proper menu.'

Harry grinned broadly and then he kissed her on the forehead. He was obviously happy his wife was willing to oblige on this occasion.

***

It turned out that in the end, Cassandra wasn't required to entertain the Becketts herself, but instead, James Wilkinson's wife, Charlotte, had insisted on throwing a dinner party for all six of them. Cassandra had yet to meet the woman but she knew enough about her to realise what a selfish, self-centred sort she really was. Indeed, the woman had once caused a rift with her and Harry because James wouldn't put any more money into Marshfield Pit because of his wife's lavish ways and the money he wanted to hold back for his children's education. Harry had expected her to pay her tea room profits into the pit funds and that, she wouldn't stand for when Charlotte Wilkson was happy to sit on her backside all day except for the times she entertained and showed her face at charity events. While, she, Cassandra Hewitt, had worked hard to keep the tea room business going. She wouldn't have given away her own profits at the expense of a woman whose only aim in life was to splash out on lavish furnishings and show her face where she felt it could do her most good. She paid "lip service" to local charities but didn't do much to really help them. So, before attending the dinner party,

Cassandra already had a bee in her bonnet about the woman's motives. And what about Prudence? What if she didn't like her either? It was going to be a fun evening, for sure.

What on earth could she wear for it? She hadn't been to such an event since the time she lived at Marshfield Manor herself. Now Charlotte was in her place as *Lady of the Manor* and she didn't want the woman rubbing her nose in it either. She had a couple of gowns left from her days there, so she'd have to wear one of those, even though they might not be thought of as high-fashion these days. No doubt, Charlotte would have a gown especially made for the event, she could just imagine it. But thankfully, if all six were to meet anyhow, then she wouldn't want the likes of her having eyes everywhere in Rose Cottage. It was a sweet place to live but very humble compared with Marshfield Manor. Cassie had seen both sides of the blanket as it were, she'd began life in a working class home but they weren't exactly poor her father had been a hard worker right up until he passed away, then she'd known wealth for some time in marrying Lord Bellingham and then she'd known poverty for a while when she'd been forced to leave the manor house after the Lord's death to pay off all his gambling debts. These days, they were fairly comfortably off and soon they'd be seeking a new house themselves.

When she told Polly and Aunt Bertha about

the dinner party later that day when she visited them at Hawthorn Cottage, Polly had chuckled. 'Go on with you, Cassie gal! You've formed quite an opinion of both Charlotte Wilkinson and Prudence Beckett before you've met either of them. Almost as though they are in league with one another. They ain't even met one another yet!' She slapped her floury hands together.

All three were in the kitchen. Aunt Bertha seated at the table as she greased a couple of baking tins for Polly's cake mixture. Polly was stood over a large earthenware mixing bowl and Cassie was seated at the table with a cup of tea in front of her.

'Polly's right,' said Aunt Bertha. She set down the cake tin for a moment and studied her niece over her spectacles. Smiling, she said, 'Give them both a chance, Cass. If after you meet them, you discover one or another is obnoxious and not nice to know, then fair enough, you're a pretty good judge of character...'

'But until then,' added Polly, 'give them both a fair trial. Go along to the dinner party with an open mind. And don't forget, Prudence has travelled a long way to a foreign country to meet people she doesn't know. We're all strangers to her. She might be homesick and in need of a good friend right now.'

Cassie nodded gratefully for the women's sage advice. They always told it as it was. Polly with her acerbic tongue and sparkling wit and Aunt

Bertha with her wealth of worldly experience.

'I don't know what I'd do without the both of you,' said Cassie draining her cup and standing to peck Aunt Bertha on the cheek. 'Thank you for the tea and your incredibly wise advice. You're both right. I need to be more open minded until I know otherwise.'

Polly nodded. 'Just glad to oblige, gal. Anything else we can do for you?'

'Yes, there is actually.' She glanced in Aunt Bertha's direction. 'I've got two lovely gowns left over from my days at the manor house and I wondered if they need taking in a little? And if one or both of you could take care of it for me?' She shot Polly a sideways glance, realising that Aunt Bertha's eyesight might make it a strain for her even though she was an extremely talented seamstress.

'You leave it to us!' said Polly. 'I'm sure we can manage between us, can't we Bertha?'

Aunt Bertha nodded eagerly. 'Yes. We'll make sure you'll look as good as those women, even better!' She chuckled.

It was good to spend time with two of her favourite people, thought Cassie. Such a tonic.

***

Cassie gazed at herself in the full-length, free-standing mirror in her bedroom. The royal blue gown Aunt Bertha and Polly had worked on together for her, now fitted like a dream. Aunt Bertha had helped a little but her eyesight wasn't good enough to do all the work herself, it was still adequate but for close work, sharper eyes than hers were required. Polly, thankfully, still had good sight and she was able to sew on a pretty pink floral corsage just beneath the cleavage area that set it off nicely. Matching flowers had been sewn to a comb that was applied to Cassie's hair after it had been swept up chignon-style with loose tendrils flowing either side. She felt she hadn't looked like this in a long time. No longer did she carry the twins' pregnancy weight around her midriff and the top of her thighs. Working at the school had thankfully, kept her continually active indeed.

'Are you ready, dear?' Harry shouted up the stairs. 'George is here with the coach!'

George was a new driver they'd recently employed as the previous one had taken on a new job in Drisdale. He'd been a good employee but as he'd explained, he was getting a little old for the job now with his arthritic hips and he'd recommended, George, his nephew for the position.

'Coming!' she shouted back down.

Thankfully, the children hadn't been settled down to sleep yet, so there was no need to keep quiet as Polly was taking care of them. She tiptoed across the landing to take a peek at Emily reading a book in her bedroom. The little girl looked up at her, so she blew her a kiss. The door to the twins' room was ajar and Cassie smiled to herself as she saw Polly playing with a train on the floor with them. Gilbert was busy kicking over a stack of wooden blocks as Ernie sat spellbound gazing at the train as Polly pushed it around the track as she made 'Choo Choo!' sounds. Deciding not to disturb the trio, she tiptoed away. There was no use in upsetting the boys before she left. Gilbert would probably be fine but Ernie could be a little clingy sometimes. Still, she was heartened at how both had grown up of late.

With a feeling of excitement coursing through her veins, she bounded down the stairs and out through the front door into the night air. Harry was already stood by the coach ready to help her to board, with George sitting in the driver seat up front.

'My, my, you do look wonderful tonight,' Harry whispered as he inhaled her sweet perfume.

Cassie smiled at him. 'Now please don't go making merry with me on the way there in the coach, kind sir!' she whispered back in a playful fashion.

***

When they arrived at Marshfield Manor, Cassandra gazed around herself, was it really only a couple of years ago that she presided here as "Lady of the Manor"?

Little seemed to have changed regarding the lawns and copious flowerbeds. Indeed, it was just as if she was still living here—hadn't left even, except the man by her side was not Lord Bellingham but Harry Hewitt.

Her stomach flipped over as the coach climbed the gradient of the drive and the driver pulled up outside of the main entrance. A fancy carriage was parked there and Cassandra's mouth dried up when she guessed it probably belonged to Tobias Beckett and his new bride. She had hoped that they would have arrived before them. As it was now, they'd be making an entrance whilst everyone else was there. Would the two ladies have coupled up with one another and be speaking of her? She wondered.

A butler and a maid stood in the large doorway, the butler to greet them and show them the way and the maid took care of Cassandra's cape and Harry's coat, hat and cane.

The first thing she noticed upon entering was that some of the décor in the entrance hall had changed. There were still black and white tiles on the floor but now there was a large ornate gilded mirror on one of the walls so people could watch themselves pass by, and a fancy crystal chandelier was suspended from the ceiling. That must have cost a pretty penny, Cassandra thought.

Lavish and exotic plants of all colours and descriptions lined the way along to the drawing room. The paintings on the wall were no longer of Lord Bellingham's family, now they were of the Wilkinsons and their children. A sweet-looking young boy smiled at them from one of the portraits. 'Who's that?' Cassandra glanced at her husband.

'That's Gerald. He's a real character, always up to mischief but in a good way. He's a remarkable lad.'

Cassandra nodded and then her eyes were drawn to another piece of artwork where James was sat astride a mighty fine looking horse; he was sporting a red jacket and jodhpurs as a pack of lusty hounds surrounded the horse, tails in the air. That was something she could not abhor: fox hunting and thankfully, Harry felt the same. There were more individual portraits of each child and then, one in pride of place of Charlotte and James, it was the biggest piece of artwork of all. The woman looking down on them seemed to have steely eyes and had a proudful look about her as she stood while her husband was seated. Her hand was placed firmly on his shoulder as if to say, "I've got my man!" This lady took no prisoners if her portrait were anything to go by.

The butler announced their arrival when they approached the large oakwood door of the drawing room. As the door swung open, Cassandra swallowed to see Tobias stood by the flickering fireplace with a brandy glass in his hand. He seemed to have aged somehow but not in a bad way, he looked more mature than she last remembered him. His long hair was now short and neat, but he still had those dark, fiery, passionate eyes which lit up as they approached and he smiled. She was about to relax a little as she thought he'd arrived on his own but then she noticed the young woman sat in an armchair further into the room. She appeared a petite, fragile creature as her jade green gown seemed to engulf her.

'Well hello, both!' Tobias stepped forward and shook Harry's hand. Harry, to Cassandra's surprise showed no reluctance, quite the opposite. He even patted Tobias on the shoulder, then as he stepped back, Tobias stepped forward to take Cassandra's white gloved hand and, looking up at her, he bowed to plant a kiss on it.

'It has been such a long time we've all been parted for and so much has happened since,' Tobias enthused. 'This is my new wife, Prudence.' He gestured at her with a flourish of his hand.

Prudence smiled coquettishly at them.

'Hello, Prudence,' Cassandra smiled at the woman. 'But where are our hosts?' Cassandra's eyes scanned the room.

'I'm not too sure to be honest with you,' said Tobias. 'We arrived here about ten minutes ago and the butler told us to wait here and handed us a drink each. You may as well have one while we're waiting.'

'Splendid idea!' said Harry. 'Brandy, Cassandra?'

She shook her head and held up the palm of

her hand in deference.

'Pru is drinking sherry,' offered Tobias, 'Would you care for one?'

Cassandra nodded gratefully. After all this time, Tobias had remembered she preferred sherry to brandy. There'd been a time when he'd arrived at the cottage waiting to see her husband about some pit business when they'd discussed such things. She couldn't remember how the topic had arisen but she'd found him easy to talk to. They could speak on any topic quite easily in fact.

His eyes glittered as he handed her the schooner of sherry and then he turned his back to the table to pour a brandy for Harry. Her cheeks flamed as she remembered their times together. Oh, nothing improper had ever happened, not until that last time when he'd kissed her and she'd pushed him away. But hadn't it been improper enough that he'd tried to cajole her into going to America with him in the first place when Rose was carrying his child? What kind of man was he really? One who was both passionate and headstrong and who could create a whirlwind when he walked into a room and opened his mouth to speak. She wondered if he'd told Prudence about his fancy for her and how he'd wanted her before he married the young woman? She guessed not. Prudence didn't appear to be giving her any sort of evil stares. She seemed to be a peaceable sort to Cassandra even though she hadn't said much thus far.

Whilst Harry and Tobias chatted amicably with one another, Cassandra excused herself and she made her way over to where Prudence was seated. She noticed another, smaller, armchair nearby so she took that. 'How are you finding it in England?' she asked.

The woman smiled. 'It's sure different to back home but I love the quaintness of it all. The small villages and the greenery.'

Cassie nodded. 'Yes, there's a lot of that. What's it like where you live in Pennsylvania?'

Prudence had a wistful look in her eyes as she spoke. 'Oh, there's quite a lot of expansion going on there at the moment, what with the railroads and the iron and steel businesses, also with the coal mining too of course...The city is the world's largest and most varied manufacturer of textile weaving too,' she said proudly in her American drawl.

Cassie smiled. 'It sounds a very up and coming place.'

'Oh, it is,' the young woman's eyes shone, 'but it's more than that, 'it's home to me. There's still a lot of farming land and the climate is mild with coastal plains and plateaus and oh, the mountains are quite magnificent and the forests too...'

For a moment, Cassie feared Prudence might start crying, but she swallowed hard and then carried on, 'but I have to make the best of it here as it's where Tobias wants us to be now as his mother is aging.'

Cassie sensed a tone of regret in her voice. 'You'll get used to it,' she reassured, remembering what it was like for her when she first moved to Wakeford.

'You said that as if you have some experience there?' Prudence angled her head to one side.

'Oh, I have, and not the best either. You see…' she lowered her voice, 'I was once married to Lord Bellingham who owned this house…'

Prudence gulped and her eyes widened. 'You were?'

'Yes, it was not that long ago.'

'Then what happened?'

'My husband sadly died but he'd accrued a lot of debts and I was forced to leave here suddenly so this house could be sold. So along with my young daughter and just a few things, we left. There was a small cottage the lord owned in Wakeford that I was allowed to keep though.'

'The one where you live now?'

Cassie shook her head. 'No. A friend has allowed us to stay at Rose Cottage until we can afford our own home. Polly, who was my child's nursemaid, now lives there with my Aunt Bertha. I decided it best to move out when I remarried.'

'Very wise,' said Prudence. 'But you indicated as if you somehow felt like a stranger too in Wakeford?'

'I did, very much so. And one or two people gave me a tough time, I can tell you. Often, I felt like packing my bags and getting out of there.'

Prudence raised her brows. 'But you stayed?'

'Yes, I did and I'm glad that I did as those who were against me back then are now for me and I feel very much a part of the community these days. I won't go into it all but it was like a test or trial for me.'

'One which you evidently passed with flying colours!' Prudence smiled which caused Cassie to giggle. She was beginning to warm to the young woman but felt it unnecessary to tell her at this point how cruel Harry's mother had been to her at the start of her journey in Wakeford. Still, these days, Edna was her biggest supporter, so she must have done something right to win the woman over. But what about Charlotte Wilkinson? Would she have to win her over too?

Chapter Ten

France May 1915

There was the sound of gunfire and exploding shells going off around him, Ernie woke in a state to hear one of the soldiers opposite him yelling out. This was common place at the hospital. Men had nightmares about their times in the trenches and as much as they spoke about it to others, if they spoke at all, these things still returned in their dreams at night.

A young man had been admitted yesterday who was behaving in a strange fashion, the like of which Ernie had never seen before. Doctor Granger had explained to him that this was a new thing for the medical profession to deal with following the effects of being in the trenches. Some men turned up at the hospital deafened or even blind from all the shelling and trauma evoked, others had swaying or sudden movements and others contracted limbs. So far there was no name for this phenomenon but it was seen more and more as the war progressed. Sometimes there seemed no explanation as the doctors couldn't find any physical damage to explain the symptoms. Doctor Granger thought along with one of his colleagues that it was some sort of stress from being around exploding shells. That made a lot of sense to Ernie. He was one of the lucky ones as although he had dreams from time to time, which he guessed was his mind processing what had happened, it hadn't taken over his life. During the day, apart from his concerns about his twin and his family back home, he tried not to think of such things, preferring to spend his time drawing little cartoons in his sketch book or chatting with other soldiers as they walked around the grounds. He did miss Marshfield Coal Pit though and he wondered how his father and Harry Hewitt were coping now they'd taken it over once again.

The young man who had been shaking and walking with an unusual gait told Ernie his name was Jonathan Campbell. A lot of the time he seemed most distressed but Ernie tried to keep up his spirits by chatting with him to calm him down and ensuring the nurses didn't pour his tea too hot in case his violent motions caused him to scald himself. After gaining his trust, he discovered the young man came from the same vicinity, in Hocklea, which was quite close to Wakeford. One day he began describing a young nurse who had tended to him at Farrington Hall Hospital and Ernie's eyes lit up. 'Alice, you say?'

'Y...y...yes!' stuttered Jonathan.

'You're not going to believe this, but Alice is

my niece! She's a Hewitt like me.'

Jonathan beamed. And it was at that moment, both men bonded and Ernie decided to look out for his young compadre.

***

Alice had not heard from Jonathan for some time and she was growing concerned about him. She contacted Eliza who was also in a similar position. They met at the same tea room in Hocklea where they'd first encountered one another.

'My fear,' said Alice as she stared wide-eyed across the table at Jonathan's sister, is that your brother is missing in action or maybe even...' she began to chew on her bottom lip, a nervous habit she'd acquired ever since Jonathan and her father and uncle had left to fight in the war.

'I know what you mean,' said Eliza with tears in her eyes. 'Mother and Father though refuse to think that way, they'd putting on a strong front, but maybe that's for my sake. Who knows what they say to one another when they're in private together. I heard Father speak of the enemy using mustard gas, that sounds horrific to me...'

Alice nodded slowly and she reached out across the table to pat the girl's hand. Who would have realised that this time last year many menfolk from Wakeford and its surrounding areas would have left to fight in some senseless war overseas. 'I have thought...' began Alice, 'to volunteer to be sent overseas myself...'

'You mean to The Front?'

Alice nodded. 'My mother won't hear of it though. She thinks I would find it too hard. You see she's a doctor herself, she works at the hospital in Hocklea...'

'Oh,' said Eliza, 'I had no idea. She must be a well-educated lady?'

'She is, but I feel it's a man's world. I think if she'd been born a male she would have gone a lot further with her career rather than working part-time at the hospital.'

Eliza frowned. 'But why do you think she objects to you serving overseas? You're already a nurse so you obviously have the heart and stomach for it.'

Alice smiled and she let out a long breath, gazing around herself, she noticed a couple of smartly dressed women sitting in the corner and to the other side of the tea room sat what appeared to be a middle-aged husband and wife. She lowered her voice before saying, 'I suppose I was what medics would have termed as a "precious baby".'

Eliza raised her brow. 'How so?'

'Before I was born my mother had three miscarriages and then there was a fourth child who lived for a couple of days...'

'Oh, I am sorry.'

'So, I was the fourth child. The one who survived. I think deep down she fears losing yet another child. That would absolutely devastate her.'

'I see,' said Eliza. 'I suppose that's what is stopping you from going then?'

'Er not exactly.' Alice began to twiddle with her lace handkerchief, immersed in looking at the intricate lace work and fine embroidery for a moment as her mind drifted, then she brought herself back to Eliza's question. 'My main reason at the moment for not going is that I want to be here if Jonathan or my father or uncle return home to the area. You see, if they are sent back right now it will be because they're injured and they might need me.'

'That's entirely understandable and very commendable of you. Maybe your vocation is to remain here as you've been helping a lot of soldiers get well enough to fight.'

'Yes, I suppose, but what am I sending them to, Eliza? It sounds like hell on earth in the trenches to me from what I've read in the newspaper. A lady I know has so far lost three of her five sons out in Ypres.'

Eliza nodded. 'Yes, it's not easy, is it?'

Alice felt maybe she was depressing the young woman with her tone of conversation so she brightened up and said, 'How about another pot of tea and a couple of fondant fancies? I think perhaps we should speak of more positive things to keep our spirits up. What do you say?'

Eliza beamed. 'Yes, please.'

It was delightful having Eliza for company and

she was beginning to feel like the sister Alice never had and that was a nice thought indeed.

**

It was a week or so later that Alice's grandmother received news from Ernest. She sat Alice down at the kitchen table and read out the correspondence to her:

My dearest Mama,

All is well here at the Chateau Hospital in Northern France it is near the Belgian border. I was sent here after having minor shrapnel wounds and it's giving me a much needed break I can tell you! The aim is to build up my strength so I can return to The Front. I'm afraid I don't have any news of Gilbert for you as we were parted but some of the soldiers arriving here are able to pass on information, so if I find out I promise I shall let you know.

I met a young soldier here called Jonathan Campbell, who apparently is a friend of Alice's! What a small world it really is. The man is well in himself but he seems to shake a lot, I help him by holding his cup of tea to his lips and ensuring the nurses don't make it too hot for him. It's my feeling he is making progress and that his tremors will pass with time. Doctor Granger here is hopeful of that. It's a new thing the doctors are experiencing and it seems to be related to the exploding shells the men are hearing going off at The Front. So please reassure Alice that her young man is safe and sound and I'm taking care of him...

Grandma paused as if to gauge Alice's reaction.

Alice's hands flew to her face. 'I can't believe they're together!' she enthused with tears streaming down her face. 'But although I'm over joyed that they're safe and sound, at least for now, that trembling concerns me somewhat. One of the doctors at the hospital where I work has mentioned that. There doesn't appear to be a specific term for it as yet.'

Grandma nodded. 'I think to be honest it's a natural reaction to the horrors they are witnessing. It's probably a little like walking on egg shells for them. A sudden noise could easily disturb them. At least that's what I read from one soldier's account that was printed in the newspaper.'

Alice nodded.

'Shall I go on?'

'Yes, please do, Grandma,' Alice urged as she waited for more.

I've sent you some sketches from the Chateau Hospital, some of the soldiers and staff there are right characters. There's a soldier there called "Jessup" who walks with a pronounced limp but sometimes he forgets which leg it's supposed to be and goes from left to right! I think he's putting it on as he wants to return home as soon as possible.

Anyhow, I hope I've reassured you that I'm doing well and so is Alice's young man.

I shall close for now and write to you again soon. I've written the hospital address down on the back

*of the sketch of Jessup so we can correspond with one
another. I'd love to hear news from home. I miss you
and Father so much.*

Your loving son,

Ernest.

Grandma handed several sketches over for
Alice to peruse. Both women couldn't resist a
chuckle here or there especially at the sketch
of Jessup with his "limp". Alice wondered why
her uncle hadn't sent any of his sketches from
the trenches but then she guessed that maybe
he didn't want to alarm them as things were
probably dire at The Western Front. There was a
possibility top security was required even when
penning what appeared to be harmless sketches.

***

A couple of weeks later, Ernie received
correspondence from home. He'd been queuing
up with the other men in "The Mail Room" as
they were handed letters, bulging parcels and
heavy Red Cross Packages.

'Got anything from home?' Asked Ernie as
he draped a friendly arm around Jonathan's
shoulders.

'Y...yes. But I don't know who would realise I
was here.'

Ernie chuckled to himself. He'd not told the
young man that he'd passed on the message that
he was here at the chateau hospital and that
either Alice or his family might now contact
him.

'Well, go and take it to the table by the window and I'll join you once I've picked up mine,' he said with a knowing grin.

Jonathan nodded at him. He noticed that the young soldier was now walking a lot better, he no longer had stiff, jerky movements in his limbs, though he did stall as he walked from time to time. It was as if he'd had to learn to walk all over again and lacked confidence in himself and his ability. The doctors had given him medication to help with his tremors so that was good, though Ernie still kept a watchful eye on him if he held a hot cup of tea, just in case it should slip from his grasp.

Ernie watched from the counter as he waited for his mail, there were now only two men in front of him. Jonathan was grinning from ear to ear as he read his letter from home. It was the first time he's seen the man smile since he'd arrived at the hospital. Any news from home was welcome for the men as long as it wasn't bad news and a definite boost to the morale.

Ernie thought it was just as well he had to wait in line as it would give Jonathan longer to relish the correspondence before he intruded into his thoughts. For Ernie that didn't matter as much as there was no sweetheart waiting for him at home, though he had to admit he had a liking for that nurse who'd attended to him at the casualty clearing station. Moira, that was her name. He'd not forgotten her with her charming smile and reassuring manner—an angel in the midst of anguish.

The staff behind the counter seemed to be having some trouble locating the soldiers' packages and mail. He'd be here for ever at this rate, but finally, they located a Red Cross parcel for each man and a few letters and postcards between them. Now it was Ernie's turn. He was handed a buff colour box containing things from the Red Cross: cigarettes, cocoa powder, soap and shaving equipment, a tin of corned beef, a bar of chocolate and other assorted items. And he was handed two letters. One, he recognised as being in his mother's handwriting from back home and the other, which did not have a stamp on it, bore his name and the hospital name. That one puzzled him. Was it sad news regarding Gilbert, he wondered? Maybe one of the commanding officers had taken it upon themselves to update him.

Unsteadily, as though almost in a dream, he took himself to a quiet corner and trembling, opened the envelope to read:

Dear Ernest,

I promised I'd write to you. I am the nurse who attended to you at the casualty clearing station back at Ypres. I hope you've settled in at the chateau hospital by now and all is going well?

Here, things are as hectic as ever, as I'm sure you can imagine, and the sights and sounds of the injured men passing through are sometimes unbearable. Many a time, I've felt like running from the tent, but something has kept me rooted to the spot. My daily prayers and my faith in God is helping me to withstand this situation I find myself in. It has been suggested that I take some leave soon, so I would like to visit you if that is permissible?

I've been asking around about your brother, Gilbert, but so far there is no news to pass on to you, I'm afraid. Quite a few men have now gone missing in action, some have turned up here at the unit, others, there is still no word of. As of yet, there has been no one with your brother's name passing through here, I keep checking the patient lists.

I'm hoping to come to visit you sometime next week if it can be arranged. I hear it's more peaceful where you are and I hope you are well rested and recuperating.

Anyhow, I have to close now as I have to begin my next shift in half an hour and I haven't eaten yet. Sometimes it's all too easy to go for many hours without thinking about food here, but if I am to work then I need sustenance.

I continue to pray for you and all the other soldiers every day.

Your friend,

Moira.

A tear trickled down Ernie's cheek and he brushed it away with the back of his hand and sniffed. To think Nurse Moira had given him as much as a second thought, meant a lot to him. He hoped she'd be able to manage to visit as it would do both of them good. He well appreciated that she'd need the peace and tranquillity of the area like a soothing balm as the sights and sounds she encountered at the clearing station must be hard to endure. She had a lot of mettle to do that particular job, his niece, Alice, too. She was another fearless creature. Thinking of Alice reminded him of Jonathan who was seated at the table by the window waiting for Ernie to join him.

**

Ernie smiled as he approached Jonathan's table, and drawing out a wooden chair, he seated himself opposite the young man. 'Who was your letter from?'

'My sister, Eliza,' he swallowed hard.

'You don't look too happy about it?' Ernie frowned. 'Although I did catch you smiling when you read it?'

Jonathan lifted his head to look Ernie in the eyes. 'I'm glad to hear from Eliza of course I am, but I had hoped...'

'You'd hear from my niece, Alice?' Ernie quirked a brow.

'Yes, that's about it.'

'I expect the letter from Alice is delayed in the post or something. We are in a war zone after all, so not all the mail will get through in a timely fashion, if at all. Or maybe it's been held up in

England for some reason.'

Jonathan shrugged his shoulders and looked so despondent that Ernie made up his mind that he'd ask his mother to tell Alice to write to Jonathan to lift his spirits next time he penned a letter back home.

'Another thing…' carried on Ernie, 'I expect Alice is very busy at the hospital, you'll see, she'll write to you soon enough…' But for some reason Ernie now had his doubts. He knew his niece to be a reliable, loyal sort, but maybe she'd now written off Jonathan as a prospective suitor, maybe she'd even met someone else who had taken her mind off him. If that was the case, then poor Jonathan. Perhaps he'd discuss this issue with Moira when she turned up next week for a visit.

***

'You're off where?' Grandma asked as she blinked several times.

'To another hospital called The Royal Victoria Hospital or Netley, it's a military hospital in the Southampton area,' Alice explained. They were seated in Grandma's comfortable drawing room, although almost summer, it was a bitterly cold day and Alice welcomed the heat from the hearth as they chatted.

'But why are you going there? I don't understand?'

Alice smiled. 'Apparently, some doctors will be researching into the strange effects the injured soldiers are enduring. I don't think there's even a name that's been put to it as yet. But lots of hospitals are now filling up with soldiers who are suffering from mental collapse and nervous afflictions after being traumatised at the battle front. They're being sent home directly from Ypres.'

'Oh, I see,' said Grandma. 'It's a good thing you're doing. How long before you leave here then?'

'I've only got another couple of days to go so I shall make the most of those once I've packed all my things.'

'But where will you live?'

'In the nurses quarters, I'll have everything I need like bed and board, so there's nothing to worry about there. It's not as if I'm being send to The Front, is it?'

Grandma shook her head. 'No, it's not but what I know of you, Alice, you wouldn't turn that down either. You're made of strong stuff, my girl.'

Cassandra smiled, the girl reminded her of herself at times, as she'd been when she was that age, wilful, strong, a determined sort. Nothing or no one would get in her way.

'Seeing as you've only got a couple of days before you leave, I think I should throw a little afternoon tea party for you here tomorrow. We can invite whoever you want. Maybe some of your hospital colleagues too?'

Alice nodded enthusiastically. 'Thank you,

Grandma,' she said rising from her seat to peck her grandmother on the cheek. 'About what time shall I tell them?'

'Three o'clock should be fine. How many are you thinking of asking?'

'Just a few nurses and one or two doctors if they're able to make it?'

Grandma nodded. 'Then leave it with me, I'll ask a few as well to make up the numbers, I'm sure Rose and Clyde will want to say farewell to you too.'

A sudden thought struck Alice, she'd been meaning to write a letter to Jonathan, maybe she'd better do it right now while her mind was on it. 'Grandma,' she said, 'would you mind if I wrote a letter to Jonathan?'

'No, go ahead, dear. All the writing materials you need are in the wooden bureau over there.'

Alice glanced in the direction of the polished wooden escritoire desk that sat in front of the open French window. She couldn't understand how often Grandma had a window or door open on a cold day, but she was one who liked to keep the house aired and loved her "fresh air" as she called it. She made her way over to the desk and drew out a chair before unlocking it and sitting down to pen a letter.

'I'll just go and see how Cook is getting on with dinner. Leave the letter on the bureau and I'll see it gets posted,' Grandma said as she wisely left Alice alone with her thoughts.

How should she begin? *My dearest Jonathan?* Did that sound as though she were being too familiar with him? After all, he hadn't even kissed her as yet. She didn't doubt for one second that had he not had to rush off to war like that, they would have spent his final few days getting to know one another. But how would she feel then? She might have been swept up in the romance of it all and wept her heart out at having being too involved with him.

Dear Jonathan, sounded much better in the circumstances.

She dipped the nib of the silver fountain pen into the bottle of ink and began to write:

Dear Jonathan,

I am so pleased to hear from my Uncle that you are together at a chateau hospital in Northern France. I hope that any injuries you might have are not too severe. I think about you often, though work is keeping me busy. Soon I am to set off for the Netley Hospital in Hampshire. I have a few days leave before then and Grandma is planning a small party at her home before I leave here. Don't worry, I will still keep in touch with you when possible.

Uncle Ernie is a kind man, I am so pleased you are together. He will lift your spirits for sure. He's very talented too. Ask him to show you his sketch books. He has been keeping me entertained in that way since I was a little girl. He never throws a sketch away and has books going back to when he was a young lad himself. I am sure he must be sketching busily away at the hospital.

I met with Eliza for tea the other day and I've promised to keep in touch with her too. She told me she plans to volunteer at one of the hospitals herself soon. She's a lovely young lady and I'm sure you must be very proud of her.

I need to close for now as I have to go home and pack my luggage ready to leave in case I end up getting called up earlier than expected, as happened to you!

One day I'm sure we'll meet again! Meanwhile, remember when you're looking at the moon at night that I'll be looking at the same one and thinking of you.

Fondest regards,

Alice

Alice slipped the folded parchment paper into an envelope, then she addressed it, locked the bureau and placed the letter on top of it. Smiling, she turned to leave the room and as she closed the door behind herself, a strong gust of wind blew in through the French doors causing the letter to fly through the air and fall on the floor between the bureau and a floral armchair. Later that evening, Grandpa took a glass of port in the drawing room as he did most evenings after work and he accidentally slid the envelope beneath his shoe under the armchair.

Grandma was so busy planning Alice's leaving party that she forgot all about posting the letter. If it had remained on top of the bureau and the French doors shut then her eye would have caught it. Alice, herself, thought no more of the letter as she was busy getting ready to go to Netley on a new adventure.

Chapter Eleven

Wakeford April 1878

Another half an hour passed quite amicably in the drawing room of Marshfield Manor as Cassandra chatted away with Prudence as Harry and Tobias spoke animatedly with one another stood by the fireplace, recounting tales of days gone by at the coal pit. Then, quite suddenly, the large oak doors flew open, startling both ladies and the men looked taken aback as the butler entered then he bowed and declared, 'Mr and Mrs James Wilkinson!'

Cassandra stifled a suppressed giggle that was threatening to emerge behind her white gloved hand. Even when she resided at the house with his lordship things were seldom that formal. It wasn't that the Wilkinsons were any kind of nobility, they'd just accrued a fine fortune over the years which had all come from Josiah Wilkinson's grandfather, Hubert, when he'd been left a small lead mine. He'd worked hard and the money accrued there had gone into several more lead mines and pits dotted around the area. Which went to show that although class was a big issue regarding fortune in Great Britain, sometimes, a little luck and hard work could pay off for the lower classes. Unusual, yes, but not totally unknown.

It seemed an age as if the drawing room scene was frozen in time as the guests waited for their hosts. Then, James Wilkinson appeared with Charlotte as he held her gloved hand high and with a flourish of his other hand, he introduced his wife. Harry, of course, already knew of her, though had not encountered her all that much when he visited the house. Indeed, he refrained from saying too much about Charlotte to his wife as he realised that Cassandra had formed the opinion that she was "well above her station" and that there was some kind of reverse snobbery going on. It seemed to her that the woman was just out to impress and show off, and by the exquisite amethyst coloured gown Charlotte wore this evening, it really did seem the case.

I bet she's had that model from a French designer! Cassandra lowered her eyelids. She glanced across at Prudence whose eyes appeared to have enlarged at the sight of the woman. Charlotte was beautiful on the outside but to Cassie she appeared ugly on the inside. And no amount of sweet talking was going to change that, she'd remembered what the villagers had said about how she loved to show her face at certain charitable events in the area, paying lip service to it all. Yet, what had she really done for those charities? Absolutely nothing. And to keep her guests waiting like she had for three quarters of an hour was rudeness itself.

Cassandra gritted her teeth as she forced a smile then she heard her husband, who had now stepped forward saying, *"Enchanté!"* as he took Charlotte's gloved hand and placed a kiss upon it. *"Enchanté!"* Indeed. Harry never even said such a thing to his own wife. Then he turned in her direction and said, 'Please let me introduce my wife, Cassandra!'

Charlotte smiled though Cassandra noticed it did not quite reach her eyes. 'Pleased to meet you,' said Charlotte with a glint in her eyes. 'I've heard *so* much about you!'

What on earth did she mean by that? Before Cassandra could think of a suitable retort, her husband said, 'All good I trust?'

Charlotte laughed but didn't answer the question directly, instead she added, 'Yes, there are so many stories flying around and about, especially when you once lived here. Of course, you'll find the house has changed a lot since your days here. The décor is very tasteful now.'

Cassandra felt as though she'd been bitten by the sharp fangs of a poisonous snake and venom was coursing around in her veins. Straightening her poise, she said, 'Yes, my late husband liked to keep the décor here as in the tradition of his father and forefathers of nobility.' She forced another smile.

LYNETTE REES

Charlotte stuck her chin in the air. 'That's all very well but when decorating a house it needs some love and attention and to keep abreast of modern times otherwise it may look a little neglected, shall we say? Uncared for?'

Why on earth was this woman goading her? How she'd love to slap that pretty little face of hers but that would be playing right into her hands. Tonight was going to prove an unsufferable, boring event for her, but nevertheless, she recognised that she had to play the game as a new three-way partnership between the men was at stake here. If she upset Charlotte then the woman might well persuade her husband to dissolve the partnership he already had with Harry. She seemed to create a lot of sway with James, any fool could see he adored his wife.

Charlotte turned her attentions on Prudence and Tobias, congratulating them on their recent marriage, then she took Pru to one side to have a chat with her thereby excluding Cassandra, who instead stood at the fireplace chatting with the men. In essence, she was more like them and felt more at home with them as she was a business person herself, not someone who sat at home in fine dresses entertaining the rich. She'd once done all of that and had got sick of it when she'd been married to his lordship. Yes, it was true, this house from the inside was barely recognisable from when she'd lived here and yet, it wasn't really all that long ago. Tobias caught her eye for a moment as James and Harry chatted.

'Are you all right?' he asked with a flicker of concern in his eyes. She'd seen that look before when he'd saved her from the clutches of Anthony Fairley that time she'd been alone with him when he'd suddenly returned to the schoolroom as she'd been about to lock up. If Tobias hadn't shown up when he had and threatened the man, who knows what might have occurred.

'Yes, I'm fine, thank you,' she lowered her voice. 'I appreciate your concern though.'

James had now taken her husband over to the bookcase where he slid out a large tome and was showing something of interest in it to Harry.

'She's a real tartar that one,' Tobias chuckled. 'Don't take any notice of her. She's all fur cape and no pantaloons!'

Cassandra burst out laughing at Tobias's description of their hostess. 'Oh, I have missed you!' She blurted out suddenly as she placed her hand on his shoulder and immediately stepped away as if she'd just burned herself—it felt too intimate, especially with their spouses in the room.

Tobias gazed into her eyes for the longest time and then breaking the silence said, 'I really appreciate what you did for my mother, Cassie.'

It seemed strange him calling her that as Harry never called her Cassie only Cassandra.

It seemed sometimes as though there were two sides to her. The Cassie working class woman and proud of it and the Cassandra Lady of Wakeford. Now in this house and being put in her place by Charlotte and reminded of the wealth she'd once had but lost, she felt like Cassie again. Her real self.

'That's all right, Tobias,' she said smiling. 'I like your mother a lot. She's been good to me so I was only returning the favour.'

He shook his head vehemently. 'No, you were not,' he said strongly. 'I know you and you have gone above and beyond to look out for her. It's in your nature.'

For a moment, it felt as though they were the only two people in the room as she looked at the flames of the fire reflected in his eyes and saw the passion in them. But what kind of passion was it really? Was it still a flame that burned brightly for her? Or was it all about his new dealings with the pit? Or even about his marriage to Prudence who seemed ever such a nice person. And indeed, would she ever find out? For things could not go on the way as they had before he left for America.

Life had changed for the both of them and to some extent, she mourned the passing away of their previous friendship.

***

Dinner turned out to be a lavish affair in the candlelit dining room. There were several courses in all and a different wine served up with each sumptuous dish. There were cheese-stuffed mushrooms as an aperitif followed by: chestnut fennel soup, and then a wilted spinach salad with warm apple cider and bacon dressing, the main course was pork tenderloins with seasonal vegetables, this was followed by a decadent light chocolate pudding with vanilla ice cream and finally, cheese and biscuits with copious cups of coffee. The dinner lasted almost two hours and although the ladies tried their best, none could keep up with the appetites of their menfolk.

Cassandra thought Charlotte was definitely making too much of an effort to impress, but why? Was it because she realised Tobias was now on the way to making his fortune? After all, if the woman disliked her that much, who else was there to impress? Prudence? Harry? It was then she realised how vulnerable Charlotte must feel to go to all this bother on their behalf. There was no substance behind her well-to-do façade. She had little education and after all, had done little with her life too.

She feels threatened by me for some strange reason! But why? I'm not after her husband and I now no longer have any claim on this house. She's jealous! She's spiteful towards me as she fears me for some reason.

Whatever the reason was, Cassandra wasn't going to get to the bottom of it tonight. Though when she had a chance at home she was going to probe her husband to see if he knew the reason why.

Breaking into her thoughts after the dinner, Tobias took her to one side and whispered, 'Can you meet me outside on the terrace in around ten minutes? Just make some sort of excuse to leave the room and I'll follow you shortly afterwards, there's something I need to ask you.'

Feeling her cheeks blaze, she hoped no one had noticed his approach, but everyone was too busy chatting, Charlotte to Prudence and her husband to James. What on earth did Tobias want to ask her? She hoped he no longer had designs upon her though if she were being truthful with herself, she had to admit there was still some chemistry there between them. The next ten minutes seemed to lag as every so often, she glanced at the clock on the mantelpiece and finally, the hands reached a quarter to ten. Was it really that late? She hadn't been up so late in ever such a long time. Spotting a maid stood in the corner holding a tray of sherry, she asked her where the powder room was.

The young girl who was probably around sixteen years of age, dipped her knee and said, 'It's just down the corridor, ma'am, to the right.' Of course she knew where it was as she'd once lived in the house and it was unlikely to have moved but she needed to cover herself, to show she needed to leave the room for a good reason and if asked the maid could back her up. From the far corner of the room, Charlotte lifted her head and stared in her direction. So she'd definitely noticed her ask the maid something. Turning her back on the maid, Cassandra quietly left the room but to her dismay, the maid was now trailing her, minus the tray.

'It's just down there, ma'am,' she called after her.

'Thank you,' Cassandra said waving her away with her hand. 'I'm sure I'll find it.'

The maid though stood looking on, so she had to enter the water closet and remain in there for some time, then finally, she peeked out through the door, and to her relief the girl had departed, so she made her way out to the terrace outside through a partially open door.

Relief flooded through her to see Tobias, head down pacing back and forth with his hands behind his back. Oh dear, he seemed a little anxious which was so unlike him. He lifted his head when he noticed her approach.

'What did you want to see me about?' she asked breathlessly as her heart beat quickened and her mouth began to feel dry.

He stepped forward and for a moment, she had a feeling he was going to sweep her up in his arms, but instead, he said, 'My mother has told me all about Sophia, my daughter. I was wondering what she's like and if I should try to pay a visit?'

Cassandra shook her head. 'Oh, please don't do that. She's well settled now with Rose and Clyde.'

131

LYNETTE REES

'That bumbling oaf!' he chuckled. 'Sorry, I shouldn't have said that, it's unforgivable of me, especially as...'

'Especially as what?'

'Especially as he's been more of a father to her than I have.'

Cassandra could hear the pain in his voice. 'You had your chance, you might have married Rose.'

'I know, but I didn't love her. You know who I really loved and she wouldn't have me!'

Cassandra's heartbeat quickened. 'It would never have worked out between us, Tobias,' Cassandra said sharply. 'You're married now and I think you ought to stay away from Sophia, and Rose too. You're married and one day you'll have more children.'

He shook his head, 'Sadly, Prudence can't carry any children.'

'What do you mean?'

'The doctor told her that her womb is ineffective. There is some sort of medical term for it which I can't remember now. But sadly, she'll never bear a child for us.'

'I'm so sorry to hear that,' she drew closer to him and took him in her arms as he wept.

'So, you knew of this before you married her?'

'No,' he sniffed. 'I feel she has deceived me!'

'But surely you don't marry someone just because they can provide you with children? For instance, if I had gone to America with you like you asked me to, I don't know if I'd have wanted any more children!' She retorted angrily, not realising she was now raising her voice.

'Sssh,' he said, closing the space between them. He placed a finger on her lips. 'You know what you and I had was special. It would not have mattered that much to me, a child with you would have been nice, but not essential.' She swallowed hard. 'That's how much I wanted you...'

Tobias removed his finger from her lips and she looked up at him to see his glistening eyes. 'We'd better return before we're missed,' she said softly.

He nodded and she wondered if he was silently crying because he couldn't have her. 'Yes, you go ahead,' he whispered. 'I know all I need to know. I'll follow on in a few minutes.'

She smiled and turning her back on him, headed back indoors. What neither of them noticed was the young maid eavesdropping behind a bush. Her mistress had sent her to find out what was going on.

Chapter Twelve

Northern France May 1915

The following week, Moira made it to the chateau hospital to visit Ernest. He was delighted to see her. Arrangements had been made with Matron for her to stay in the nurses' quarters for a few days, though she was not expected to work as she was taking several leave days. Ernest and Moira spent their days walking around the large grounds and picnicking in the nearby woods where there was a large lake. Though they were warned by officials not to stray any further in case they accidentally wandered into enemy territory. How delightful it was for the both of them to hear the birds in the trees, see the sun rise and set and to feel safe in their own little world. Ernie found himself drawing close to Moira and by the third day, he had taken her hand as they walked along with a wicker basket towards the woods. She had looked up at him and smiled and he felt his heart skip a beat. He never wanted this feeling to end, ever.

When she laid the tartan rug on a nice clear spot just behind the lake, shielded by pine trees, he knelt beside her and before they knew it they were kissing one another. Oh, it felt good to feel someone so soft and vulnerable in his arms instead of a wounded soldier crying out for his mother. Moira smelled of honeysuckle and jasmine and he sensed a strong stirring for her. 'You know there's a possibility that you and I might not come out of this war alive?' he whispered.

She nodded as he stared at her Revlon painted shiny lips and then he was lying on top of her probing that beautiful sweet mouth and she wasn't resisting at all. It wasn't the first time for him. Although Ernest had never had a serious girlfriend, he had been with one or two women of a nefarious nature that he'd have been ashamed to take home to his parents. They had served a purpose as he was a man after all. Gilbert, though, hadn't taken the same path. He'd been fortunate to meet the love of his life as a young man and had remained with her ever since, though Ernest guessed that maybe his brother had been tempted a time or two.

Now, he was running his hand up and down Moira's leg as she gasped wantonly. Was she a virgin he wondered? To be honest, he didn't much care whether she was or not, he just had to have her but needed to be gentle if he was taking her virginity. And before they both knew it, he was fumbling with his trouser buttons and she was removing her silk underwear and then he was inside her, moving up and down as she moved her hips below him in a rhythmic fashion. She seemed to know what she was doing, so he relaxed. For a time all thoughts of war and death left him, there was no battlefield, no enemy, only peace and love as he planted his seed inside of her and both of them lay gasping on the ground, spent, but happy and carefree.

**

It was now June and Cassandra and Harry were having a drink in the drawing room one evening, when Harry got out of his favourite chair and putting down his glass of port on a nearby occasional table said, 'This armchair's feeling a bit wobbly of late, maybe one of the castors is working loose…'

He pushed it a little backwards and was about to tip it up to check as he knelt on the floor when something white caught his eye. 'What's this?' He slid it towards him and standing, showed it to his wife. 'It appears to be a letter of some kind, unopened at that. It's addressed to someone called "Jonathan" at the same chateau hospital in France as our Ernest!'

'Oh, my goodness!' Cassandra's hands flew to her face. 'A few weeks back before Alice left for Netley, she wrote a letter and I told her I'd post it for her, but as everything was so busy, I was planning the leaving party for her at the time, I totally forgot about it. I thought she'd left it on the writing bureau. I'm sure if she had I would have spotted it and remembered. I can't imagine how it got under your armchair!'

'It's quite simple,' Harry smiled. 'You're always leaving windows open, I expect a gust blew it on the floor and it somehow ended up getting pushed under my chair. I'll put things right and go and post it this very moment. Poor Jonathan will think Alice has forgotten all about him!'

His wife nodded gratefully. 'I should hate that to happen. The sooner he receives it the better, though in a few weeks anything might have happened, he might even have been sent back to The Front.'

'I know, my dear. Let's hope it wings its way to him in time. Those men need all the morale boosting they can possibly get. What did Ernest say about him in his last letter, I've forgotten?'

'I've got it here.' She rose and unlocked a drawer in the writing bureau and extracted a few envelopes all tied together with a red ribbon. She had written as often as she could to Ernest and had received four replies so far, although she continued to write to Gilbert too, up until now, there had been no word and that bothered her. Swallowing down her grief that one son was obviously missing, though there was no official word as yet, she studied the date marks on the envelopes and selected the most recent and chose a three-page letter that was elegantly written in his stylish penmanship dotted with little cartoon drawings here and there. 'I'll read the part where he speaks of Jonathan.

Jonathan's condition is improving daily though he still has to see the hospital psychiatrist and will be assessed soon to see if he is well enough to return to active service, if not, then it's expected that he may return to Great Britain to finish off his convalescence. Although physically, he appears to be much better, I do however fear for his mental state as there are days when he just sits in the corner and seems in a world of his own. The horrors of this war are so hard for some to take.

She paused and trembling with tears in her eyes looked at her husband. 'This war is dreadful, isn't it? It's taken our men and boys away from us, and for what?'

Harry nodded slowly. 'Ernie is a strong character though, Cassandra. Remember what he was like when he was born? He almost died at birth but he obviously has a fighting spirit inside him.'

'Yes, you're right about that. But what about Gilbert? There's still no word from him and I hate the thought of our boys being parted, Harry.'

Harry drew near to her and took her in his arms as she wept. 'Who knows where he is right now, but we must conclude, at least for time being that no news is good news until we hear otherwise.'

Cassandra swallowed a sob, knowing in her heart that her husband was absolutely right. Tomorrow she was going to visit Emily, her eldest child, at least she was still close to home.

***

Emily and her mother were seated in the rambling garden behind Trevelyan House. The roses were in bloom in fragrant shades of scarlet red and, soft white and a jaunty yellow which was pleasing to the eye. Gazing around, Cassandra realised her only daughter had done well for herself. She'd always been ahead of her particular age group at school and her teachers had noted this from a young age that she'd go far someday. As a result, Emily had trained as a doctor like her aunt, but Emily was working full time. She'd never had children of her own and her parents had never questioned this. It felt too personal a question to ask.

'So, you mean to say there is still no word of Gilbert?' Emily poured some homemade lemonade into two long ice-filled tumblers and added a sprig of mint to each.

Her mother shook her head. 'Sadly, no. The latest word from Ernie is that he's heard absolutely nothing at all since being transferred to the chateau hospital in Northern France.'

'I see,' said Emily setting down the large glass jug on the dark green wrought iron table. 'Cake, mother?' Emily pushed a slice of Victoria sponge cake towards her mother.

Cassandra waved a hand as if to indicate no, but Emily directed it further towards her mother. 'Look, I know you're upset about this as indeed we all are, but Mother, you must eat.'

Cassandra forced a smile, the truth was she felt so helpless with both her sons on foreign shores and a granddaughter miles away in a military hospital, at least she had Emily though. Emily's husband, Benjamin Smallbrook, was a well-respected lawyer whose services were very much in demand. Nevertheless, he had indicated that he might well go and serve overseas and Cassandra dreaded the thought that he might take Emily along with him for her surgical skills.

'Well at least for time being, no news is good news,' said Emily sagely.

Her mother smiled. 'Do you know, that's exactly what your father said to me only last night.'

'It's just something people say I suppose...' Emily shrugged, 'but it is true as you haven't been informed otherwise. There's been no telegram sent to Marissa as yet.'

Her mother supposed that was true and until they knew any better, they just had to hope for the best. 'That is some comfort for time being, at least.' She took a sip of the cool lemonade and set her glass down once again. 'Have you heard from Milly?'

Emily smiled and it warmed Cassandra's heart to know she did absolutely the right thing years ago in accepting the child as her first husband's love child, into their home. It wasn't exactly easy at first realising he'd been cheating on her with the barmaid from The Crown and Feathers so soon after their marriage and that his daughters were born just weeks apart. Emily first and then Milly a fortnight later. But it all made sense as it was after the wedding night when he'd taken her forcefully in the marriage bed that he never went near her again. It had been a relief at the time. Over the years, the half-sisters had formed a close bond. These days, Milly was happily married herself and living in Drisdale with her husband who was a carpenter by trade. Milly stayed at home to keep house and care for their three children. Her mother, Jess, had married a good man who'd taken on the child as his own.

'Yes, she's coming over for Sunday dinner tomorrow with all the family.'

Cassandra folded her hands beneath her chin, with her elbows on the table, to gaze at her only daughter. 'That's lovely.'

Emily frowned. 'Oh, I didn't think of inviting you and Father, would you like to come?'

Her mother chuckled. 'No, indeed. You literally have enough on your plate and it will be nice for you to spend some time with Milly.'

'Very well. How's Alice settling at the Netley Hospital?'

'Good by the sound of it. She's keeping busy. She told us in her last letter that she won't get a full day off for another fortnight, so we're going to visit her then. She's been speaking about "the talking cures" that are going on there, by all accounts, it's doing wonders for some of the traumatised men.'

'That's interesting,' said Emily. 'I'm glad that something is being done for those men. It seems to me that the mind is as important as the body, so it all makes sense.'

'From what she said about one poor fellow he was traumatised from having to shoot at the enemy and he actually killed a young German soldier. She said every time he drifted off to sleep he'd see the soldier's eyes staring at him!'

'How dreadful!'

'Anyhow, the doctor there as well as using talking therapy has been getting him to relive the event with a real rifle, not loaded of course, and re-enacting the scene with someone dressed up in German military uniform. The idea was to demonstrate to the man that he had little choice and was in fact, a hero, as his action had saved several lives.'

***

After leaving the chateau hospital, following a few days break on returning to the casualty clearing station at Ypres, Moira was later dispatched back home after discovering she was pregnant. The Front was deemed a most unsuitable place for a pregnant woman. Moira made the difficult decision to keep the news of her pregnancy from Ernest. After all, what would the point be? He might be forced back to The Front to fight for his country. So instead, she intended at some point to write to inform him that she'd been sent to work at a hospital back in Britain and would continue to correspond with him whilst she still had his address at the hospital in France, but if he should be moved from there, she'd appreciate a forwarding address as a point of contact. The thing that bothered Moira was how people would react to the fact she was unwed and with child. Her father had passed away some years since, so her mother after being told the news, sensibly suggested she go to stay with her aunt and uncle in the country, which was far away from Moira's family home in London. It would create some "breathing space". And who knew? If the war suddenly ceased as many hoped it would, then Ernest would be informed of the situation and hopefully, he'd make Moira his wife.

***

It was more than three months since Moira had visited Ernest at the chateau hospital. Parting had been, in the words of Mr Shakespeare, "Such sweet sorrow" for them both. They had clung on to one another in the hospital grounds as a military truck lay in wait ready to whisk Moira back to The Front. At the same time, several of the recovered soldiers at the hospital would be taking a ride in that truck too, including Jonathan and Angus. Although Jonathan seemed fit and well, Ernie had concerns for the young man going back into the situation that had caused his neurotic behaviour in the first place. He also realised that no word from his niece, Alice, had impeded the young man's recovery. He'd since learned in a letter from his mother that a letter Alice had penned had somehow got misplaced and only recently posted. Ernest had taken it upon himself to ask the people in charge of the mail room to watch out for it and to give it priority should it show up with a view to forwarding it to Jonathan at The Front. Whether he'd receive it or not was quite another thing but at least, Ernest felt he'd have tried his best to help the situation.

The following day, early in the morning, an order was sent for himself and three other privates to be interviewed in the commanding officers' boardroom. There, he sat in front of a group of people which included military officials, doctors and nurses. The interview was thorough as he was bombarded with questions, 'Do you think yourself fit enough to return to combat?', 'Do you think you are of sound mind?', 'What's your view of this war?', 'What date is it today?', 'Who is the prime minster of Great Britain?' By the time they'd had a break half way through, it was evident to Ernest that they were testing his state of mind. Of course, he didn't want to return to The Front and keep fighting, not now he could see the soldiers were being used as fodder to feed the enemy. But if he returned then at least he might have a chance to see Moira again as he'd received no word from her, and that alone,

made him decide to declare himself fit enough to
return to active duty.

***

Cassandra had received a letter from Alice:

Dearest Grandma,

*Thank you so much for forwarding Jonathan's
letter. I am glad he is getting on so well and is with
Uncle Ernest. My hope is that he'll now receive it and
it's not too late. I do hope he doesn't think that I
don't care for him because nothing could be further
from the truth…*

As she read the letter, Cassandra bit her
bottom lip and tears welled up in her eyes. Oh,
it wasn't really her fault that the letter had
got mislaid, no one was blaming her, but if
she hadn't been so busy with that going away
party for Alice, her mind wouldn't have become
distracted and she'd have posted that precious
letter. Now she felt like she'd let down both Alice
and Jonathan, who she'd never even met.

*I met another Netley girl called Bronwen at the
station when I arrived here. She's from North Wales
and we drove up in her father's motorcar and sent
the two lots of boxes on the cab that came to meet
me! Matron met me at the hospital and although
seemingly fierce, deep down she is a good sort: firm
but fair.*

*I am sleeping in what is known as the Stalls. It is
a large room divided into eight sections and is just
across from the laundry which is useful, so you can
imagine there is no fear of my being cold at night*

with the heat that comes from there! They really are awfully nice stalls, and the bed is a very comfy one, but I'm so glad I had the electric torch with me that you gave me before I left as sometimes I need to pass from one block to another at night to use the conveniences and it's not very well lit!

I am in a ward known as B Ward with two other smaller wards attached to it called A and C. Yesterday, a regimental band played here and they also put on a variety show. There was a magician, a comedian, a couple of singers and a dancing troupe. All the patients were taken into the large day room where a make shift stage had been constructed. The ones that could not move were put on stretchers on the floor and the others were sat in chairs. They enjoyed themselves but sadly a few were in such a bad way that they couldn't make it to the show.

The new nurse, Bronwen, and I, only saw a small part at the end as we had a lot of dressings to prepare, and Matron apologised but she said we were needed in the treatment room. From the hoots of laughter and cheering we heard, it must have been an amazing performance. The Tommies were kept entertained and I'm sure it has boosted morale.

How are you both getting on? I hope all is well in Wakeford?

Your loving granddaughter,

Alice.

PS: Looking forward to seeing you both when you pay a visit soon!

Cassandra sniffed and swallowed as she gazed

at the letter in Alice's familiar penmanship through misted eyes, how she missed her only granddaughter and wished she were here right now. Her presence would help put soothing balm on the internal pain she felt at both sons fighting overseas and the knowledge that one of them might be wounded or even dead. This not knowing what had happened to Gilbert was slowly killing her.

***

It had been decided that Ernest was to become an ambulance driver instead of returning to the trenches for time being. If all went well, then in a month or so he'd return to active duty but for time being he helped the stretcher bearers load up his vehicle and as fast as possible he transported the wounded to the casualty clearing station at Ypres. This was ideal for him as now he thought he would be reunited with Moira. He had fallen for her fast and hard, that's what war did for you as for tomorrow, there were no guarantees what that day would bring, if it brought anything at all.

After dropping off his first patients which was a young lad who had shrapnel wounds and an older man who he suspected had trench foot, he went in search of Moira. He was pleased with himself that he'd been able to reassure the young soldier that his wounds would soon heal as he'd had the same thing happen to him. The older man though, it was harder to reassure as everyone knew that trench foot as it was termed, more often than not led to an amputation.

He caught a nursing sister, who had just emerged from a tent through the double flaps. She smiled when she saw him. 'Can I help you, private?'

'Yes please, Sister. I'm now working as an ambulance driver until I can return to the trenches, you see I had shrapnel wounds which were treated...' he paused.

She raised a concerned brow. 'And they're not healing?'

'Oh, no, nothing like that,' he waved his hand. 'They've healed very well. It's just that when I was here I met a nurse called, Moira, who was ever so kind to me.'

The sister's eyes seemed to cloud over at the mention of Moira's name. 'Moira Watkins, you mean?' she sniffed loudly.

Something was wrong, he could feel it. 'Y... yes.'

'She's no longer here,' she said curtly.

'But why ever not? Has something happened to her?'

'Er, not exactly. She's not ill or anything like that. Look,' she paused and then as if thinking better of it laid a reassuring hand on his shoulder, 'I'm not really at liberty to tell you but I will say this, she's perfectly well and she has returned to England, I was under the impression she'd written to a friend to say she was back home, but if that person was you, maybe you didn't receive her letter?'

Ernest felt his heart sink down into his muddy boots, he shook his head. 'No, I've not received anything from her at all. England? How can that be?' In one way he was glad that now she'd be safe from all harm but in another, he couldn't bear it if he never spoke to her again.

The sister sighed, then taking him by the arm, she led him into another tent which he recognised as the one he'd once found Moira in when she'd been looking for laundry. 'I can't say too much as I might get into trouble for it...' she whispered.

Ernest's eyes grew large and he swallowed hard. 'Trouble?'

'Quite what was Moira to you, Private, er..?'

'Hewitt. Private Ernest Hewitt, ma'am. Moira is my sweetheart, she came to visit me at the chateau hospital a couple of months ago.'

The sister nodded knowingly. 'Then I shall tell you as it is in your best interests to know but you haven't heard a word from me, understood?'

He nodded. 'Of course. I just want to know what's happened and where she is so I might contact her.'

'This might come as a shock to you but Moira is pregnant and I'm guessing the child is yours?'

Ernest nodded blankly. 'Y...yes. But I didn't know she was pregnant?'

'Well, she is. Once she found out, for obvious

reasons she couldn't remain on The Front, it's far too dangerous for a pregnant woman. So a decision was made for her to return home.'

'I see,' said Ernest shaking his head. 'Please, do you have a forwarding address for her?'

'I do, Private Hewitt. I have to go now as we'll be setting up for an operation shortly, I'll jot down Moira's address for you and when you're here next, I'll pass it on.'

'Thank you, Sister. Sorry, what's your surname?'

'Sister Shaw.' She smiled at him in a reassuring manner and then she turned on her heel and was gone.

Moira pregnant though? He could hardly believe that. She was pregnant with his child. He didn't realise it would be so easy to get someone pregnant, he always believed it took a lot of time. Gilbert and his wife had tried for ages for Alice. The truth was after that time he'd made love to Moira in the woods, he'd remembered that day with such love and fondness for her that a possible pregnancy was the farthest thing from his mind.

'Oi, Ernie!' Tom, one of the stretcher bearers, summoned him. 'Come on, we need to get back for the rest of the casualties.

Ernest nodded. Who knew what deaths and injuries they'd see by the end of the day? One thing was for certain, it was still a hundred times better than being in those awful trenches.

Chapter Thirteen

Wakeford April 1878

As the guests were departing from the dinner party and Charlotte and James were waving them off from the top step, the young maid hovered behind the pair, then as the final coach pulled away from the drive, Charlotte turned and stared at the girl whilst her husband left them to speak with the butler.

'What is it, Martha?' Charlotte asked, she wasn't in the mood to deal with anything right now as it had been an exhausting evening as she'd presented her best self to them all. That Cassandra one had irked her quite a lot during the evening as she seemed so calm and self-assured, almost like one of the men as she'd spent most of the evening chatting with them, instead of making herself more available to her and Prudence. Prudence, though, she'd found amicable enough, if not a little dull at times.

The maid dipped her knee and speaking in hushed tones mumbled something that sounded like *"Were near the bushes, ma'am..."*

Charlotte frowned. 'Speak up, girl. Please stop mumbling.'

The girl's face reddened as she tried to form the words that appeared to be difficult for her to say. 'Ma'am, you asked me to keep an eye on Mrs Hewitt...'

'I did indeed. So?' Charlotte folded her arms across her chest as she glared at Martha.

Martha's mouth dried as she tried to formulate the words, realising this could put her in the mistress's favour for some time to come. 'So, ma'am, when she went to visit the powder room, I followed her when she came out and she ended up walking to the terrace near the bushes...'

What on earth was the girl telling her this for? 'So? Maybe she was trying to cool off as it was quite a warm evening.' Charlotte made to turn away as she had plenty to do, she needed to thank Cook for the fantastic evening and to tell the housekeeper she wanted the dining room well cleaned by morning.'

'But ma'am...' Martha persisted. 'It's what happened after that what I was coming to...'

Charlotte immediately turned back to face the girl. 'And?' She arched an interested eyebrow.

'Mr Beckett was already there as if he'd been waiting for her and they were deep in an interesting conversation that I think you should know about.'

Charlotte smiled. This was delicious news for her and her eyes glinted with mischief. 'So, what was their conversation about?'

Martha appeared to hold a breath and then

released it, almost as though this information was too hard for her to hold on to any longer, she was excited by it. 'Mr Beckett went out to the terrace as if she was expecting him and then...'

'And then what?' Charlotte drew in nearer to the girl.

'And then, Mr Beckett asked Mrs Hewitt something about a child he has over here. A little girl called, Sophia...'

'I didn't know he had any children!' Charlotte's eyes widened.

'But that's not all, he asked if he might see her and Mrs Hewitt didn't seem to think that a good idea. He mentioned that he hadn't loved the child's mother named, Rose, but that there had been someone he'd loved and he'd wanted to take her to America with him.'

Charlotte Wilkinson was on tenterhooks now, drawn in by Martha's dramatization of the whole situation. 'But who was this person? Did he say?'

'Er, not exactly, ma'am, but it became obvious that he was speaking of Mrs Hewitt and he drew very close to her. I thought he was going to kiss her but she suggested they go inside.'

'Very interesting,' said Charlotte. 'Very interesting indeed.'

'That's not all though, ma'am...'

'You mean there's more, Martha?'

Martha nodded. 'I heard Mr Beckett say his wife couldn't have any children and that he didn't find out until after they'd wed.'

'Martha,' said Charlotte, 'you've done very well tonight, thank you. When is your next full day off?'

'Not until next month, ma'am.'

'As you've given me that information I'm going to give you a whole day off this Saturday on the proviso you say nothing of this information to anyone else, understood?'

Martha dipped her knee again. She understood all right and would not be so foolish as to break the mistress's trust in her. 'No, ma'am, I most certainly will not and thank you for allowing me a full day off but what shall I tell the other staff about that day off, they might think it's odd.'

'Leave that to me, I'll have a word with Mrs Bailey, she draws up the rosters. I'll think of some sort of cover story for you.'

'Thank you, ma'am.'

'Now perhaps you can go and help Cook in the kitchen as there's a lot of clearing up to be done and tell her I'll be along shortly to have a word with her. She did a splendid job this evening.'

'Very well, ma'am.'

Charlotte watched the young maid head off in the direction of the kitchen then, she, herself, walked off with a spring in her step. It had been a magnificent evening which had just got even better.

***

It was a few days following the dinner party when Cassandra attended a special charity afternoon with her mother-in-law, Edna, in Drisdale at the local church hall. It had been set up by her husband and James Wilkinson to honour the widows and orphans of the area. It was something Harry had now insisted on doing once a year in memory of his father. William Hewitt had been a benevolent sort towards members of the community and he had a particular affiliation for widows and orphans which Cassandra found totally ironic when he'd gone after the Widow Lizzie Butterworth and produced his own "orphan" in Clyde. But, nevertheless, she didn't say so to Harry nor to Edna. They both had their own individual crosses to bear regarding that fellow.

The church hall was buzzing when they arrived. There were tables set out selling all sorts of arts and crafts: beautifully embroidered tray cloths, paintings by local artists, knitted garments, rag dolls, dolls' clothing, wooden toys and there was even a gentleman who was in the process of cutting out silhouettes of folk using black card and a scissors as they posed in a chair beside him. Then afterwards, upon their approval, he placed their black silhouette mounted on white card, in a silver-edged frame, for a fee of course.

At the far end of the hall was a long table set up which sold refreshments. Polly and Jess were manning that along with Aunt Bertha. The tea room had been closed for the afternoon and now all the stock of scones, French fancies, currant buns, iced slices and apple tarts were being sold to eager customers. While Jess dished out the cakes, Polly manned the tea urn and coffee pot whilst Aunt Bertha's job was to pour the homemade lemonade from a couple of large jugs at the end of the table. All appeared to be going well, so Cassandra whisked Edna over to the silhouette artist and asked her to pose for a portrait as she'd love to buy one for her husband as a surprise.

Edna beamed with pride. 'Cassandra, that is most kind of you. I would be honoured of course, but only if you allow me to pay for you to have your future told!' she insisted.

Cassie startled for a moment, she hadn't noticed the gypsy fortune teller who had a curtained area set up in the corner of the hall. In fact, she was surprised the vicar had allowed her to be there at all. But wasn't it all supposed to be in good fun to raise funds for the widows and orphans of the parish? It wasn't that she objected to having her fortune read of course, but it reminded her of that time when Mrs Beckett had read her tea leaves and been very accurate indeed. Besides, she didn't want to upset Edna by turning the woman down, so she nodded and forced a smile. She paid the man a sixpence for Edna to have her portrait done and Edna slipped several coins into Cassie's palm for the fortune teller. 'See how good she is first, cross her palm with the silver sixpence to begin with,' she chuckled.

Nervously, Cassie made her way through the throng towards the gypsy's curtained off area. The young woman was well tanned and had the most amazing jade green eyes Cassie had ever seen. She was so pretty with her long dark hair that fell in waves on her shoulders. A natural beauty if ever there was one.

'May I have my fortune told, please?' Cassie asked nervously and the young woman beckoned her with her hand to go behind the curtain. Once behind the voluminous, billowing curtain that was adorned with half silver moons, stars and suns, she took a seat beside a small table on top of which was set a large crystal ball. She'd never actually set eyes on one before but she knew what it was as she'd once read a story in a romance book about one and there was an illustration of it.

The gypsy girl smiled and took a seat opposite her. 'My name *eez* Marina,' she spoke softly in an accent Cassie did not recognise and she wondered if it were real or if she was faking it. Still, it was all in a worthy cause, wasn't it?

'Now place your hands on *zee* magic crystal ball, *pleeze*,' she instructed, 'and then close your eyes, do not open *zem* yet. I want your thoughts to roam freely into *zee* universe…'

Cassie did what was asked of her and then she closed her eyes trying to blot out the sounds that were arising of folks' chatter from behind the curtain.

'*Zat eez* good,' said the girl. 'Now remove your hands and I will see what *zee* crystal ball has to tell you...'

Cassie nodded, then she handed the girl a silver sixpence to cross her palm.

'I see large whirlwind,' Marina said peering intently into the ball, 'it eez like tornado and *eez* heading your way!'

Cassie's eyes opened and she gasped as her hands flew to her chest as though she'd just suffered a heart attack. 'Oh, no!'

'Please don't alarm *zeeself*,' said Marina. '*Zee* magic crystal ball tells of things that may happen. It *eez* not definite...'

Cassie frowned. 'What do you mean?'

'What I mean *eez* that *zee* ball can foretell what happen not what definitely will. You have *zee* chance to change course of destiny *zeeself*.'

'Oh, I see,' said Cassie now relaxing.

'*Zee* tornado headed your way *eez* made by one person.'

'Really? But who?'

Marina shook her head. 'I have no name for you but it *eez* a woman of around your age. She has some power and she *eez* jealous of you. Avoid her at all costs if you are to survive *theez* whirlwind of energy she *eez* forcing on you. She *eez* out to destroy your life as she desires what you have.'

Cassie laughed nervously, this was all nonsense, but she found herself saying, 'Please continue.'

'I also see someone from overseas who has a yearning for you, an unrequited love.'

That made Cassie sit up straight in her seat. 'Yes, nothing has happened there.'

'I see *zat*,' said Marina as she raised her head to look directly into Cassie's eyes. 'He wants something to happen but you have resisted so far but you are in danger of falling under his spell once again...'

'So, you're telling me there are two people I need to avoid?'

'Yes, precisely. Now, it *eez* not all bad news for you. I see you doing very well in your career and you will climb ladder to top but won't happen for few years. I *zee* lots of children surrounding you, you work with *zem*?'

'Yes,' said Cassie feeling amazed the girl could see that. 'Yes I'm a ...'

'Please do not tell me, allow *zee* magic crystal ball to say what it sees through me...' The girl looked at her intently, then she gazed back into the confines of the ball. 'You are teaching *zees* children and they like you a lot.'

'Could the woman who is going to cause trouble for me be another teacher?' Cassie enquired.

'No, it is nothing to do with your teaching, *zee* woman *eeze* someone within the community who has how you say? Social standing. She likes to make impression on people but there *eeze* little substance to her.'

'I think I understand who that might be now,' said Cassie as an image of Charlotte came to mind.

'Avoid her at all costs,' said the gypsy girl. 'Then she slipped something into Cassie's hand. '*Eeze* a lucky charm of a black cat, carry it around with you always.' Marina smiled at her but now Cassie felt unsettled and she wished her mother-in-law had not sent her to have her fortune told at all. What utter nonsense!

By the time the session had finished, Edna could be seen admiring her portrait as Cassie approached. Peering over the woman's shoulder, Cassie said, 'He's caught you to a tee there, Edna.' And the artist had, he'd somehow managed to produce a silhouetted image with Edna's small button nosed features and tucked in chin with her feathered hat on top of her head.

Edna beamed. 'Yes, he has. I hope Harry will like it.'

'I'm sure he will,' smiled Cassie.

'How did the fortune telling go?' The woman's blue eyes sparkled mischievously.

How could she tell her she wished she hadn't gone to have her fortune told? She decided on a partial lie for time being to satisfy the woman's curiosity. 'Oh, it was the usual thing, travel and an unexpected visitor arriving!' She chuckled.

The truth was she'd already seen the unexpected visitor and she wouldn't be travelling with him any time soon.

Suddenly, Edna narrowed her eyes. 'I can't bear that woman!' She seethed as her gaze seemed focused on someone behind Cassie.

Cassie turned and noticed Charlotte entering with Prudence by her side. Now they appeared to be best friends of sorts. Charlotte seemed quite flighty with friends, she was always in different company as far as Cassie could tell, apart from one or two long-time friends. 'What is it about her you don't like?' Cassie whispered behind her gloved hand.

'Just something about her I don't trust,' sniffed Edna, 'the woman's poison. She flounces around these sort of charitable events like she's cock of the walk!'

Cassie nodded, realising she knew exactly what Edna meant.

Chapter Fourteen

French/Belgian Border June 1915

A narrow shaft of early morning sunlight projected in through a gap in the barn door as Gilbert raised his head and groaned and looked at the young soldier beside him who was still fast asleep on the hay. They'd both managed to escape the pursuing enemy when they went up over the trenches that day and fought on The Front. Both had got lost in the mist and mayhem that ensued as their comrades fell like a pack of dominoes all around them. Somehow in amongst all the shell fire, the threat of loaded bayonets and the smoky haze, they'd managed to find some sort of clearing, and headed towards it, where the fighting seemed to fade away behind them and then they were on an open road headed who knew where. All Gilbert knew for certain was that it would be foolhardy to try to get back to the trenches, that would mean certain death for the pair of them. So as soon as he noticed some approaching woodland, he decided they must take that route to keep them under cover from the enemy. It had been cool and shady in those woods and they were able to sit and rest near a mountain stream where they washed their faces and hands and simply drank the refreshing water which to them both was like nectar from the gods.

They'd slept for a while and then decided to make tracks, the young soldier, who he was to discover was named Davy Johnson, was limping slightly, so from time to time, Gilbert helped to support the lad by draping Davy's arm around his shoulder. They must have walked for a couple of miles before Gilbert smelled smoke and thinking there was a farmhouse nearby, became excited until he heard voices and in a clearing some two hundred yards away, noticed a group of German soldiers who had started a fire and were seated on the ground roasting sausages with a pitchfork over the flames. They appeared to be in a merry mood and he guessed with beating heart that they might be consuming alcohol too, so he'd quietly ushered Davy well away from the area but in their haste the lad had fallen and there was the sound of snapping twigs. Gilbert could speak fluent German as he had been taught Latin, French and German at Oxford. He heard one of them say in his mother tongue: 'What is that?'

Another then laughed and said, 'It's probably a forest animal, a deer or something like that!'

But the soldier had become spooked and wouldn't let it drop. 'I think we should check it out, Hans!' he declared standing and staring around the area with the palm of his hand to his forehead as if seeking out the offending creature.

'Harald, I think we might be able to get some venison!' another joked, but he did not see the funny side.

Gilbert held his index finger over his lips to warn Davy to remain as quiet as possible. After what seemed an age of holding his breath, Gilbert released it as one of the soldiers distracted Harald by saying, 'Look, we haven't much time, let's eat and get going!'

All the others murmured in agreement and then slowly, Gilbert and Davy walked away hidden behind bushes and trees being careful not to trip or fall over any broken branches or step on any twigs that might alert the enemy to their whereabouts. It seemed an age until they could no longer hear the German voices behind them and now darkness was falling fast and Gilbert had no idea where he was going. Then he spotted it in the distance, some sort of barn, they were nearing farmland. That would do to spend the night. Now geed on, he slapped Davy on the shoulder and led the way, excitement mounting with each step he took.

That barn had been their home for the past few weeks. The farmer didn't seem to be using it for some reason and it was well away from the farmhouse itself and other out buildings. They'd managed to survive the following weeks trapping hares and rabbits near the forest and even shot a couple of wood pigeons, there were also plenty of berries in the woods and Davy had discovered some sacks of oatmeal in the barn, no doubt being stored there for future use. They'd even managed to take a couple of eggs now and again from the henhouse, though not too many, not to arouse suspicion. And when once, Gilbert had daringly managed to milk one of the cows, when the family living in the farmhouse were asleep, they'd had milk for a day or two and cooked some oatmeal for breakfast. Although they had no sugar, they'd used some wild blueberries to sweeten it and Gilbert had to admit, it was the nicest breakfast he'd had in a long while.

Now though something was different, the narrow beam of light was getting wider. Someone was opening the barn door!

**

There, standing silhouetted in the doorway, was a young girl of around sixteen years old. She wore her long dark hair in two braids, coiled on both sides of her ears, on top of which was some kind of white linen cap. Her dress was of a blue-check sort, covered by a hessian apron. She stood frozen to the spot for a moment and her hands flew to her face. Fearing she might scream at the very shock of it all, Gilbert said softly as he raised both hands as if in enemy surrender. 'Please do not fear, we will not harm you...'

Then realising the girl might not speak English, he said, *'Excusez-moi, mademoiselle. Nous ne vous ferons pas de mal. Nous venons de dormir ici, c'est tout...'* He hoped he'd said to her to excuse him and they would not harm her but they had just been sleeping here. His French was a little rusty but it was the best he could do.

Whatever he'd said must have been correct or at least, she understood him as she nodded and stepping forward, closed the barn door behind herself as if realising they might be in danger if discovered. 'Ah, you are English,' she said as she took in their uniforms and her eyes caught Davy's. The poor lad wasn't much older than her.

'Yes, English soldiers,' said Davy. 'We got caught up in some cross fire at Ypres and managed to make it here through the woods but there were some German soldiers and I think if they'd caught us, we'd have been shot or taken as prisoners.'

She shook her head sadly. 'It is dangerous here. I work for the family and they not how you say, trustworthy. I think they may help the Germans. I not know for sure but a German officer was at the farmhouse just last night.'

Davy gulped and he exchanged glances with Gilbert. 'How often do they call at the farmhouse?'

'A couple of times a week, maybe. I think you need to leave here but go when it gets dark.'

'B...but where can we go? We don't even know

where it is safe.'

'I can help you,' said the girl smiling. I know of a place where it will be safer than here, but you must wait until nightfall, I'll be back then. Have you how do you say, *mange* today?'

'Eat you mean?' asked Gilbert. The girl nodded. 'No. Not yet, we only just woke up.'

'Then I will fetch you something,' she said.

'Please, what's your name?' asked Davy.

'It's Greta. I'll be right back with something for you. The farmer won't come to the barn today because he's off to market. I was just sent to fetch some eggs.'

They both thanked her and then Davy turned to Gilbert and whispered. 'Do you think we can trust her? What if she brings the farmer back with her or even German soldiers?'

Gilbert smiled. 'I think we can trust her. It seems evident to me she dislikes her employers and it is her who distrusts them.' Davy let out a breath of relief.

Greta was true to her word and returned later with two buttered baguettes of bread with thick slices of cured bacon inside and a pot of coffee with two tin mugs.

'Just leave the coffee pot and mugs inside the door and I'll fetch them later,' she reassured, 'it's best no one asks me where they are--that might arouse some suspicion.'

Gilbert nodded gratefully. The smell of the bacon was making his mouth water and the

167

aroma of the fresh roasted coffee was divine. It would be the best breakfast they'd had since that oatmeal with blueberries no doubt.

At the first sign of nightfall, Greta turned up with a man who had a cart. 'This is Louis,' she introduced. 'He will take you further into France as you are just on the border here, it will be safer for you.'

'But where will he take us?' Gilbert blinked.

Louis looked at him sternly. 'Please do not ask too many questions as we are both risking our lives for you. You will be taken to a safe house run by sympathetic French people.'

Gilbert nodded. 'I understand.'

'It is not safe here in Belgium but it will be safer in France for you. Here we are on the borderline, Greta and I are of French origin but the farmer and his wife are Flemish. It is our belief that they are spies for the German army. You are lucky it was Greta who found you and not them.'

Gilbert released a breath as he exchanged glances with Davy. 'I don't know how we'll ever be able to repay you both for your kindness,' said Gilbert gratefully.

'There is no need,' Louis said with a wave of his hand. 'It is payment enough for us that we help you escape, we've had enough of those pigs around here!' He spat on the ground. 'Now we better get going. You both need to get on the back of the cart under the tarpaulin and Greta will place some wicker baskets of fruit and vegetables on top of you in case we are stopped along the way.'

Gilbert and Davy both nodded and they shook hands with Greta, Davy then took her hand and held it to his lips as he looked at her. Gilbert smiled to himself as he could see the young lad was smitten with her. 'Now drop Greta's hand and let's be on our way!' he said jovially. Davy did as told and both of them clambered onto the back of the cart and pulled the tarpaulin over them, leaving a little space to breathe. They felt the baskets being loaded on top of them and then the cart started to move as it jerked forwards as the wooden wheels rumbled into motion. They were on their way but who knew where to? At least they were leaving a dangerous area behind them, thought Gilbert as he closed his eyes as he planned to sleep on the way in case he needed the energy later if they were suddenly stopped by the Germans and needed to run. He'd rather lose his life running away than be tortured for any information that would put the British Army at risk. He'd heard all about that, men being tortured, giving away valuable information under duress and then, losing their lives anyhow in front of a firing squad. It didn't bear thinking about.

***

Gilbert and Davy arrived at a "safehouse" in a French town two and a half hours later. They were not given the information of where they were taken to but they were looked after by a French married couple, who ensured they were well fed and had proper beds to sleep in. The couple did not ask any questions, and it was evident from their tone, they did not expect to be asked any questions either. After all, the pair was risking their lives of which Gilbert and Davy were aware of and supremely thankful for. They were then moved around from house to house every few days, before finally, they found themselves at a port which Gilbert immediately recognised as Le Havre. It was the port where the British Expeditionary Army first landed and where he'd spoken in French to two men who turned out to be English like him! How he and Ernie had laughed over that one. It was only a few months ago, yet, it seemed a life time. He wondered what his twin was doing right now.

The guide sent with them was dressed in a black beret, corduroy jacket and matching trousers, he handed them some folded paperwork. 'A fishing boat will show up here in about three quarters of an hour,' he said in a quiet manner so not to be overheard by any passers-by. 'The boat is called "La Fleur Blanche" and the captain's name is Pierre Gusto. Show the papers to him and all will be well, he'll get you safely to England, but you will have to pose as fishermen for a few days.'

Gilbert and Davy were now dressed in civilian

clothing, their army uniforms had been burnt on the advice of the French organisation, whose name they had not been told, and replaced with more suitable attire.

'For time being as you wait, you do not wish to draw attention to yourselves, so I would go to that bar over there.' He pointed with his index finger towards what looked more like a street café to Gilbert than any bar he knew back home. Small tables with red and white checked table cloths and white chairs were arranged outside the venue and a red and white striped canopy drawn down to provide customers with shade.

Gilbert nodded. And then their guide handed him some money. 'This will pay for your drinks —ask for two beers in French and to be seated at a window seat inside. The owner will then know who you are and watch out for you. Do not get into any conversation with customers in the bar in case they trip you up. I understand you speak a little French?' He angled his head in Gilbert's direction.

'*Oui, un petit peu,*' Gilbert said nodding.

'But only use French,' continued the guide, 'if you absolutely have to. On the documentation I have given you it says you are two Fisherman from Dieppe and your names are Michel Martin,' he glanced in Davy's direction and the lad nodded. Then he turned back to Gilbert, 'And your name is Sacha Piaf. Understood?'

Gilbert nodded. 'Yes.'

'You are waiting for La Fleur Blanche to dock where you will join the captain and his men on a fishing trip for a few days where you will stop off at several locations to deliver your catch which is sold to various markets and restaurants around the coast of France.'

'Yes. We understand,' smiled Gilbert. 'And thank you, Monsieur?'

The guide shook his head. 'Believe me, it is better you don't know my name. It might put you and me in danger if you are questioned under duress. Now I am just going to shake hands with you as old friends do in case we are being watched by the Germans. They are very clever, they sometimes pose as French civilians and some French and Belgian people work as spies for them. Oh, and use those code words with the boat's captain too. If he doesn't hear them you won't be allowed aboard.'

Gilbert gulped. He realised there were spies of course, but hearing it for himself, brought home to him what a dangerous mission this was. If he and Davy should fall into enemy hands, it didn't bear thinking about.

'Au revoir!' said their guide as he shook hands with them, 'May God be with you,' he whispered under his breath. Then he turned his back on them to walk away. Gilbert felt like shouting a loud thank you to him but realised that would put both them and him in danger as what exactly would that mean to enemy ears?

'My legs feel like jelly now he's gone,' whispered Davy. Gilbert understood exactly what he meant, they were on their own now and not home by a long chalk even though they'd moved miles across country.

'Let's get over to that bar in case we look out of place here,' Gilbert suggested.

Davy nodded and they set off at a normal pace not to draw any attention to themselves. Their clothing looked authentic, they'd been given berets, thick waist coats and cotton shirts and corduroy trousers to wear. The clothing itself appeared well worn and going by the mustiness and creasing of the garments, Gilbert guessed maybe they'd been worn by real fishermen.

Chapter Fifteen

Wakeford June 1878

Cassandra noticed that whenever she came across folk, whether it was stood in line at the post office, some other such queue, or even mothers waiting by the school gates as she allowed their charges to go home to them, that she got the distinct impression they were talking about her. It was almost as though they knew some secret about her that she wasn't privy too. There was the odd exchanged knowing glance here or there, the whispering behind a palm, a smirk or a lowered voice. Surely it couldn't be her imagination at work? It was beginning to remind her of when she first moved to Wakeford and she was a marked woman for becoming involved with Lord Bellingham while his poor wife lay on her death bed. And all this, even after she married the fellow himself and she should have had a modicum of respectability shown towards her.

At the time, Edna Hewitt's involvement hadn't helped one iota, but Edna had seen the folly of her ways and had in recent years shut anyone down who dared to criticise her dear daughter-in-law. So it was with some surprise that all this had started up again.

Later that day, when Cassie called in to Hawthorn Cottage to speak with Aunt Bertha and Polly with a view to mentioning it to them, Polly poured a cup of tea for Cassie as she seemed to be quite distressed. 'If you ask me no one would dare speak ill of you in front of myself or your Aunt.'

Aunt Bertha nodded enthusiastically. 'No, they wouldn't,' said Aunt Bertha in a fearless manner as she lifted the poker from the hearth. 'They'd get this whacked around their heads.' Then smiling, she replaced the poker in its rightful place in its metal stand where it stood with a pair of coal tongs. 'But are you sure you're not imagining things, dear?'

Cassie shook her head and then stirred her tea which was sweet and strong, just how she liked it. 'No, at first I thought it was pure imagination but now I'm convinced that something is going on.'

Polly narrowed her eyes. 'It's not Edna reverting to her old ways, is it? She gave you a tough time of it a couple of years back.'

Cassie smiled and shook her head. 'No, definitely not Edna. She defends me these days.'

'Look, I'll tell you what I'll do,' said Polly as she stretched her hand across the table to pat Cassie's, 'I'll keep my ear out at the tea room to see if anyone gossips about you.'

Cassie nodded. 'I appreciate that,' she said.

The truth was neither one of the three knew where the gossip had originated from and what it was about even. They didn't have much to go on and that was the problem.

***

It was a full two weeks later that Polly called around to Rose Cottage to see Cassie. She'd left Doris in charge of the tea room. Cassie was washing the dishes in the old sink and she'd glanced through the kitchen window for a moment to see the woman headed towards her, rosy-cheeked and out of puff, her bonnet askew on her head and her shawl lopsided on her shoulders. It was evident to Cassie that she'd arrived in a rush. She wiped her soapy hands on a towel left by the side of the sink and opened the door for her.

'C...Cassie,' Polly said breathlessly as she entered the kitchen, 'I've found the source of the gossip and what's been said about you!'

'You'd better come in,' said Cassie frowning. She led Polly over to the kitchen table and poured her a glass of water from an earthenware jug. 'Take a few sips to calm yourself, you look as if you rushed to get here.'

Polly nodded gratefully and did as told, then she said as Cassie sat opposite her, 'Yes, I came as soon as I heard them mocking you...'

'But who?' Cassie gazed at the woman. Who could possibly want to mock her these days? No one in the village seemed to give two hoots about her and his Lordship these days.

'Charlotte Wilkinson and her cronies!'

'Oh!' Cassie's hands flew to her face in surprise. Charlotte was the last person she'd have suspected as she hardly knew the woman. All right, it was evident there was no love lost between them but that seemed to be a jealousy thing. 'What exactly did you hear?'

'She don't know me from Adam of course, so I was able to eavesdrop on their conversation. She used your name so me ears pricked up fine style! I hovered about by their table and then instead of Doris taking their order, I did. She started off telling her friends how you'd been at her house and how she'd sent her maid to spy on you.'

'Oh, my goodness!' Cassie felt the blood drain from her cheeks. What could the girl have seen or heard? 'Go on,' she urged after a few seconds.

'Apparently, the maid followed you out onto the terrace and hid behind a bush and she said you were quite intimate with a man. Of course, the women then wanted to know who that man was and then she lowered her voice to say, 'Tobias Beckett, he's come half way around the world with the woman he married to take you back to America and he's going to dump poor Prudence with his mother!'

'What stuff and nonsense!' Cassie shook her head.

'That's not all,' said Polly, then she took

another sip of water, 'she reckoned that you and Tobias are going to snatch his child from Rose and take her to America with you!'

'That woman is insufferable and what a load of lies!' Cassie said narrowing her eyelids as her mouth dried. Oh, what she would like to do to that witch right now!

'Obviously, I know none of it is true,' said Polly sagely. 'I mean you told me previously all that transpired and I believe you. You rejected his advances and that's why he left for America. I felt like telling them so but then I thought they wouldn't believe me.'

Tears welled up in Cassie's eyes. 'What am I to do, Pol?'

'Well, I reckon you ought to somehow put those bunch of old busy bodies straight and I know just when and where you ought to do it!'

'You do?' Cassie sniffed incredulously.

'Yes, I do. There's another charity function coming up for the Ladies of Wakeford and Marshfield soon. I heard them say so, it's going to be held in the community hall at Marshfield. I reckon you ought to go over there and put them straight in front of everyone. Maybe take Mr Beckett with you so you can both meet them head on. After all, both your marriages may be at stake with that kind of gossip.' She wagged a finger in Cassie's face.

'Not mine,' said Cassie confidently as she knew her husband trusted her implicitly, but then she bit her bottom lip, 'but Tobias's might be at stake if Prudence gets wind of this!'

And so, a couple of weeks later, Cassie found herself at "The Ladies of Wakeford and Marshfield's Summer Fayre" where she offered her services as one of the speakers. Her name seemed to have drawn a large crowd who no doubt were there to tittle-tattle about her but Cassie had other ideas and had a trump card up the sleeve of her dress!

Throughout the afternoon, there had been various speakers. It was a particularly warm day so a makeshift platform had been erected outside the community hall and rows of chairs placed facing it. Ladies sat enthralled, some holding their summer parasols over their heads while waitresses took their orders for tea, coffee or cool beverages as they listened.

The first speaker was the vicar from All Saints Church in Marshfield and he spoke of the need to help your fellow man and then at the end he told them that all were welcome to come along to services. Then Doctor Bryant spoke about his surgeries held in Marshfield which Cassie found interesting as he gave the back story of his life and how he'd been born in India to British parents who had brought him back to England to complete his education. His talk of elephants and rajahs was so interesting that Cassie almost forgot why she was here in the first place. Then Charlotte Wilkinson took to the stage, all eyes upon her and it was evident to Cassie that she must have shipped in yet another exquisite gown from either London or Paris for the event. She spoke about the ladies' organisation and the good work it was doing but Cassie found her voice tiresome and there seemed to be little substance behind her words as far as she was concerned. She guessed too that the women had jumped at the chance to have her as a speaker as Charlotte intended to humiliate her, but no, she was about to turn the tables on the woman.

'And now,' said Mr Morrison, the compere for the event, 'we have Mrs Cassandra Hewitt, local school teacher, owner of the Wakeford tea room, wife of Harry Hewitt who is part owner of the local pit here in Marshfield, and mother of three young children...'

There was a ripple of hesitant applause from the audience. Then Cassie rose from her chair and made her way to the stage where she became aware of hushed voices and shaking of heads. Half of this lot wanted her to fail, she could feel their eyes boring a hole into her back as she stepped purposely with every footfall. It reminded her so much of when people were against her at Lord Bellingham's funeral so that a surge of fury propelled her forward.

Standing on the stage she stared at the crowd and heart beating wildly, she began, 'I've been living in Wakeford now for a couple of years and have got to know most of you one way or another. You may be a parent at the school where I work or you may pop into my tea room from time to time. I've worked long and hard to get where I am right now. When I first arrived in Wakeford I was an outcast!'

There was an audible gasp from the audience, it was evident they were not expecting this manner of speech.

'Yes, an outcast. Most folk had turned against me apart from a loyal few. I strove hard over the months to regain a good reputation and I did achieve that, even those who were against me became my biggest backers. But now, alas, it's happening to me again. I hear there is tittle-tattle circulating around the village that comes from one source...'

People began to look at one another in puzzlement.

'Yes, one source and there is no foundation to it whatsoever. The lady in question is making out that I am about to run off with Tobias Beckett, who most of you will know once worked at Marshfield Coal Pit but then he decided to seek his fortune in America, and very nicely he has done for himself too. So nicely in fact, that he has returned home and is now part owner of the same pit where he once worked as a young collier!'

There were several gasps from the audience.

'Yes, so nicely he found himself a lovely wife and brought her here with him. Now, do you think a man in that position would wish to return to America with the wife of his colleague, who is part owner of that very same pit? And do you think my husband would go into business with him if that was the case? These are all lies without foundation. The truth was before Mr Beckett's departure for America, he was a regular caller at our home as I was teaching him to read and write and now, very accomplished he is and all.'

Eyes were turning now on Charlotte and her face began to flush red as she was being made to look foolish. As if a rush of anger finally took over her, she stood and facing the crowd yelled, 'Well, what is he doing back in Wakeford then when he has a pit in Pennsylvania?'

At that, heads turned as Tobias himself, who was looking sombre as he strode purposefully down the aisle and took to the stage besides Cassie, was then followed by Harry as all three stood on the stage as people's mouths popped open in surprise.

'And can't I change my mind and return home?' Tobias asked.

'What with the lifestyle you had out there!' screamed Charlotte. 'There's only one reason you returned home and she's standing beside you!'

'You mean Cassandra?' Tobias glared at Charlotte.

'Yes, of course I do!' Charlotte's lower lip was trembling now.

'Well, let me fill you in, Mrs Wilkinson,' said Harry who had been silent up until now spoke, 'Tobias returned here because he'd made money by selling his share in the pit in Pennsylvania and he also wished to return for a woman. Yes, a woman! But that woman was not my wife it was Mrs Beckett Senior, the man's mother!'

'You see,' said Tobias, 'you need to get your facts straight!'

'That's not what you told me!' shouted a woman at Charlotte. 'You made out there was some big affair going on and the man was going to run off with Mrs Hewitt as she could give him a child as his wife can't!'

More people joined in until finally, Charlotte held her hands over her ears and fled the occasion, leaving the audience in a state of bemusement.

'Come along, everyone,' said the compere trying to calm the situation, 'I think we've all seen enough of the floor show and now fully understand the evils of gossip mongering!'

For a moment, Cassie felt as though she had caused problems for the man as now there was an awkward silence as though the audience didn't know whether to leave or stay. She soon solved that by taking to the stage once again to say, 'Now all that is over and it needed to be said for obvious reasons, both my husband, Harry Hewitt, and his partner, Tobias Beckett, would like to have a word with you about the future of Marshfield Coal Pit.' She stepped aside for the men to speak and there was a quiet ripple of applause.

Tobias had lost none of the fire in his belly and he spoke with conviction about the good the employers had done for their workers and how fair practices were now carried out to ensure child workers only worked above a certain age. A fair day's work for a fair day's pay had always been his motto. Both men spoke of the future of the pit though of course, the third partner was missing, James Wilkinson. Which was ironic as the men spoke fondly of him to the audience and about his family's history in the area whilst his meddling wife was now running away in tears.

***

The following day, James called around to Rose Cottage to see both Cassie and Harry, apologising profusely for his wife's actions. 'I don't know what's the matter with her!' he exclaimed as they sat taking a glass of wine at the dinner table when the children were asleep.

'Don't be too harsh on her,' Cassie said generously, 'for some reason she appears to be envious of me, for what I've achieved in life.'

'You can say that again,' said James briskly. 'Usually, I take her side or defend her, but not this time. I can see Beckett's an attractive proposition for the ladies in this area as he's handsome and wilful and now he has money too! But really? Why would she assume that you of all people would run off with him?'

Harry caught her eye for a moment and she felt herself blush.

'Yes, why indeed,' she said taking a sip of wine and hoping it might cool her down.

***

There was no consoling Charlotte after the incident in which she had been greatly humiliated by Cassandra Hewitt. She was angry and began taking it out on the staff who knew nothing of what had gone on. She particularly became angry with the young maid, Martha.

'I could box your ears!' Charlotte said when she'd cornered her in the drawing room as the girl was tidying up.

'Sorry, ma'am, I don't understand?' said Martha furrowing her brow. Why was her employer so annoyed with her?

'You gave me that information the night of the party and I believed it to be true but you must have made it up?'

'No, ma'am. I did not. I know what I heard.'

Charlotte picked up a steel poker from the fireplace and held it above the girl's head. 'I've a right mind to thrash you now for what you've done to me and my reputation!'

The girl trembled but she couldn't lie. 'I am telling the truth, honest I am! That Mrs Hewitt was quite intimate with Mr Beckett and he spoke of how he'd like to have taken her away with him.'

Charlotte looked down at a small puddle on the floor between the girl's legs. She'd wet herself with fear. Is this really what that Cassandra had done, humiliated her and caused her to turn on a member of her staff? Maybe there was some truth in it all, a half-truth? She replaced the poker in the fireplace and smiled at the maid. 'We'll say no more about this for time being, now you'd better clean up that mess and change your clothing. I do believe you, Martha. I'm starting to see that I've been deceived and it's not you that deceived me! It was *her*!'

Feeling confused that now the mistress was being nice to her, Martha dipped her knee and went to fetch a cleaning cloth and a bucket of soapy water to mop up the floor then she was going to rush off to her quarters to change her urine sodden bloomers and stockings. She'd have to get a move on else the housekeeper would be on her back too. Sometimes working in this place made her feel so anxious that she wished she was back at the workhouse. At least there, she knew where she stood and wasn't messed around all the time.

***

Belgium August 1915

Ernest much preferred his position as an ambulance driver as he felt he was doing something far more productive than bayoneting or shooting at the enemy as he had done previously from the trenches.

There had been a bit of a stalemate going on as the second battle of Ypres had ended in May of that year. A large scale use of poison gas had been employed on The Western Front. Troops were taken by surprise and they suffered heavy losses due to their lack of protection against the gas. The German army did not press on further forward. The battle began to breakdown into a see-saw pattern of attack and counterattack. Entente forces retained control of Ypres. The city though was reduced to rubble. The enemy lost around 35,000 men in the offensive compared to 69,000 Entente troops. The heavy losses amongst Entente soldiers were primarily due to the initial lack of protection against poison gas. Ernest had lost count of the men he'd witnessed who had suffered from those gas attacks. Some survived but many did not.

Thankfully, he had the sort of personality where he was able to reassure and calm the sick and wounded or even give a kindly word with the promise of informing relatives when someone was due to pass away. Oh, when would this bloody war ever end?

Moira was never far from his thoughts and although he'd written her a couple of letters, he never received a reply. Was she angry with him for consummating his passion that time in the woods of Northern France, he wondered?

But no, surely not as she appeared at the time to feel the same way as himself but he did however, accept that war did funny things to folk and cause them to live in the present without looking too far ahead. All he could do now was hope and pray that someday he would see her again and he'd be reunited with her and their forthcoming child.

Jolting back to reality, he jumped as he heard the fire of several shells and screams and shouts which never failed to cause a shiver to run down his spine. Then all was silent, too silent maybe, there was a space of time when it was considered safe to see to the injured. There were clouds of earth, limbs of men and debris out there. Who knew who he'd encounter today? Maybe he'd even find his twin brother injured or dead in the course of his work and that he could never bear.

**

At the bar at Le Havre, Gilbert found the landlord and said the code words in French as given to him. 'Two beers and a window seat, please.'

The landlord nodded and he glanced shiftily to his left and right to ensure they weren't being watched but thankfully, no one seemed at all interested. There was a man and woman sat near the window and three fishermen sorts playing cards at a table, who didn't even lift their heads that engrossed in their game they were as they smoked foul smelling thin cigars and supped full-bodied red wine.

The landlord beckoned Gilbert and Davy to

follow him through the bar and out into the back room through a thin curtained off area. There, Gilbert was amazed to see the couple who had put them up originally at the first safe house when they'd arrived in France.

'Hello, we came to wish you a safe passage and to give you this,' said the woman as she handed Gilbert a sealed envelope.

'Hello again!' Gilbert nodded at her and her husband while Davy stood quietly hovering in the background. 'But what is it?'

'It's a letter of explanation for the both of you to give to your British Army when you arrive home so they don't think you deserted your posts!' said the husband.

Gilbert gulped. Of course, they might be held for a court martial back in England if it was thought they had deliberately absconded from their line of duty even though they had risked their lives running from the enemy and the bombardment of shell fire. There had been little choice as to try to return to the trenches would have meant death and to be caught alive might mean torture and persecution.

'Thank you both,' he said shaking the man's hand.

'But,' carried on the man, 'if you encounter the enemy on your travel home destroy the letter. Keep it safe, it's too dangerous for it to slip into enemy hands. It is very thin rice paper which you can digest quite quickly if captured.'

'You both look in need of a drink,' said the landlord kindly and both Gilbert and Davy nodded with some relief, they weren't out of the woods yet by a long mile. He uncorked a bottle of brandy and poured them a small drop each.

Gilbert lifted the glass to his mouth and took a sip then knocked it back in one go. It had been a long time since he'd drank any alcohol and it warmed him to the core.

The fishing trawler, *La Fleur Blanche,* was twenty minutes late pulling into port and both men were never more relieved in all their lives to see it, now all they had to do was get on board and hope it pulled away quickly from the dock.

'Before you go,' said the landlord, 'take these bags with you to look like proper sailors who will be away for a few days!' He handed them a bulky duffle bag each which appeared to have items inside.

'Thank you. What's in them?' Gilbert grinned.

'Oh, the usual sort of thing a sailor might take to sea for his ablutions, a bar of soap, flannel, small towel, razor and blades, tobacco, that kind of thing.'

Tears welled up in their eyes. 'You're all so kind!' Davy shook his head.

'Now go on with you!' said the woman, 'in case the boat won't wait. They've been helping others to get away so the captain might be a little how you say...' she paused as if to think of the right word.

'Cautious?' asked Davy.

'Yes, that is it! Precisely. Now go!' She ordered the men who didn't need asking twice. They shook hands with everyone and hastily departed with their duffle bags slung over their shoulders and their papers inside their jackets.

As they approached the dock, the captain looked up at them from down below. '*Bonsoir*!' he called to them, then Gilbert remembered the codewords their guide had told them.

'Two beers and a window seat!' he shouted in his best French and the captain laughed and beckoned them to descend the stone steps leading down to the boat. Soon they would be on their way, leaving Le Havre and France behind them.

Chapter Sixteen

Wakeford September 1915

There was still no news of Gilbert and little coming from Ernest either. Sometimes their mother felt bereft if she dwelt too long on the situation. Ernest was in such a dangerous place and for Gilbert, she knew all too well that *missing in action* might well mean, *killed by the enemy,* but if that had occurred then his body was yet to be discovered. She imagined her poor first born buried in a ditch somewhere with no one to care for his grave. An unmarked grave in a strange land.

'What's the matter with you this morning, sweetheart?' Harry dipped his head to peck his wife's cheek as she sat at the breakfast table in the dining room. She'd hardly touched her breakfast and was pushing her food around on the plate with her fork.

She let out a long sigh. 'If I only knew!' she exclaimed loudly.

Harry furrowed a brow as he took his seat opposite her as they did most mornings. 'Only knew what?'

'Where both *my* I mean *our* sons are and what

they're both doing right now?'

Harry frowned. He hated to see his wife this way and realised he must gee her up. 'Now you know very well that Ernest is all right as he only wrote to you last week?'

She nodded. 'Yes, but when did he write that letter? He didn't date it, that might have been written weeks ago!'

'And as for Gilbert...' he carried on, 'he always was a survivor, they both are in fact. No one has told you any differently about him.'

'I suppose so!' she said, pushing her plate away. At that point their maid of all work, Hattie, entered and placed a silver pot of steaming coffee down on the table for them.

'Thank you, Hattie!' acknowledged Harry. Usually his wife would say that or similar to their maid but her mind seemed far away this morning.

'I can't shake the feeling that we're about to get some news of Gilbert,' she sighed, 'and I just hope it won't be bad news either...'

Harry sprinkled a spoonful of sugar onto his coffee. He hoped the same thing but he wasn't about to say so. Instead, he paused, and looking across at his wife, said, 'I really don't think it will be.' Beneath the tablecloth, he crossed the fingers of his free hand and hoped it would be good news for a change.

***

Once aboard *La Fleur Blanche,* Gilbert felt a

sense of relief that soon they'd be on their way headed home. He glanced at Davy who had bagged himself a hammock in a small cabin they were to share for their journey.

The Captain summoned all the men, including them onto the deck, as he always did on a fishing expedition, he was in the middle of speaking with the crew. Gilbert could pick our snatches of the French conversation and roughly translated it for Davy. 'He's saying something about being at sea for several days and how many ports we'll be docking at along the way...' He was about to say something else when he glanced up at the quayside to see several men in army uniform marching towards it. His stomach lurched and he nudged Davy, whose demeanour had changed to a putrid shade of puce.

One of the sailors informed the captain. At the head of the soldiers was a blond-headed man who stood out from the rest as he wore a long trench style coat, and no hat. He appeared to be in charge.

'*Achtung!*' He shouted at them. Then he spoke quite quickly in German and then French and the captain nodded at him.

'He says they're coming aboard to search the vessel,' Gilbert hissed at Davy. 'Keep your cool remember we have documentation. We're French fishermen.'

Davy swallowed hard and nodded.

The man and the soldiers who had rifles slung

over their shoulders, made their way down the stone steps and onto the boat. Three of them went below deck to search the rooms and several minutes later appeared back on deck. Gilbert could make out that the man in charge was asking them if they'd found anything and they shook their heads. Then the man turned towards the crew. 'Papers, now!' he yelled in French.

The sailors seemed unconcerned but Davy looked ready to pass out. 'Hold your ground,' whispered Gilbert. 'Get your papers ready.'

Both men retrieved them from the inside top pockets of their jackets and the man held his hand out. He spoke to Gilbert in French who seemed to answer him very well as the man studied the papers and handed them back to him, but then he approached Davy. The man asked him a question in French as he studied his papers which Davy couldn't answer. Then Gilbert butted in and said something. The man nodded and smiled and returned the papers to Davy. Once all the men's papers were checked, including the captain's, Gilbert and Davy heaved a sigh of relief. They watched the man and the soldiers clamber back off the boat and leave via the quayside steps.

'We'd better get going while we have the chance,' said the captain good humouredly in French to Gilbert in case they were overheard. Gilbert nodded with appreciation.

Once down below in the cabin both men were

assigned, Davy looked at Gilbert and said, 'I thought I was a goner then when that man spoke to me, I didn't have a clue what he was saying but you stepped in and said something on my behalf?'

'Yes, I did,' smiled Gilbert. 'I told him you were a deaf mute!'

Davy's jaw slackened and then his face broke into a grin. 'That's positively genius!' he said, slapping Gilbert on the back. 'You certainly saved my bacon!'

Gilbert smiled ruefully as he realised it wasn't only Davy's bacon he'd saved by being quick witted but everyone else's bacon on that boat too.

***

Alice was enjoying her work at the Netley Hospital, the doctors there were very innovative in their methods. Major Arthur Hurst, who had volunteered for service with the Royal Army Medical Corps, after establishing a neurology department at Guy's Hospital in London, was instrumental at this hospital. He'd been to France to study what the doctors there were doing with men diagnosed as suffering from "hysteria" and he'd returned to England to put new treatments he'd learnt into practice. Hurst helped men at the Netley and other hospitals get well again, by introducing forms of hypnosis and talking cures. There was occupational therapy and writing too, by even producing their own hospital magazine, with a gossip column called, "Ward Whispers". He filmed the men so he could see what their walking gait was like so improvements could be viewed at a later date. Some of the men on entering the hospital had stiff, jerky movements but Alice could see the improvements to them as the days went by and a new film was made of now and then as a comparison. It really was astonishing. Alice found Major Hurst's treatment and findings intriguing and whenever he was around she asked Matron if she might participate or if she was on free time, just to sit and observe the great man at work. Ninety percent of shell-shocked soldiers were sometimes cured in just one session.

One of Hurst's methods was to take the men out into the countryside and to help out on a farm where they got good clean fresh air and a break from their worries of war. Other times, he persuaded them to relive the battlefield of Flanders on Dartmoor by encouraging them to attempt firing a rifle again. Major Hurst's methods were viewed as ground breaking as before this, military treatments had been harsh and some soldiers placed in solitary confinement. Even electro convulsive therapy and disciplinary treatment had been enforced, whereas Major Hurst concentrated more on the men's whole-being by introducing dietary changes and massage, employing a more holistic approach to healing, which seemed to work very well in most instances after all they had suffered on the battlefield.

Today though, Alice was having a break from work as her grandparents were arriving to take her out for the afternoon. She'd bathed and washed her long dark hair in a special herbal shampoo Bronwen had gifted her with her from Wales and she'd slipped on the only pretty floral gown she'd brought with her that was suitable for a trip out, as all the others were more serviceable sorts and the rest were her nursing uniforms. Still, what with the straw bonnet with pink ribbons Bronwen had loaned her to set off the outfit, she looked highly presentable and was glowing with excitement to be reunited with her grandparents once again. It had seemed an age since she'd left Wakeford and during that time she felt she'd grown up a lot. She'd managed to keep in touch with Eliza, but unfortunately, there was no word of her brother Jonathan. She didn't want to dwell on that, so today, despite that fact and the realisation her own father was still missing in action, she pushed all negative thoughts from her mind as she emerged through the hospital gates with a spring in her step.

***

Davy was heaving again and he slumped back down in his hammock as high waves lashed up against the side of the trawler—Gilbert sympathised but was aware that he needed to keep his wits about him for all he knew there might be some sort of spy aboard the boat itself in the guise of a fisherman. People were too quick to pass on information, especially if money was handed over. They needed to keep to themselves as much as possible.

'I'll see if I can get you some water,' Gilbert offered.

Davy let out a long groan, his face pale. Some people just weren't good travellers. Luckily he and Ernest had never been that way. He managed to find one of the sailors on deck and in his best French asked if there was any possibility of getting some water. The sailor looked at him, grinned and shrugged, then said in French, 'Who needs water when we have whisky on board!'

'No, no, whisky, please,' Gilbert shook his head. 'My friend needs water as he has an upset stomach, he's not a good traveller.'

The sailor held up a finger and walked off. At first, Gilbert thought the man was just being rude in walking away but then he returned with a leather pouch. 'Water in here,' he said pushing it towards Gilbert. 'You keep it for your friend for the rest of the journey.'

Gilbert nodded his thanks at the man and took the pouch from his outstretched hand, hoping upon hope that soon, Davy would recover. He needed him well as if any more Germans got on board to search the vessel at the next fishing port, it might well draw attention to them both.

But he needn't have worried as by the time they'd reached the next port, Davy was up to the mark again and back in the land of the living. He was even beginning to feel hungry but they had to make do with the supplies given to them by the man in the café as the sailors seemed to be working in shifts, catching the fish, drawing them in with their big nets and the others down below were asleep or at the whisky, Gilbert suspected. Doesn't anyone eat around here? He wondered.

***

Alice's grandparents took her to a charming tea room where they chatted about all sorts of things like what it was like working at the Netley Hospital, Alice couldn't wait to fill them in on all the details, how stern matron could be and what a hoot her Welsh friend, Bronwen, was. It was an enjoyable afternoon and then they took an omnibus into Southsea. Along the way, Alice gazed out from the top deck onto the amazing picturesque views across the Southampton Water and the ships that passed by. Although it was early September, it seemed more like summer as it was so hot that day, thankfully, Grandma had brought a spare parasol for Alice which she was grateful for. She hated breaking out in freckles from the sun, it had bothered her ever since she was a child.

As they walked linking arms with Grandpa strolling some distance behind them, Grandma said, 'You know there's still no word from your father, don't you?' She paused at that point to peer into Alice's eyes as if to gauge her reaction.

Alice swallowed hard. 'Yes, I know and I also understand what that might mean too...'

Grandma nodded. 'We must never give up hope though.'

Alice sniffed loudly, it was funny when she was busy on the wards either bedbathing patients, pushing them in their wheeled chairs, serving them meals, cleaning their wounds or whatever, she rarely thought about what might have happened to her father, it was at times like this she was forced to think about him, or when she lay awake in her bed at night. Where was he and if he was still alive, what was he doing right now? She had no idea how her mother coped either. Although she had her part time work at the hospital to contend with, lying awake herself at night in the half-empty bed must be difficult for her.

'Shall we go down to the sands?' said a voice behind them. For a moment, Alice had almost forgotten her Grandpa was with them as in the main he was quite a quiet man but she loved him for it.

'Yes, I'd like that,' said Alice turning back to smile at him and he tipped his straw boater in her direction.

'I think,' he said, 'you ought to try one of the donkey rides!'

Alice burst out laughing not because she couldn't imagine herself sitting on a donkey but because he was treating her exactly had he'd done years ago when she was just a little girl. It was good to be back in the company of her grandparents once again.

All too soon though, it was time to return to the hospital and she hugged them both for the longest time, wiping away her tears with the large gentleman's handkerchief Grandpa offered her.

That night in her bed as she stared out of the window at the starry sky, she wondered when she'd see them again or if she'd ever be reunited with her father?

**

It was a week or so later of living onboard the trawler that the captain forbid both Gilbert and Davy to go offshore as he deemed it too dangerous. Both men had been holed up before in that barn in Belgium but had to admit even though they were receiving sustenance in the form of the odd piece of bread and hunk of cheese here and there, a slug of whisky or water from time to time or even strong cups of coffee, in some ways it had been better for them in the barn. At least there, they didn't have to put up with the stink of rotting fish and strong sweat from the toil of the fishermen, not to mention the constant rocking back and forth of the vessel as heavy waves lashed the sides of the trawler. So it was with some relief, one day they were told they were meeting with another vessel mid the English Channel to be transported back to England. Davy was beaming from ear-to-ear, but Gilbert still erred on the side of caution as he feared something could still go wrong for them both. So it wasn't until they were firmly ensconced on "The Happy Jack" that he felt able to relax. Gilbert explained to Davy that a fishing trawler was a commercial fishing vessel designed to operate fishing trawls by actively dragging or pulling a trawl of fish through the water behind one or more trawlers so it would be the perfect cover for them both.

The skipper told them how he was part of the rescue mission to meet certain French fishing vessels to transport people to safety back to England. He kindly reassured both men that they'd have no problem when they reported to their superiors back home. Further transportation was arranged once on dry land at Dover to return them to barracks.

***

After meeting with officials following a full debriefing, arrangements were made for them to have leave of absence so they could be reunited with loved ones. Davy was all for that and as Gilbert wanted the young man to enjoy the moment, he didn't mention to him that when that was over they'd be expected to re-join the army and would probably once again at some point, be posted overseas. The war was still on, it wasn't over yet, not by a long chalk. No matter how short his leave, Gilbert intended to make the most of it and couldn't wait to see his wife and daughter once again and of course, his parents too. There was only one other person he was desperate to see and that was his twin brother.

***

As Cassandra walked at a jaunty pace from her house, a wicker basket over the crook of her arm, in the distance, she noticed a soldier headed towards her. That familiar gait, those broad shoulders, no, it couldn't possibly be, could it? She dropped her basket in the excitement and ran hurtling towards him.

'Hey now, Mother, don't take on so!' She buried her head in her son's chest and wept tears of joy to be reunited with him as he cradled her in his strong embrace.

When they finally pulled away from one another, Gilbert held his mother at a distance, it was so good to see a familiar face at last and none more so than his dear mother's. He had planned on finding his wife first as that was the proper thing to do, but there was no sign of her at the house, so he'd rushed over to his old family home in the hope that his mother and step father would be around.

'Let me look at you a while longer,' his mother said with tears in her eyes.

In the months since he'd gone, he could see she'd aged a little, there were worry lines etched on her face and her hair was now peppered with grey at the temples, something he hadn't noticed before he'd left. A pang of guilt hit him that she'd probably been pining for both of her sons.

'You look grand, son,' she said, 'but tell me, what happened as you were reported missing in action?'

He smiled broadly, it was so good to be back home with someone he was very familiar with, no matter how many folk had helped him and Davy on their mission back to Britain, none had known him as well as his mother did. 'It's a long story that I'll need to tell you over a cup of tea…' he said hopefully.

She smiled at him, 'Then what are we waiting for,' she said turning and they walked back in the direction of home along the leafy, tree-lined street. The shopping could wait, she retrieved her basket and linked arms with her son.

The house hadn't changed at all from the outside since he'd been gone which was reassuring, she led him into the kitchen and putting her basket down on the table, set the kettle to boil.

He took a seat at the table and removed his cap. 'Has there been any word from Ernest?' He asked hopefully.

'I haven't received a letter from him for a while, have you heard anything?'

He shook his head. 'The last I heard when I arrived back was that he'd been working as an ambulance driver at Ypres.'

'Yes, that's correct. Your brother was wounded, not too badly but he had shrapnel wounds and was moved to a military hospital in Northern France.'

'Oh?' Gilbert quirked a puzzled eyebrow. 'I never knew. All I was able to find out was about what he was doing now, no one mentioned he'd been wounded, I did wonder why he hadn't gone back in the trenches but I suppose it can be fairly dangerous driving an ambulance to the front line.'

His mother nodded and swallowed. 'Yes, of course...' She reached out and touched Gilbert's hand. 'I'll make us both a nice cup of tea and you can tell me everything that's happened to you since you left here.'

'Everything?' He laughed.

'Yes, as much as you care to say anyhow.'

It was going to be difficult for him reliving it all but it wasn't all bad, he supposed he and Davy were both the lucky ones to escape with their lives.

***

Being treated as a hero wasn't something Gilbert was expecting, nor did he feel like one. In fact, he felt like a fraud because although that day on the battlefield it would have been impossible to return to the trench without being fired at and he and Davy had sought escape, he did wonder why he should have tried. Then a little voice reminded him he would have been a real hero then lying on his back with sightless eyes, one of many who lost their lives with honour that day. Instead, he had chosen the escape route which had undoubtedly saved his own life and the skin of young Davy too. His mother had sought to remind him how Davy's parents would be thrilled that their son was safely home again on English soil. But for how much longer? He asked himself. Davy was fit and young and would undoubtedly be sent as fodder once again. At least if he himself died, he had seen a lot of life, been married, had a daughter, but Davy hadn't achieved any of that thus far.

'Come on!' A voice said as he was patted on the back. 'What are you having to drink? Can't let a service man home on leave go buying his own pint!' He turned from the wooden bar to see old Jake McCarthy stood behind him. Jake was a local farmer, too old to fight for his country now and at any rate, even if he were years younger, he would probably be allowed to stay home as the country needed farmers to provide its folk with food.

Gilbert nodded and shot the man a wan smile. It had been the same thing this past few days, either men in pubs offering him drinks, so many that first night home, he could barely stand and had to stagger back with a troupe of men singing his praises, ensuring he arrived safely home. Or if it wasn't the men, then it was the women folk. They all seemed to want to mother him and bake cakes for him. Polly from the tea room had already popped around with a "Welcome Home!" fruit cake, covered with marzipan and a thick coating of icing. Even their next door neighbour, Maggie, who hardly passed the time of day with him had turned up on the door step with a plate of jam and cream scones. People were so kind but they just didn't understand. He didn't feel like a hero. After all, what had he really done? Just escaped by the aid of the French from a God forsaken hole of a battlefield in Belgium. No, he'd much rather be treated as he was before, respected by folk but not overly praised.

He wondered how Davy was doing right now? No doubt, he'd enjoy all the attention, the lasses would be flocking at his feet to attend to a young, handsome war hero.

Jolting back to reality, he heard Jake say, 'What's it to be? A pint of best ale or something a little stronger?'

He could hardly cope with another session like the other evening so he smiled and said, 'The ale, please!'

In any case, Marissa wouldn't be best pleased if he got plastered again. Alice was due home tomorrow and he couldn't wait to see her. She'd been allowed special dispensation to visit her father and would be home for a few days. He was so proud of her and all they'd achieved. Marissa, though, he was concerned about. She didn't seem herself since he'd returned. She was distracted somehow and in many ways he didn't feel that she was really pleased to see him. He hoped it was his imagination playing tricks.

Chapter Seventeen

Wakeford July 1878

Cassandra realised she'd made an enemy of Charlotte but she bore the woman no ill will whatsoever as she wasn't that sort of person, having a forgiving nature and she hoped the incident where the woman had been put in her place at the local charity function, would end all the speculation and gossip. Naively, she'd thought so.

So it was with some surprise that she received a visit from Prudence one day at Rose Cottage. The family were now ready to leave any day to move to their new house and most of their items were packed into wooden tea chests that somehow Harry had managed to acquire for her.

She stood in her kitchen looking around herself thinking of all the memories attached to the cottage like the time she'd first visited Jem and Clyde here and how initially Clyde had seemed wary of her but had eventually taken to her. There was the time when she went into labour while her husband was discussing business with James Wilkinson at a hotel and there'd been no one around to help her, and thank goodness Polly had turned up out of the blue as she'd have been in a right pickle otherwise as things did not go so well for the twins' birth, it had been touch and go when Ernest was being born, but he'd been a fighter and Doctor Bryant had been sent for in the end.

Then there was the time Tobias Beckett had walked up the path and she'd spotted him from the window and when she'd spoken to him she'd wondered who the young, handsome and headstrong man was. It turned out that he was a rabble-rouser of sorts who worked at her husband's coal pit. The attraction between herself and him had been almost instantaneous but now she realised although there was something there still between them, and maybe there always would be, it was all a dream, a fantasy.

So absorbed was she in her thoughts as she lifted a pretty pink china cup from a set that Harry had once bought her as an anniversary gift, to make herself a cup of tea, that she almost failed to notice the light knock on the door. The person on the other side was someone who wanted to make themselves heard so they knocked louder. With the teacup in her hand she made her way to the door. Who on earth could be knocking so urgently and at this hour too? It was still early, the twins were sound asleep in their little beds upstairs.

She unlocked the door and opened it to find

Prudence stood there, her eyes glistening with tears. 'Is it true what they've been saying about you and my husband?' she asked in her American drawl.

'W...what have people been saying?' Cassie's mouth dried up as she wondered when this situation was ever going to end as she thought people had been put straight after they'd all taken to the stage at that charity function.

Prudence lifted her chin as if in defiance. 'That you're planning to leave your husband and run away with Tobias?'

Cassie's heartbeat thudded in her ears. This couldn't be happening. Not to her. 'No, it most definitely is not true!' She shook her head in disbelief. 'You'd better come inside and discuss this.'

Prudence nodded and followed Cassie inside to the kitchen. 'I'm afraid I'm in a bit of a mess as we're moving house this week.'

'Oh?' said Prudence as if astonished by that.

Cassie smiled. 'Now, I'd hardly be moving house with my family if I planned on leaving Wakeford with your husband, would I?'

Prudence shook her head and she let out a long breath. 'I'm sorry, Cassandra. It's just something I was told last night.'

'Now let me guess, Charlotte told you that?'

Prudence bit on her lower lip. 'I'd better not say, sorry.'

'Look,' said Cassie kindly, 'come and sit here

at the table and I'll make us a cup of tea, I've already boiled the kettle and I'll explain what's been going on.'

Both women chatted at the kitchen table as Cassie explained as best as she could what her relationship had been like with Tobias before he left for America and how Charlotte had for some reason decided to make mischief and the fact she might now have mentioned this to Prudence as she'd been humiliated at the local charity event.

Prudence nodded thoughtfully and then took a sip of her tea and set it back down on its saucer on the table again. 'I think I understand,' she said. 'But I have to ask you, are you in love with my husband?'

Cassie shook her head vehemently. 'No, most certainly not. Back then before Tobias left here, I admit to feeling a little confused, yes. Harry was working a lot and when he was home he never had much time for me so Tobias and I grew close to one another. But in the end, I realised it was my husband I genuinely loved and I'm sure Tobias is no longer in love with me either! It was pure infatuation, I believe!'

'It's just that...' Prudence looked away for a moment as she blinked hard.

'Just what?'

'That I can never give him a child...you see the doctors have told me I will always be barren. That's why I thought maybe the gossip about you and him might be true as you can give him something, I cannot.'

'I see,' said Cassie. 'But doctors aren't always right, are they?'

'Maybe not, but I wished I'd told him of this before we married.'

'If Tobias really loves you then you will be the most important person for him not the fact you can't bear him a child. In any case, of what I know of him, he's very interested in pit business and Marshfield Coal Pit will be his baby if you like, his obsession.'

Prudence smiled through her unshed tears. 'I'm so glad I came to see you, Cassandra,' she said.

'Call me Cassie. And if I were you I'd stay away from the likes of Charlotte Wilkinson, well when you're not with your husband as obviously we have to mix as the three men are in a partnership. Go to her fancy dinners with Tobias by all means but don't let her corner you as otherwise she'll inject her venom into you.'

Prudence nodded. 'I agree, wholeheartedly, what a spiteful person she is!'

Cassie nodded, she couldn't disagree with that.

***

Cassie's twin boys were now just over two-years-old and had really found their feet, so much so at times she was glad when their elder sister, Emily, was around to help run after them. Ernest was much faster on his feet than

Gilbert. Gilbert, though not lazy, seemed a more contented child. He'd quite happily play with a set of blocks for ages, creating towers and all sorts, but Ernest had a quick, active mind and he was the one who disturbed his brother's peace leading him off to play with something else; it was then Cassie had to keep an eye out in case the boys got into any danger. Unlike James Wilkinson's boys who were that much older and attended private school. From what she could tell, Dominic and Gerald had been molly coddled by their mother.

In an ideal world, she and Charlotte would be the best of friends as their husbands worked closely together but instead, they were sworn enemies. At least Cassie could reassure herself that none of it was of her making, quite the opposite, she had been prepared to stretch out an olive branch towards the woman but it was quite obvious that Charlotte had an axe to grind against her and other than jealousy, she couldn't see what else might be making her so malicious.

Fortunately, she now had Prudence onside and a lot of other villagers now understood after she'd stood up for herself at the charity function, supported by Harry and Tobias, Charlotte Wilkinson was not to be trusted.

***

'Now you be sure to listen in on their conversation this evening, Martha,' Charlotte was instructing her maid. James had invited

Tobias and Harry to the house for some business talk over a light meal, undoubtedly with lots of alcohol, that his wife was not invited to.

'Yes, ma'am,' Martha curtseyed. The young maid was now very wary of her mistress after that ticking off she'd received as she believed the girl had lied to her about the conversation between Tobias and Mrs Hewitt. But Martha had been telling the truth and finally convinced Mrs Wilkinson of the matter, now the woman was being overly nice to her, but Martha, not being anyone's fool, was waiting for the sting.

'You bring back some good information to me, and I shall reward you!' Her mistress smiled at her. 'Shall we say a whole Sunday off and a couple of extra pennies in your pay?'

Martha smiled nervously. 'Thank you, ma'am!'

'You may go now,' her mistress dismissed her.

As Martha headed off to find the housekeeper, a shiver coursed the length of her spine. If she didn't get the required information, what would her mistress do to her? Dismiss her? She badly needed this job and didn't want to end up back at the workhouse so she'd better keep her lugholes well and truly open.

***

That evening at the dinner party, Martha hovered around and was attentive to the guests offering them a glass of whisky each when they arrived as a pre-dinner aperitif. Then she helped the butler serve up the food. Most of the talk between the men was innocuous and boring during dinner and it wasn't until afterwards when they retired from the dining room to the drawing room for port and cigars that their tongues loosened somewhat and when James had departed the room, she heard Mr Beckett say something to Mr Hewitt. He'd deliberately lowered his voice to speak in hushed tones and Mr Hewitt had to lean forward in his armchair to hear what exactly was being said to him. It was obvious to Martha that whatever was being spoken of wasn't something that either man wanted their host, Mr Wilkinson, to overhear. She thought she caught the gist of their conversation as Mr Beckett mentioned something about Mrs Wilkinson fleeing the charity function and being disgraced. No wonder her mistress had been so testy of late!

'I wonder if she told James?' Mr Beckett said, louder now.

Mr Hewitt shook his head and then, noticing Martha's presence said, 'I think this would be better discussed at a later date!'

Martha stood near the drinks trolley just focusing her gaze on the pretty floral arrangement on the sideboard, appearing not to be listening to or noticing either gentleman.

'Yes, you're right,' said Mr Beckett. Mr Hewitt's words seemed to have sobered him up a little.

When her master entered the room, there were no more hushed tones just bellows of laughter and good natured banter, so it wasn't until both guests were leaving that Martha hid behind the fountain outside the property as both men spoke briefly before climbing aboard their prospective coaches.

'Let's just hope,' said Mr Hewitt as he addressed Mr Beckett, 'that his wife is contrite after that charity function incident.'

'Better leave *shhhleeping dogsh* lie then, eh?' Mr Beckett slurred his words.

'Yes, I think so. Hopefully, she's learned her lesson as have we all. I used to see you as a threat to me, young man. But not any longer!'

Mr Beckett chuckled.

'At least you did the right thing in allowing Rose to marry Clyde without interfering.'

Mr Beckett appeared to have cleared his head. 'I still miss my little girl, though! I need to tell my wife about Sophia and what happened with Rose, but she may get very upset as she can't have any children of her own.'

Really? Mr Beckett hadn't mentioned to his wife that he'd once fathered a child? Martha hoped they'd speak more of the situation, but then both men just shook hands and said goodnight. If what she'd heard was correct, then Tobias Beckett wasn't being truthful with his wife, he was lying by omission! Martha smiled broadly, maybe she'd get that extra Sunday off plus a few extra pennies after all!

When Martha returned to the house she went

in search of her mistress, but she was nowhere to be seen, eventually, she found her sitting in the drawing room with her husband. They both faced one another in high backed winged armchairs near the fireplace, both with a drink in their hands, she hovered in the doorway, so that they were unaware of her presence.

'Did either mention that awful incident at the charity function?' The mistress blinked.

The master shook his head. 'No, hopefully that will be an end to it all. I can't afford to fall out with these men, Charlotte, they're my business partners and you can't say you didn't have it coming to you. Why on earth do you dislike Cassandra so much?'

'I just think she's too full of herself, that's all.'

James gave a scornful laugh. 'Or is it because she's everything you're not, my dear?'

That was all too much for her mistress, who set down her glass with some force on the table and she began to flounce out of the drawing room in disgust.

Martha backed away from the door and began walking in the opposite direction towards the hallway as if she had some business to attend to.

'Martha!' her mistress called after her.

Martha felt her neck shrink down into the collar of her dress, but she turned and dipped her knee at her mistress. 'Yes, ma'am?' It was evident that the master wasn't standing by his wife's side regarding the Cassandra Hewitt matter.

Her mistress drew near and with a gleam in her eyes said, 'Is there anything you'd like to tell me about this evening?'

***

'Well, come on, girl!' The mistress folded her arms across her chest with a sly look upon her face. 'What did you pick up? Anything?'

There was something about the mistress's demanding demeanour that Martha did not much care for. Did she really need that extra Sunday off this month and those few extra pennies in her pay packet? The answer was, yes, she did. So, swallowing hard, she began to relate what she'd overheard.

'It appears that Mr Beckett hasn't yet informed his wife, who can't bear him any children, the fact he already has a love-child!'

The mistress narrowed her eyes. 'And you're quite sure that's what you heard?'

Behind her, Martha could hear the loud ticking of the old walnut grandfather clock that had stood loud and proud in the hallway for many a year. The repetitive sound seemed to intensify the tension between them.

The mistress fell silent for a moment as if mulling things over in her mind. 'Very good,' she said soberly. 'Anything else to report?' She glared at Martha with cold beady eyes.

How could Martha tell the woman what she'd heard Mr Beckett say to Mr Hewitt when the master was out of the room? So, instead, she said,

'Nothing much more was said of interest, ma'am. Except...'

'Go on?'

'Except I heard them mention "the charity function incident" ...'

'Oh, did they now!' She raised her voice an octave as her eyes enlarged.

'Yes, ma'am.' Martha could feel the perspiration on her palms and she feared how all of this might pan out for her.

Charlotte Wilkinson smiled at the maid, 'Martha, you've done very well. Take this Sunday off and as promised, there'll be more money for you next pay day.'

Charlotte watched the girl bob a curtsey and as she walked away she noticed her wiping the palms of her hands on her dress. A nervous habit she expected. Or was Martha afraid of her? Well, if she was, it might not be a bad thing as she could use her again. As she made her way back to the drawing room to sit with her husband, she vowed to say no more about the incident tonight, she'd bide her time as there were plenty of ways to skin a cat or two and Tobias Beckett and Cassandra Hewitt had it coming to them. Prudence, she felt desperately sorry for, but the woman wasn't really her sort, not simpering enough. Charlotte's friends were in reality hangers-on, the sort who were sycophantic by nature. She chose wisely and carefully as she didn't want anyone to outshine her. *And that's why Cassandra Hewitt is no friend of yours....a* little voice within informed her.

***

It was a bright, fine day, storm clouds had cleared overhead when Cassandra set off walking on the path that led into the village. They were due to move house the following week and she needed some cleaning products from Mr and Mrs Lowe's hardware store. The store had everything in it that someone could possibly need for a house, whether it was a ball of string, a set of dusters, a bag of nails—if the Lowe's didn't have it to hand then they could certainly acquire it from somewhere within days. She'd once asked them what was the strangest thing that anyone had ever asked for and Mrs Lowe had smiled and whispered in her ear.

'Never!'

Mrs Lowe's eyes had glittered with amusement. 'It's absolutely true, he'd asked for a chastity belt for his wife while he was on business in London!'

Cassie hadn't known whether to laugh or cry as obviously it was funny but not so funny for the wife. Why didn't her husband trust her anyhow? 'And did you manage to get one for him?'

'We did,' Mrs Lowe had said nodding her head. 'Arnold had to go over to Small Heath to a blacksmith he knew and he returned with a new one, complete with key!'

The store sure was a cornucopia of curiosity!

Today, she didn't need anything as complicated as a chastity belt, it was cleaning products she was after. Beeswax polish to clean up the wooden doors and frames of the cottage, brass polish for all the ornaments that were being left behind as they belonged to Jem and Clyde and dried lavender to give the place a nice welcoming fresh odour. Oh, she was going to be busy for the next few days.

Chapter Eighteen

Wakeford August 1878

Clyde watched his wife sweep into the hallway, her bottom lip atremble with tears streaming down her face as she gulped back great sobs.

'W…what's the matter, Rose?' He hadn't seen his wife like this in a long time not since she'd had all that bother with Tobias Beckett before he left for America, so now he feared the man had been hounding her again.

Rose was unable to say anything for a time as she tried to compose herself. Clyde dipped his hand into his inside jacket pocket and drew out one of his best silk handkerchiefs and proceeded to wipe away his wife's tears, dabbing gently at them. Then he took her into his arms and held her tightly before she broke away.

'Rose,' he repeated, 'what's the matter?'

She looked up at him through glazed eyes. 'It's f…folk…' she said and she took in a deep composing breath and let it out again.

Clyde furrowed his brow. 'Folk? What do you mean f…folk?'

'People coming on to me and saying Sophia's

not your child, Clyde!' She burst into tears again. 'It wasn't supposed to happen like this, most people didn't know.'

Poor Rose was inconsolable, so he led her to the drawing room and when she removed her cloak and sat down and composed herself, he asked the maid to send them a pot of tea. While she was gone, he looked at Rose from the opposite armchair. 'We didn't want people knowing I'm not Sophia's father, but does it really matter when you think about it?'

Rose twisted Clyde's handkerchief between her fingers. 'Yes, it does to me but it's worse than that, Clyde...'

'How?'

'Somehow, they know who her father is!'

Clyde clenched his teeth. 'But he was only here recently visiting Sophia and he p...p...promised he'd not tell anyone he was the father!' Clyde stood near the mantelpiece and gazing at his own reflection, bunched his hands into fists. 'I... I've a good mind to go around there and punch his f...flamin' lights out!'

'What good will that do?' Rose sniffed and shook her head sadly.

He turned to face his wife. 'Maybe n...no good at all but it will ma...make me feel a lot better!' He raised a fist.

'No, you must not do that, Clyde. We don't know for sure that it's Tobias who said so anyhow.'

'True,' said Clyde, relaxing his stance. 'Maybe it's that wife of his?'

Rose narrowed her gaze as if that thought hadn't occurred to her.

'W...who were the folk who mentioned it to you anyhow?'

'Maisie Wren and Christina Peters!'

'They're a f...fine flippin' pair!' Clyde sneered. 'So they were gossiping together, were they?'

Rose shook her head. 'No, I encountered them separately, Maisie yesterday at the tea room and Christina just now at the end of the road.'

'That's odd though,' said Clyde, 'that it should come out right now.'

'How do you mean?'

'Tobias has been back here for several weeks, y...you'd suppose if he or his wife were going to say anything about the situation that they'd do so before now. In fact, I'm not entirely sure h... he's mentioned it to Prudence as yet as he did say that first time he called here that he was looking for an appropriate moment to tell her.'

'But why?' Rose sat forward in her armchair.

'Because the poor woman can't have any children of her own and he doesn't want to hurt her.'

'If that's the case then you must see Tobias privately, Clyde. No fists, no violence, just find out the facts.'

Clyde nodded. 'Yes, I intend to and I promise no v...violence.' No one was going to speak malice to his wife like that, no one. He intended finding out who was behind it all.

***

Charlotte was in the rose garden collecting long stemmed yellow roses for a dinner party she was throwing that evening. She couldn't help smiling at the thought of how she'd deliberately put the cat amongst the pigeons at one of her afternoon tea parties, the day before yesterday. She'd told Maisie Wren that Clyde was not Sophia's father, Tobias was and not only that but the man's poor wife couldn't conceive herself. Then she'd put both her hands to her mouth as if she shouldn't have said anything at all. That would set tongues wagging in Wakeford, she was sure of it. Now at next week's afternoon tea which was at Maisie's house, she'd let it slip that she suspected there was something going on between Cassandra and Tobias. How she hated those pair, in her book they deserved one another.

Charlotte snipped a stem and placed another yellow rose in her basket. This was all shaping up nicely.

'Excuse me, ma'am!'

Charlotte turned her head to see Martha stood behind her.

'Yes?'

'The master wants to see you in the study. I'll take those back to the house for you, if you like?'

Charlotte smiled with uncertainty. Had James

got wind of the recent gossip? She hoped not. 'Thank you, Martha,' she said placing the basket of roses in the girl's hands. 'Take them to the dining room for me and fill my best vase with water, I shall arrange them myself later. They have to look just right for tonight.'

Martha dipped her knee and carried the basket in both arms in the direction of the house, realising that at last she'd found favour with the mistress and was a valuable asset to her, a situation that she could exploit, perhaps.

Charlotte hovered in the doorway before entering the study but she needn't have worried as her husband stood there near the French Windows and when he turned to face her he had a big smile on his face.

'What's going on?' she asked.

'I've heard the most marvellous news!' he enthused.

Charlotte couldn't possibly guess what it might be.

'Tobias only told me last night, Prudence is having a baby!'

'B...but that can't possibly be so!' Charlotte stood rooted to the spot, astounded by the news.

'Why on earth not?'

'Because she's barren.'

'Evidently not. Tobias took her to see some sort of medic in Harley Street and they ran some tests and now she's pregnant.'

Charlotte felt the wind being taken from her

sails. She'd been about to dine for weeks on the knowledge that Prudence's husband was taking up with Cassandra as his wife couldn't bear him a child and the fact that Clyde wasn't Sophia's father, now this information would make her look like a liar.

Where was that servant girl! Someone needed paying for this news! She gave a weak smile at her husband. 'Yes, that's wonderful news!' She forced out the words but inside she felt as sick as a dog.

***

Cassandra hated to see how upset Rose was about the circulating gossip and she knew without any doubt who was behind it. 'Look,' she said kindly, 'as Rose sat in a discreet corner of the tea room whilst Polly, conveniently busied herself stacking away the crockery behind the counter, 'it's not really you and Clyde who Charlotte is gunning for it's me and Tobias.'

Rose's jaw slackened. 'But why does she dislike you both so much? I don't understand. Neither of you has done anything to her, have you?'

Cassie shook her head as she stirred her cup of tea. 'No, not really, but I suppose we kind of humiliated her when we all spoke out against her at the charity function.'

Rose narrowed her gaze. 'All?'

'Yes, I explained to everyone what had really gone on and invited Tobias and Harry onto the stage to back me up. All eyes were on Charlotte and her face went bright red, she obviously didn't know where to put herself and could take the humiliation no longer, so she stood and fled from the place.'

'Oh, I see,' said Rose smiling. 'Seems like she got her comeuppance then. I suppose she must be jealous of you for some reason?'

Cassie nodded. 'Oh, I believe so. But while she's making an enemy of me, she could be making a friend. It's such as shame as now Tobias is partnered with her husband and mine. It's a pity all three wives haven't formed such an alliance.'

'But what of Prudence though?' Rose lifted her cup and took a sip of tea, and then set it back down in its saucer.

'Prudence is fine, she's a very nice lady but I have warned her to stay away from Charlotte. Charlotte was trying to include her in her inner circle, but it seems obvious to me she's no friend of Pru's.'

Rose shook her head and tutted. 'What a shallow person Charlotte really is.'

'Yes, but how do you feel now it's all out in the open that Clyde isn't Sophia's father?'

Rose shrugged her shoulders. 'At first I felt awkward about it as people would have realised I had relations with Tobias out of wedlock, but now, well, it's nine days talk, isn't it?'

Cassie nodded. 'You're right,' she said, 'you're far better off rising above it. One day that madam will get her due, you see if she doesn't.'

Rose nodded. 'Hopefully,' she said wistfully.

To change the topic on to a more positive one, Cassandra said, 'You'll have to come around and visit soon. We're all settled in the new house now.'

'Oh, that's good. Clyde said you'd moved out of the cottage and left it far cleaner than when he and Jem left it for you!' Rose giggled.

'Aw, it wasn't all that bad when we moved in, nothing a bit of elbow grease didn't sort out at any rate. Believe me, Harry and I were so grateful to them for allowing us to live there. It's made me appreciate our new home even more so as it seems huge in comparison.'

'Do you have a name for it?'

'Yes,' Cassandra nodded smiling, 'we're going to call it "Valley View" as it has a splendid view of Wakeford and beyond...'

'That's a lovely name. You're right though, our houses on this side of the valley on the hillside have beautiful views. I still wander around the house in awe sometimes after being brought up in a small cottage with my brothers!'

Rose really was a lovely person and Cassie felt she didn't deserve to be treated in such a fashion by Charlotte, after all, she'd done no harm whatsoever to the woman. What kind of a monster was Charlotte Wilkinson?

***

Tobias was happier than he'd been in a long time. To think his darling wife was now pregnant with his baby, it was far more than he could wish for and far more than he really deserved. He realised he'd done wrong by Rose but he was younger back then, more headstrong and foolish. Tonight, he realised he was going to have to confess to his wife that he already had a child even though she wasn't a part of his life and that wasn't going to be easy for him, or her, he supposed, especially as Clyde had called around to tell him about the circulating gossip that had upset Rose and now folk knew he was Sophia's father. No woman liked to think that the man they loved had been that intimate with someone else before marriage to leave his own spawn behind. How would Pru take it though? He hadn't a clue, but he knew someone else who would be happy about this new baby and that was his dear Ma. It was so good that now he was home she was taking care of herself once again. He hadn't realised how badly she'd neglected herself as she'd pined for him whilst he'd left for distant shores. It was Cassie he needed to thank for helping her seek medical assistance, in fact, he had a lot to thank her for.

Things were going well at Marshfield Coal Pit of late, the alliance with James and Harry was working out very well indeed. Not only that but his old pals who worked underground were delighted to have him back onboard, albeit in a different capacity these days, but they knew he understood them far more than the other two bosses did as once upon a time, he'd been one of them.

He turned to see his wife enter the drawing room and he smiled. 'Please sit down, Prudence, there's something I have to tell you...' he said with uncertainty.

Prudence raised an enquiring eyebrow and seated herself near the fireplace while Tobias poured himself a large brandy from the crystal decanter on the sideboard. He was just about to ask his wife if he ought to send for a tray of tea for her, when the drawing room door opened and Mr Blenkinsop, the butler, stood there with a letter on a silver platter. 'There's a lad outside who's waiting for a reply, sir,' he said lowering his head as he pushed the tray towards his master.

Tobias nodded and then stepping forward he removed the unsealed envelope from the tray, extracted the letter and placed the envelope back on the tray. He frowned as he read it.

'What's the matter, darling?' Pru asked.

'There's trouble afoot at the pit, I have to return to sort it out. The men will only listen to me!'

'Yes, of course you must, dear,' Pru said softly.

Tobias went in search of his long frock coat and top hat but Blenkinsop already had them waiting for him. 'I've told Kendrick to bring the coach to the front,' he smiled.

Tobias nodded at him, the man was worth his weight in gold. What he had to tell Pru would have to wait for another time, the miners at the coal pit needed sorting first.

Chapter Nineteen

Wakeford September 1915

The novelty of being a hero had well and truly worn off for Gilbert. He was grateful for the appreciative pats on the back and the foaming tankards of ale offered him, but, he just didn't feel as though he deserved any of it and that's why he wanted to return to The Front. His parents, though, thought he should remain in Wakeford for a while after the trauma he'd been through but none of his trauma compared in his mind to what poor Ernest had been going through. Wounded by shrapnel and then back out on the front line as an ambulance driver, he was right in the thick of it.

Marissa hadn't been herself of late and he wondered if her mental illness was returning as she'd been that way for some time after she'd given birth to Alice, though she had recovered and worked part time at the hospital, he realised something was up with her. She was so quiet of late, mostly speaking when she was spoken to and seemed in a faraway place. He ventured to ask her brother, Alfred, about it one day, but Alf had just shrugged his shoulders and acted as though he didn't want to get involved which made Gilbert highly suspicious indeed. Being parted from his wife for months, he would have expected her to make a lot of effort like his parents had when he returned home. Even Alice was making a journey home to see him.

It wasn't until a few days later that he discovered the truth. Marissa informed him herself that while he'd been away, she'd feared he'd never return and in a moment of madness, had formed a relationship with a doctor at the hospital who was widowed—so there was nothing to lose for him. Marissa was now confused over what she ought to do and the stigma of it all if and when folk found out. Gilbert had flown into a fit of rage at hearing that, to think that whilst he was ducking and diving the artillery fire from the enemy, his wife was engaging in some sort of romantic liaison with a man who wouldn't have the possibility of having his head shot off if he raised it above the parapet! Well not in the conventional sense anyhow. He felt betrayed as even though they weren't exactly a close couple of late, he'd once trusted her, now his life lay in tatters and he didn't even think he could speak with his parents about it nor Alice of course. There was only one person he'd have liked to have confided in right now and that was his twin. He just had to return to The Front to see him again and escape this desperate situation. Maybe in some sort of silly way it would clear his head for him. Dicing with death shouldn't be a way to clear one's mind, he realised that but getting away from Marissa and Wakeford might be the best thing. But before he left, if the authorities allowed it, he was going to see his beautiful daughter and he wondered what she was doing right now.

***

Alice had bed bathed her final patient that morning, some of the men on the ward had varying degrees of injury, a few were amputees, others suffered mental trauma, whilst some had shrapnel wounds or stomach injuries. Matron had already told her she could take her morning break when she noticed a couple of ambulances drawing up outside. No time for a break as some new patients had arrived and Matron was clapping her hands to summon the nurses to attend to them. Thankfully, the medics aboard both vehicles told them there was no one with serious injuries, well nothing that needed operating on fast, so she helped one soldier who was on crutches off the ambulance and into an awaiting bed on the ward, she was about to turn away to go for her break as one of the other nurses was going to book the men in on the ward, when something beckoned her back to the vehicles. There was one final vehicle that had a patient on a stretcher inside.

'Sssh,' she soothed to the whimpering man. 'The medics and nurses will attend to you shortly, I'm just leaving for my break but I can wait with you until they arrive, if you like?'

'P...please,' said the man as he gulped back sobs.

As she took a seat beside him on the wooden bench, she gazed at his face, it couldn't be, could it? 'Jonathan?'

The man's eyes flicked open as he stared at her. 'Alice?' He began to sob gratefully as she took his hand as the memory of all she'd once been to him came to mind.

'I never thought I'd ever see you again,' she said softly as she held his bruised hand to her face, allowing tears to trickle down her cheeks as she realised at that moment just how much she cared for him as her heart swelled with love.

'Nor I you.' He smiled at her, the love in his eyes for her mirroring just how he felt too.

But he seemed to have aged this past few months since going away. Before that he seemed bright and breezy, a chipper sort of chap.

Alice frowned. 'But what happened to you?'

'I ended up in a military hospital in Northern France with your uncle.'

'I heard about that and I sent you a letter.'

'I didn't receive it and it broke my heart, so the first opportunity I had I asked to go back to The Front. I thought I was no longer on your mind, Alice.'

'Of course you were, you always were. The letter got delayed as my grandmother lost it and forgot to post it at the time, but it was eventually sent to you. But what happened after that?'

'I got wounded in one of my legs. The doctors may have to amputate...' he began to weep. How could she leave him at a time like this?

***

Over the next couple of days, Alice spent as much time as she possibly could at Jonathan's bedside. Drat that letter not being posted on time. It wasn't really Grandma's fault of course, it was a set of freak circumstances that had caused it to flutter from the writing bureau and find its way beneath the armchair until Grandpa discovered it under his shoe a few weeks later after it had somehow revealed itself, probably when the armchair moved further back when sat upon. But if that set of circumstances had not occurred, causing Jonathan to believe she'd forgotten all about him, maybe after he'd been injured, he wouldn't have been so quick to volunteer to return to The Front and he wouldn't be in a military hospital with the threat of an amputation looming over his head.

Whichever way she looked at it, somehow it felt as though it were her fault. She might have posted that darn letter herself and not asked Grandma to do so on her behalf.

Jonathan had drifted off to sleep as he was medicated with heavy painkillers amongst other things. She took this as an opportunity to ask Doctor Bartholomew what he thought of his condition. She found him in his office at the end of the corridor and gingerly, she rapped on the door with her knuckles.

'Enter!' a voice from within boomed and as she did, she noticed Matron tidying up some paperwork behind him. She seemed to be spending a lot of time with the man of late, but then again, Matron was unmarried and the doctor had lost his wife to consumption the previous year.

Matron raised her brows as if surprised to see Alice stood there.

'Yes, nurse?' Doctor Bartholomew smiled, his rheumy blue-grey eyes creasing at the edges. For his age, he was quite a handsome, distinguished-looking fellow with silver-grey hair and a matching pencil-slim moustache. His eyes twinkled wickedly, she noticed at times and she suspected he had a good sense of humour that couldn't prevail that often in a ward full of sick patients and the pressure he was under.

Alice cleared her throat. 'I'm due some leave home tomorrow for a few days, Doctor,' she glanced at Matron for her approval, who nodded and smiled. 'But I'm concerned about our new patient, Jonathan, I knew him back home and I just wondered...'

'Whether he has to have that gammy leg amputated?'

She nodded. 'Yes, Doctor.'

'No decision has been made as yet,' he said

as he stroked his chin as if in contemplation. 'There'll be a ward round first thing tomorrow morning and a decision will be made then. The antibiotics seem to be working quite well and as far as I can see, the infection is clearing up nicely.' He closed the space between them and laid a hand of reassurance on her shoulder. 'Have no fears, my dear, go home and enjoy your leave as I understand your father, the war hero, is home?'

'Yes, Doctor,' she smiled weakly.

'It's my guess though I can't be a hundred per cent sure, as no one is in these matters, but I believe your young man's leg will still be there when you return. But don't tell him I said so as I don't want to raise his hopes and dash them again if something untoward happens meantime. I'd say though that I'm ninety nine percent sure we won't need to amputate.'

Alice heaved a sigh of relief, now she could return home with the reassurance all would be well. Though it would be bitter sweet for her as now she'd found Jonathan, she didn't want to be parted from him. Still, the five days home would probably fly past for her.

***

Alice was home and Gilbert couldn't wait, he flew out of his armchair to greet her when she walked in through the door. 'I've really missed you, sweetheart!' he said as he held her in his arms and swung her around.

Alice hung on to her hat, feeling out of breath,

241

until finally her father put her down. 'It's so good to see you, Father!' she exclaimed.

He held her at arm's length. 'Let me take a look at you. My, how much you've changed. You're a proper lady now by all accounts and I'm so proud of your work as a nurse at Netley!'

She grinned at him. 'I'm having the most marvellous time there but some of the cases there are quite sad...' She looked deep into her father's eyes. 'But you, how are you? Haven't you lost some weight?'

Her father patted his stomach. 'I suppose I must have but I feel fit as a flea! A performing one at that!' He enthused.

Alice's eyes looked beyond her father for a moment, 'But where is Mother? Isn't she here?'

'She is, she's just popped next door to Maggie's to borrow a jug of milk to make a cup of tea as she knew you'd want one as soon as you came in.' He held his breath for a moment and released it.

Softly, she touched his shoulder and searched his eyes. 'What's the matter?'

'Oh, nothing,' he shrugged. 'I'm just not used to being back on civvy street...'

Alice supposed that might be the case as she'd nursed so many soldiers home from The Front but this, she felt, was something else entirely. Her father seemed so much older somehow and weary worn as if something was troubling him greatly, but before she had the opportunity to ask anything further, her mother burst into the room with a jug covered in a tea cloth in her hands, she almost dropped it in her haste to get to Alice, but Gilbert, ever the dutiful husband took it from his wife's hands, saying, 'Here, let me, Marissa.'

As Alice hugged her mother, she became puzzled. She, too, appeared different—slimmer, spindly somehow, almost gaunt. What on earth was going on for her parents? Maybe it was the stress of the war though with both herself and more recently, her father being away, perhaps those issues had taken their toll. Although an excellent doctor, Alice realised that sometimes, her mother got herself in somewhat of a "fragile state of mind" and that was why it might never be a good idea for her to work full-time.

After a slice of apple pie and a cup of tea, the trio settled down in front of the fireside. Mainly, it was Alice telling them tales from Netley about how she suspected Matron was having some sort of a liaison with Doctor Bartholomew, she noticed her parents exchanging glances once or twice with one another throughout and she wondered what that was all about.

Then after running out of steam of reminiscent tales and hospital gossip, she rose to her feet and looking at them both said, 'I'm going to call over to see Eliza, Jonathan's sister, to tell her about her brother being at the hospital. I promised him I'd do that much for him whilst I was at home.'

'That's all very well,' said her father, 'but you haven't long since got here, why don't you settle down for the evening and wait until tomorrow?'

Alice shrugged. 'I think the sooner his family know of his progress the better, don't you?'

Her father nodded slowly. 'I suppose you're right, my dear.'

'In any case, I want to go before it gets dark. I'll take the omnibus.'

Her mother smiled. 'Of course, you must go, Alice. I would want to know as soon as possible if you were in hospital.' She glared at her husband who didn't appear to notice her annoyance with him.

'I'll have all day to spend with you both tomorrow though,' Alice enthused. 'That's the other reason I want to go right now.'

***

Eliza and her family were thrilled to know that Jonathan was safe at Netley, Alice had toyed with the idea of maybe not informing them about his gammy leg, but her conscience got the better of her in the end, so she told them all that Doctor Bartholomew had said about how he thought they could save the leg but there was a possibility of amputation and she'd find out if that was the case upon her return.

Mr and Mrs Campbell had borne the news well but Eliza had left the room in floods of tears.

'Come and sit down, dear,' Mr Campbell, who was a tall, smart dressed man, invited. 'This is supposed to be your leave from the busy hospital and you're doing sterling work from what Eliza has told us.'

Before Alice had a chance to give her reply, Mrs Campbell laid a reassuring hand on her shoulder, 'Please do as my husband says, he is right. Eliza is upset by the news of course she is, but the way Wilfred and I view it is, we're glad to have our son back in Britain even if it means losing a limb. Some haven't been so lucky.' She smiled at Alice, who nodded.

Alice took a seat by the fire place and Wilfred summoned the maid to bring a pot of tea for them all. By the time the maid had returned with a tray of tea and generously buttered slices of fruit loaf, Mrs Campbell and her daughter had returned to the room to join them. Eliza's eyes looked red and puffy and she sniffed loudly as she took an armchair opposite Alice whilst Mr and Mrs Campbell took the settee.

The talk was subdued for some time as Wilfred tried to keep everyone's spirits up and Eliza dabbed at her watery eyes with her lace handkerchief, but finally, the air cleared and they were all able to discuss everyday things such as what Alice's job entailed, how Eliza herself was getting along working at the local hospital and the state of the war in general.

Finally, Alice thanked them for the refreshment and stood to leave.

'But where are you going to, dear?' Asked Mrs

Campbell.

'I'm going to walk down the road to see if I can hail the omnibus back home,' she said, surprised.

Mrs Campbell shook her head and smiled. 'Now you sit back down, Wilfred will give you a lift home in our motorcar.'

Alice gasped. She'd only been in a motorcar once before and that car belonged to Bronwen's father when she'd first arrived at the hospital. Her father though had been speaking about purchasing one before the war.

'Iris is right,' said Wilfred. 'Why do you need to go out in the dark when I can give you a lift home? After all, you've put yourself out to give us some good news, our Jonathan is still alive. Will there be any chance of us seeing him, do you know?'

'Thank you, I would appreciate a lift,' Alice smiled. Then she nodded at Wilfred. 'Yes, there's every chance if I enquire for you. Meanwhile, before I left I know Jonathan wrote a letter to you all, you should receive it any day now. I could have offered to bring it home with me but Jonathan didn't realise that when he gave it to a medical orderly to post that I was due leave. But let me tell you, despite everything, he's in good spirits.'

'I've just had a thought,' said Wilfred, 'you're not the same nurse who cared for our son whilst he was in hospital here before going to fight for his country?'

'Yes, the one and the same!' Alice glanced at Eliza surprised the girl hadn't informed her parents of the matter but still, maybe Jonathan had told her to keep it quiet for some reason.

'Thank you,' said Iris. 'We'll never forget what you've done for him. When he came out of hospital and he should have been home for a few days, except he was called up early, he did nothing but speak of you!'

This was turning out to be a pleasant evening for Alice because although it was difficult bearing what might potentially turn out to be sad news if the amputation went ahead after all, the Campbells were reassured that their son was still alive.

Later, as Mr Campbell's car drew up outside her home, Alice sensed that there was something wrong. There were lots of lights on inside the house and as she peered through the window she saw Grandma and Grandpa. Grandma was slumped in an armchair with her head in her hands whilst Grandpa appeared to be consoling her as he stood, gently rubbing her back.

Alice looked at Wilfred. 'Thank you, Mr Campbell. I better get inside, there's something wrong!' she said with great alarm.

Wilfred nodded sombrely at her. 'If you need anything, just let us know and I hope that nothing bad has happened,' he said as he turned to walk back to the car.

***

Alice burst into the living room as all heads turned in her direction. Her grandmother's eyes appeared watery and swollen.

She was right, something was wrong.

'Oh, no!' She gasped as realisation set in. 'Uncle Ernest?'

Her father nodded grimly and then walked towards her with his arms outstretched and took her into his embrace. They hugged one another silently until quite naturally, they broke apart. And then, her father tipped up her chin with his thumb and forefinger to gaze into her glazed eyes.

'Yes. Your grandparents received a telegram earlier this evening when you were out...' He swallowed hard and then she heard his voice crack with emotion. 'Your Uncle Ernest is dead, my dear.' He choked back a sob.

'B...but how? I thought he was on ambulance duties not fighting in the trenches?'

'He was. We don't know the full details yet, just that he was killed in action.'

Uncle Ernest dead though? It didn't bear thinking about, he was her father's twin and she'd been almost as close to him as she'd been to her own father. In some respects, there were things she'd been able to tell Uncle Ernest that she hadn't felt able to confide in her own parents in case they made a fuss.

Grandma's shoulders were now heaving with emotion, so Alice rushed to her side and kneeling on the fireside rug, she took her hand and wept openly with her.

***

It was several days before an official turned up at Cassandra's and Harry's home to explain that it was whilst Ernest was driving a field ambulance that a German aircraft had dropped a bomb killing or wounding twenty men.

The ambulance which was parked in a courtyard was being used as an advanced dressing station which was a way of treating the wounded before they were moved to a casualty clearing station further from The Front. Heroically, Ernest had left the vehicle to attend to a wounded soldier who was lying on the ground, severely injured, when he was caught in the cross fire of the opposing sides and died instantaneously.

The official said he'd been killed outright and as a result, wouldn't have suffered too greatly. A tin box containing some of his personal items was returned to his parents which held some of his sketch pads that he'd been using both at The Front and in the military hospital, his battered pocket watch, and a few postcards from home.

'Thank you, for calling here,' Cassandra said to the man, realising it couldn't be easy for him knocking on strangers' doors to deliver the bad news.

'Won't you stay for a cup of tea? Harry offered.

The man shook his head, and standing, he

replaced his hat on his head which had been resting on the table. 'I would have liked to have stayed longer but there are several calls I need to make. There's another family in Wakeford and two in Hocklea I need to speak with. This job never gets any easier for me...' He sighed as Harry showed him to the door and shook his hand.

Pausing at the threshold, the man looked Harry squarely in the eyes and said, 'Your son really died a hero, you know!'

With a lump in his throat, Harry nodded and then he watched as the man turned and walked down the path towards a chauffeur driven motorcar—he reflected on what a difficult job it must be for him to visit families as sometimes he would be first to inform them of a loved one's death as there wasn't always a warning telegram like they'd had, he'd disturb families who had just been going about their normal duties, doing everyday things and that one knock on their door would change their lives forever.

Chapter Twenty

Wakeford August 1878

Prudence had been milling around the house, quite happily humming a song to herself. Life was good—she was with child and the man she loved, what more could she possibly want?

Tobias was at Marshfield Coal Pit today, he seemed to love being in the thick of it all and was far more fired up here than when he'd lived in Pennsylvania. Oh, he was passionate there of course he was, but there was something about him being back home in Wakeford that brought him to life once again. Last night he'd had to deal with some sort of a dispute and had helped calm the situation down, if it hadn't have been for the men having so much trust in him there might have been a pit strike for the bosses to contend with.

She liked Tobias's mother a great deal and the rest of his family too. One of his sisters, Meg, had offered to be around for the birth of the baby to help out. Prudence patted her swollen stomach, it was a little early to feel any movement as yet, and when that did happen she knew she'd be over the moon about it.

So, it was totally unexpected when she turned and something white caught her eye on the door mat in the hallway. That was odd? Had her husband dropped something on his way out of the door this morning? Tobias had left home about an hour ago, he'd kissed her goodbye and told her to rest up. She hadn't noticed anything then.

Stooping, she picked up the envelope. It was addressed to her—Mrs Tobias Beckett.

Locating a silver letter opener from the desk drawer in the study, telling herself it was probably some kind of invitation for them both as there seemed to be various activities lately going on for the wives of Wakeford regarding charitable events, afternoon tea parties and other social occasions.

Her hands trembled as she slipped the letter out of the confines of its envelope, unfolding it to read:

Congratulations on your pregnancy. Your husband will now have a second child. Ask Rose and Clyde about it!

The letter wasn't signed, she couldn't believe what she'd just read. Gasping for air, Prudence's stomach lurched. This couldn't be happening to her surely? She'd awake sometime soon in her own bed to discover it had all been a nightmare. Her head seemed light as if she were in a dream and the room began to spin for her, and then, all turned black.

**

Cassandra had decided to call on Prudence that morning to bring her a bottle of tonic as Tobias had informed Harry his wife was extremely exhausted and nauseated in the mornings. Cassandra had been given the tonic pick-me-up by a friend when she too, had developed an upset stomach. All she knew what was inside of it was stem of ginger and some sort of herbs, but it had helped. She stood outside the house with her wicker basket, containing the tonic, over the crook of her arm and then she rapped three times on the door.

There was no immediate answer so she tried again. Feeling concerned as Prudence knew she'd be calling, she left the doorstep to peer in through the window with the palm of her hand shielding her eyes. Nothing and no one there. She was about to rap on the door once again when she stooped to peep through the letter box to glance inside the hallway to see Prudence sprawled out on the floor. Dropping her basket in alarm, she tried pushing the front door handle and fortunately, it opened. She stepped over the threshold and knelt beside her friend. The woman was out for the count. Gently she patted her cheeks. 'Prudence, come on, it's Cassandra, are you all right?' she asked gently.

Prudence mumbled something as she stirred and then her eyes flicked open. 'Oh, thank goodness,' said Cassandra as she assisted the woman up onto her feet. 'What happened here?'

'It was the l….letter!'

The colour drained from Prudence's face as she pointed to the opened letter on the hall table.

'May I read it?' Cassandra asked.

'Yes, please do. It upset me so much.'

'Well first,' said Cassandra, 'we need to get you seated and I'll fetch a glass of water. Did you hurt yourself when you fainted?'

'No, I don't think so.' She shook her head.

'Come on then,' Cassandra led the woman into the parlour and encouraged her to sit, fetching a glass of water from the kitchen for her, and then she went in search of the letter.

Gasping, she read its contents. How dare someone write such a thing and stir up a hornet's nest!

She realised that as yet, Tobias had not informed Prudence of the fact he had already fathered a young child, he was going to choose the right time he'd said, but when would that have been?

It was a pity he hadn't already told Prudence as then the letter would have lost its impact as it was truly shocking for the woman to read especially when she was alone, but then again, when was the right time to tell her the news at all?

As if Charlotte Wilkinson hadn't already stooped so low, this was an altogether different level of malice—this was malice with intent against a lovely woman who hadn't done her any harm whatsoever just to get back at her husband.

***

Tobias paced the living room with his head down and his hands behind his back. This time, Charlotte Wilkinson had gone a step too far to upset Prudence like this. He paused a moment to glance at his wife on the sofa as Cassandra held her limp and pallid hand. The poor thing looked completely wretched, so wan and pale. If anything should ever happen to either the woman he loved or the baby, then he didn't know how he'd go on living.

He gritted his teeth. James Wilkinson needed to take that malicious wife of his in hand. He glanced at Cassandra who was soothing his wife's brow as Prudence reclined on the sofa with her eyes firmly shut.

Cassandra looked up at him and shook her head. He indicated with his thumb that he needed to speak with her in the hallway.

She nodded and then, whispering to Prudence, she told her that she'd be back soon.

Once the door was closed and they were both in the hallway, Tobias shook his head. 'I can't believe that ruddy woman has done this to my wife!' He said angrily.

'I know,' said Cassandra softly, laying a hand on his shoulder, 'but what we must concentrate on now is to ensure Prudence is taken care of.

It wouldn't be a bad idea if you brought Doctor Bryant here to check on her condition as she's pregnant.'

He nodded soberly. 'Would you wait with her while I see if he's available?'

'Yes, of course. I'm not going anywhere.'

'Thank you, Cassie. I'll run over to his surgery right away.'

She nodded at him. Thankfully, Tobias's new home was a stone's throw away from the doctor's house which housed his surgery in one particular wing. With any luck it ought to be the end of his morning surgery, so Tobias was leaving at the best time.

***

Doctor Bryant was quite optimistic that Prudence's condition was nothing to be concerned about.

'I've seen it before,' he smiled as he spoke to Tobias and Cassandra in the hallway. 'Because Mrs Beckett isn't eating all that well at the moment due to the severe nausea she's experiencing, it's bound to make her light-headed on occasion which can lead to a fainting spell—"syncope" it's known as in the medical profession. A syncopal episode is triggered by a sudden and temporary drop in blood flow to the brain, leading to a loss of consciousness and muscle control which in turn may cause the person to fall over, allowing the blood flow to return to the brain, this allows the person to regain consciousness once again. Thankfully, the episodes tend to be short lasting.'

'I see, Doctor,' said Tobias stroking his chin. 'But might a stressful event also cause such a thing?'

Doctor Bryant furrowed his brow and then, Tobias handed him the offending letter that had been addressed to his wife.

The doctor quirked a brow as he read it through his gold-rimmed round spectacles, narrowing his gaze from time-to-time as if he couldn't quite believe what he was seeing. 'A poison pen letter by the seem of it? And this was read just before Mrs Beckett fainted?'

'Yes,' said Cassandra. 'I arrived shortly afterwards and found Prudence collapsed in a heap on the floor, she told me she'd just read the letter and how much of a shock it all was, next thing she fainted.'

Doctor Bryant exhaled a long, slow breath. 'It's difficult to tell as a fainting spell during pregnancy can be quite common. But tell me, has this happened to her before?'

'Never,' said Tobias. 'You see, the contents of the letter are true, I do have another child that my wife didn't know about...'

The doctor smiled and nodded at him, then placed a hand of reassurance on his shoulder. 'It's all right, young man. I did know about you fathering Sophia. I was called to the delivery where Rose and Clyde mentioned it to me then. I haven't told a soul of course, it's not my place to do so either, but now, it seems the cat is out of the bag as it were. This, in a strange way, might be the best thing to happen for all concerned. Now there are no more secrets—the pressure is off you all. Mrs Beckett will get over it, and, it did happen before you even knew of one another's existence!' He smiled and left Tobias with that thought standing in the hallway with Cassandra in silence.

Tobias exchanged glances with her. 'Do you know, Doctor Bryant is absolutely right! There are no more secrets between Prudence and myself—that Charlotte Wilkinson might have done us a favour!'

Cassandra nodded and smiled, wondering all the while if she'd be so quick to forgive the woman? One thing was for certain, even if this incident had backfired for her, Charlotte wouldn't stop her campaign any time soon, not until she got her revenge. And maybe she was coming for her next? Being humiliated at the charity function in front of all her friends and neighbours had appalled the woman and now she was trying to turn the tables on her accusers.

Chapter Twenty One

Wakeford September 1915

There was no funeral for Ernest as he was laid to rest in a burial plot quite close to the casualty clearing station in Belgium, and his family were informed of his place of burial.

A special memorial service was held at St. Michael's Church the following month in September for the families of the fallen of Wakeford and the surrounding areas.

A sea of black-hatted men and women thronged the church where the hymns, *Abide with Me* and *The Day Thou Gavest Lord is Ended* were sang by the choir and congregation. Several people rose to walk to the pulpit to speak. The mayor and other local dignitaries, and representatives of the families concerned.

The saddest thing for Alice was the realisation she'd never see Uncle Ernest again and she sobbed bitterly throughout the service.

Jonathan was making satisfactory progress at the Netley Hospital. The doctors had managed to save his leg though it had left him with a nasty limp as the infected tissue healed but Doctor Bartholomew was confident that given time, he ought to walk normally once again. The good news for him though was that for the foreseeable future he would not be required to return to fighting at The Front and for that, Alice was extremely grateful. But there was one person who would return there soon and that was her father.

**

Gilbert couldn't leave home without resolving the issue hanging over his head—that of his wife, she had been unfaithful to him and understandably had created somewhat of a schism between them.

'Marissa,' he said as he waited for the army truck to transport him to Southampton. 'Do you think we have anything worth saving here at all?'

She smiled and with watery eyes, she shrugged her shoulders. 'I just don't know, Gilbert…'

He turned and picking up his belongings, went outside to wait for the truck, in that moment, she'd told him all he needed to know. Not only had he lost his twin brother, he also felt as though he'd lost his wife too. To all intents and purposes, she was dead to him. With resolve, he realised going back into battle that he didn't much care about anything anymore except for his daughter and parents.

When the army truck arrived, for a split second he thought he saw Marissa's face at the window and that she'd appear immediately at the doorway and then come rushing out at any moment to take him into her arms and kiss him as soldier's wives were expected to do. But she didn't, maybe he'd imagined her looking at him through the pane of glass because it was what he wanted to see. Who was he kidding?

He'd said his goodbyes to his parents last night and to Alice the previous week, before she returned to Netley.

***

Gilbert ended up fighting in The Battle of Loos which took place from the 25th of September to the 8th of October 1915, in France, on The Western Front. It was the biggest British attack of 1915 and the first time that the British used poison gas and the first mass engagement of New Army units. The British gas attack failed abysmally.

Cassandra and Harry finally received a letter from their son in November:

Dearest Mother and Father,

Hope all is well with you both?

Early on in October, we left Mazingarbe to march back to the war. The amount of shelling bombardment from both sides was terrific! There was a little respite as we marched through some very pretty villages on our way where the people were friendly and waved to us and treated us like heroes. Unfortunately, there were very few trees or hedges and no buildings for shelter. It was about another half a mile before we arrived at the first captured German trench.

What we discovered sickened us to the pits of our stomachs! The bodies of soldiers laying in all sorts of positions. I just could not believe my eyes!

These soldiers were all dead and wearing kilts. Their bodies were badly bloated and their faces and hands were as black as coal. We were to discover the cause was gas, not German gas used earlier at Ypres, but British gas. Young Scottish men who had rushed unknowingly into the gas they were supposed to follow. It upset us all no end. Yet, here I am alive to fight another day. Something or someone is watching over me and bodes me well!

Your ever loving son,

Gilbert

Another letter arrived before Christmas:

My dear Mother and Father,

I hope my festive greetings will reach you in time. I send my good wishes to you for a Merry Christmas and a Happy and Peaceful New Year! I suppose Alice will be home? I'm getting on all right here but I don't expect the food in the trenches will be as good as yours! What I wouldn't give to taste a roasted goose with apple sauce and all the trimmings. The thought of crisp roasted potatoes, lots of vegetables and a flavoursome gravy poured on top! The best we can expect here on the day itself will be tins of bully beef and potatoes I should hazard a guess! Christmas out here isn't desperately bad but it doesn't differ very much from other days of the week, one day runs very much into the other. Christmas day will arrive and maybe we'll sing some Carols and exchange greetings with one another I expect. I can't believe I have now been back out here for three months. Time passes so quickly over here. This is not really war at all but for us in the trenches, it feels like some sort of target practice carried out by overly keen gunners engaged in what I think is termed "Artillery Duel".

I must close now as I am being summoned for a meeting with the other men soon.

Your ever loving son,
Gilbert.

***

Christmas 1915

That Christmas, Alice was required to work through the festive season but she was allowed leave home during the period 29th December through until January the 4th, where she looked forward to spending time with Jonathan who had now been discharged.

One afternoon, they were out walking in Hocklea, strolling through the park and taking in the wintery sunshine, when Alice decided to purchase two mugs of hot chocolate from the wooden stall there leaving Jonathan seated alone on a park bench. She patiently waited her turn in the queue and thought how wonderful it was to be alive that day and with the man she really loved at her side. As she was about to be served, some shouts and raised voices drifted towards her which alarmed her, turning her head, she noticed a small group of well-dressed women who appeared to be shouting insults at Jonathan. One was raising her fist and another pointing at him as she spoke.

Puzzled and appalled, she left her place in the queue to rush back to his side, bunching up the sides of her skirts as she ran.

Out of breath, she watched one of the women remove a large white feather from her handbag and she tried to hand it to him.

'Hey, what's going on here!' she yelled at the women.

'This man is an utter disgrace!' said the woman, 'an idle lay-about in our opinion who should be overseas fighting for his King and country!'

Alice lifted her chin in defiance at the group. 'For your information...' she raised her voice, 'this gentleman has fought in the Battle of Ypres not just once but twice over! He was wounded in action both times and almost lost a limb and I should know as I was his nurse at the Netley Military Hospital! Now get out of here, you evil meddling witches!'

The shouting had caused quite a scene as

people crowded around to see what the fuss was about. Then the crowd, realising that Alice spoke the truth broke into spontaneous applause and one or two even cheered as the group of women made off with their heads down realising the folly of their way.

'That should never have happened to you,' said Alice as she touched Jonathan's shoulder. He seemed to tremble as she did so. How she cursed those women as they may well have set back his progress made since the shell shock.

'I...it's a...all right...' he said eventually. 'They were m...mistaken that was all. It only happens when I'm on my own.'

'You mean it's happened before now?'

'Yes, several times. I've got used to it. Women are worse than the men in making false assumptions. At least the men give me time to explain myself and when I do, they want to buy me a pint of ale!' he smiled.

***

May 1916

Life without one of her sons, just wasn't the same for Cassandra and she plunged into a deep depression. It might not have been as bad if Gilbert had not decided to return to fighting overseas at least then she'd have had some comfort from someone as bonded to Ernest as herself. She found some of Gilbert's correspondence deeply disturbing as she thought of the contents of his recent letter from France. That poor Scottish regiment that had been accidentally gassed and at the hands of their own men—it didn't bear thinking about.

She reflected back to the time of Ernest's birth and how it had been touch and go for his survival. If Polly hadn't arrived when she had and then Harry not summoned Doctor Bryant, who was able to arrive immediately at the scene of the birth, who knew what the outcome might have been? Maybe she nor the twins would have been alive to tell the tale.

As she stared out of the parlour window, she noticed a young woman passing by with an infant in a shawl cradled in her arms. For a brief moment, she saw herself in that young woman comforting her child, and tears slid down her cheeks. She found her handkerchief in her dress pocket and dabbed away at them.

That young mother wasn't from around these parts that much was evident. She appeared to be lost the way her head was turning this way and that as if seeking out the correct residence to visit. Drawing herself out of her reverie, Cassandra headed for the door and began to walk along the garden path but when she opened the gate and looked both ways up and down the dirt track road outside, the woman and infant were nowhere to be seen. Shrugging her shoulders, she made her way back indoors.

**

For some reason, Polly couldn't take her eyes

off the young woman with an infant on her lap who were seated in the corner of the tea room. Every so often, she fed him little bits of bread dipped into a cup of milk. Polly smiled remembering that her mother used to do that too and referred to it as "milk sop"—it was a way to start weaning young children onto solid foods.

The woman's dark lustrous hair was drawn into a bun which was secured at the nape of her neck and a large-brimmed lavender hat was set at a jaunty angle on her head—it slightly overshadowed her face but when she looked up from the child to take in her surroundings, Polly noticed she had the most vivid cornflower blue eyes she'd ever seen. She estimated the woman to be in her mid-twenties maybe. Her dress matched her hat but she wore no gloves or at least, if she did have them, she had put them out of sight to attend to the child.

'What yer staring at?' Doris's voice broke Polly out of her reverie.

'That young lady in the window seat...' whispered Polly as she nodded in her direction. 'I've not seen her before around these parts, have you?'

Doris shook her head. 'Likely she's just passing through the area, visiting or something like that. Perhaps she has relatives living here.'

'Maybe,' said Polly thoughtfully, and then a steady stream of customers began emerging through the door as the bell tinkled and tinkled over again, keeping her busy at the tea urn and when she next glanced at the corner of the room, it was empty, both woman and infant had departed.

***

It wasn't until the following day when Cassandra called to the tea room that Polly mentioned the woman and baby to her.

Cassandra chewed on her bottom lip. 'It sounds as if it's the same young woman and child I saw that day. I glimpsed them out of the window and she appeared to be lost so I rushed outside to see if I could help but when I got there, they'd vanished.'

Polly smiled but there was a concerned frown on her face. 'Yes,' she touched Cassie gently on the forearm. 'I just felt there was something about her as if she needed help. I wish now...'

'You wish what?'

'Well, that I hadn't been minding me own bleedin' business for once and had asked her outright what she was doing here in Wakeford.'

'I don't know though, Pol. Maybe you'd have upset her, who knows?'

***

It was around a week later when Cassie was out strolling in the park with Polly that they encountered the same young woman and child seated on a bench, beneath the sweeping arms of an oak tree.

The local Salvation Army brass band, which

was comprised mainly of women except for a couple of elderly men as the rest were signed up overseas fighting, was playing hymns at the bandstand while people sat or stood around listening and generally enjoying the music while a couple of the women marched back and forth with tin buckets to collect pennies from them.

It was a beautiful spring day, the sky was a deep cerulean blue with hardly a cloud overhead. The leaves on the trees were fresh and green and new buds were growing everywhere. A small group of children raced after a large wooden hoop, laughing and shouting excitedly as they went along. A family were flying a kite and people were queuing up to go on the rowing boats.

'Hello,' said Polly as they approached the woman.

She glanced up at them and forced a smile in their direction. It was evident from her swollen, puffy eyes that she'd been crying for some reason. 'Hello,' she sniffed, then she bounced the young child on her knees as if to soothe him.

'I noticed you in the tea room the other day,' Polly said softly.

'Oh?' the young woman seemed surprised but then again, it was Doris who had served her at the table and not Polly.

'Yes. I was serving the teas,' Polly chuckled. 'Sometimes I can't get away from that big silver urn...'

Cassie cleared her throat. 'And I spotted you from the window of my home, you appeared to be searching for someone?'

Much to Cassie and Polly's dismay, the woman began to weep profusely, her shoulders shaking with emotion.

'There, there,' said Cassie, 'let's get you out of here, we were about to return to the tea room, come along with us and we'll make you a nice hot drink.'

Once back at the tea room, Cassie settled the young woman and child, who was asleep in his mother's arms near the fireplace, whilst Polly brewed up a pot of tea at the urn. The little boy, who Cassie estimated to be around three or four months old, began to wriggle and then he opened his big blue eyes and let out an almighty yell as his mother looked on, her face weary and worn.

'Here, allow me,' said Cassie taking the infant from her arms. Surprisingly, as he was handed over to her, he immediately ceased crying and Cassie cradled him to her breast, soothing him and jiggling him up and down as she sang *Golden Slumbers*, a well-known lullaby to him. Her rich melodic voice seemed to calm him down.

'Thank you so much,' the young woman said.

Realising she didn't know her name, Cassie asked, 'I'm Cassandra or Cassie for short and the other lady's name is Polly. What's yours?'

'Moira,' she smiled.

Polly approached the table carrying a tray containing three china cups of tea, a bowl of sugar and a plate of jam tarts. 'Made them fresh this morning,' she smiled. 'Help yourselves.' She handed Moira a cup of tea.

Cassie exchanged a reassuring glance with Polly realising they were both doing a good thing for the woman and her child.

Polly persuaded Moira to take a second jam tart and then she poured her a cup of tea and took the baby from Cassie. 'What's your baby's name?' asked Polly, 'He's such a handsome young fellow.'

'Michael,' Moira smiled.

'And what brings you to Wakeford?' Cassie seated herself at the table.

Moira took a sip of tea and set her cup back down again. Then she let out a long breath. 'It's a long story and I hope you won't think too badly of me?'

'Not at all!' Polly shook her head. 'We ain't 'ere to judge folk, believe me, with this war on people are capable of anything at all as tomorrow ain't promised to no one!'

Little Michael was fast asleep so Polly laid him down on the only settle in the tea room and she sat beside him to save him from rolling off. 'No, go on,' Cassie urged. 'Do tell us.'

Moira's cheeks reddened. 'I was a nurse on the Western Front...'

Cassie and Polly exchanged glances of

admiration. 'Well, I never,' said Polly.

'Yes, it was a tough job and someone had to do it. Anyhow, one day a soldier was brought into the casualty clearing station where I was posted. He'd been wounded with shrapnel and I helped to nurse him. He was handsome and very nice and I found myself attracted to him and he to me...'

Polly quirked a curious eyebrow. 'And?'

'And he was transferred to a chateau hospital in France. I was allowed to go there to visit. We became very close one day and went for a picnic and got even closer, if you understand me.'

Polly chuckled as she tapped the side of her nose. 'Oh, I'm understanding you all right, gal!'

'Anyhow, I returned to my life as a nurse at the clearing station and then discovered I was pregnant, without telling him as I didn't want to upset his life as we'd made no promises to one another. I was then ordered back to England due to my advancing condition. The Western Front is no place for a pregnant woman and to be perfectly honest with you, I was relieved as I didn't want the baby's life put at risk...' She glanced at Michael who was still sound asleep on the cushioned settle as Polly kept a careful watch.

'Oh, that's perfectly understandable,' Cassie smiled. 'But the baby's father...have you been able to trace him to tell him he has a child?'

The lines of worry on Moira's face relaxed as

she let out a long, slow breath. 'Well, I was unable to do that through official channels. My mother thought it best I went to the country to stay with my aunt and uncle as I'd been residing in London before the war took hold. She thought it would be a good idea as then no one need know I was pregnant back home—I think she thought the man I'd fallen in love with might return and marry me and then all three of us would be together...' she smiled wistfully.

'I see what you're saying,' said Cassie as she poured another cup of tea for Moira. 'But to be realistic, that might not happen...he may never return.' Behind her, Polly was shaking her head as if she realised the truth of the situation.

'So you never got any word from your young man ever again?' Polly asked.

Moira shook her head. 'No. I did though receive a letter from Sister Shaw at the casualty clearing station.'

'Oh?' Cassie arched an eyebrow. 'You mean she knew of your young man's whereabouts?'

Moira nodded. 'Yes. You see he went in search of me afterwards and Sister Shaw kindly gave him my address when he showed up and informed him of the situation.'

'So, your young man knew then that you were carrying this one,' smiled Polly.

Moira smiled through glistening eyes. 'Yes, and I'm so glad of that.'

'But didn't he write to you then?' Polly

273

frowned.

'He did yes, but as Mother and I had left for the country, it was a couple of months later that I received the letter telling me how much he loved me and although he was surprised by the impending birth it was the best thing ever that could happen to us and not to worry because as soon as he got leave, he'd be returning home and in search of me. I've tried to find out where he is but as I'm not an official next of kin I'm not allowed that privileged information,' she said sadly. The only thing I thought I could do is to write to Sister Shaw and see if she could contact his brother for me as he was also serving at The Front.'

'But the thing I don't understand,' said Polly, 'is why you're in Wakeford unless your young man is from these parts?'

Moira nodded. 'He was, he told me all about the place and how his life was living here, I feel I know it all so well, particularly the tea room.'

'The tea room?' Cassie's brow frowned in puzzlement. 'Then if he was a regular customer in here surely Polly and I would know him? In any case, Wakeford is a small community. Would you like to tell us who he is or would you rather not just in case it causes some embarrassment for him?' She knew all too well the way people judged one another and maybe the young man if they were reunited would rather folk not know his business at least not until he'd married Moira and made an honest woman of her.

'No, it's all right, I'll tell you both as you probably would know of him. I came here searching for his parents. He told me all about them and his twin brother too…'

'Twin brother, did you say?' Cassie heard Polly's voice in barely a whisper behind her and then she felt a lump grow in her throat as she swallowed hard. This couldn't be Gilbert's sweetheart and baby boy as he was married, unless of course he'd had some sort of affair whilst overseas which she very much doubted.

'Yes?' Moira was now looking at Cassie in a curious fashion.

'What's your sweetheart's name?' Polly was saying behind her but it all seemed unreal.

'Ernest. Ernest Hewitt…'

Cassie's cup rattled in its saucer as she laid it down and then she was out of her seat with open arms in front of Moira who rose to her feet to meet with the embrace. Tears rolled down their cheeks as Cassie whispered in her ear, 'I'm Ernest and Gilbert's mother…'

It was several minutes before either woman pulled away and now Polly was on her feet too. 'I think this calls for another cup of tea,' she said firmly. 'Watch Michael for me, won't you?'

Cassie nodded slowly as she took her chair near to the sleeping infant, her grandson. No wonder Moira had reminded her of herself at that age as now when she looked at him, she saw the strong resemblance to Ernest there as a child in Michael. That little cherubic face which was smaller than Gilbert's had been. Ernest had been a gentle soul indeed but now she was faced with the dilemma of how she'd break the news of his death to Moira, but it needed to be done, and she'd give the young woman and her grandson all the love and support she possibly could from the depth of love she had for her youngest son. They'd be welcomed into the Hewitt family and into the village of Wakeford with open arms.

Chapter Twenty-Two
Wakeford August 1878

When Harry spoke to his wife after returning from Marshfield Coal Pit, he shook his head in disbelief. 'You mean to say that bloody woman has caused trouble yet again?' he said as he removed his coat and hung it on the hallstand.

'I'm afraid so, darling,' Cassanda said with a note of resignation to her voice. 'Tobias is most upset about it.'

'I should say I'd be too if you'd received a poison pen letter revealing some sort of secret about me and then you'd collapsed!' He stepped towards his wife and taking her by the shoulders he pecked a kiss on her forehead and then stepped back.

'So, Prudence is all right now?' he asked holding her at arms' length to gauge her answer.

Cassandra nodded. 'Yes, fortunately she is. Tobias went to fetch Doctor Bryant who confirmed all was well, and of course, it can be normal for pregnant women to faint anyhow but I do feel the letter was the cause of it.'

'I shall have to have a word with James, this

can't go on,' Harry shook his head. 'We've spared his feelings for far too long regarding that wife of his!' He marched off in the direction of the low occasional table beneath the French window and poured himself a small glass of brandy from the decanter into a cut glass tumbler, turning, he asked, 'Would you like one, my dear?'

Cassandra shook her head. 'Oh, no, it's far too early for me, Harry. So, what do you plan to do?'

'I shall summon James to a meeting with Tobias and myself first thing tomorrow morning...'

'But what if that threatens the partnership between the three of you?'

'Then let it do so!' He said forcefully as he placed his glass on the table. 'Let it do so!'

***

If James Wilkinson was surprised that a meeting was being summoned between the three of them then he wasn't letting on. The elderly office clerk, Arthur Brown, brought the men a tray of coffee and then he mumbled something to them about heading off to post some correspondence. Arthur was a bright fellow, he knew when the bosses didn't want him around, although at the same time, he also realised he was trusted enough not to pass on anything he overheard from them.

'What's this all about?' James asked nervously as Harry handed him his cup and saucer and then another to Tobias before taking one for himself from the tray.

Harry and Tobias exchanged glances with one another. 'Well...' Harry let out a long breath. 'It's more for Tobias to say than I but...'

'But the thing is,' interjected Tobias, '*your wife* has been upsetting *my wife* and that's not on especially as Prudence is pregnant.'

James furrowed his brow. 'What on earth do you mean by *upsetting*? I realise Charlotte can be quite forthright at times and Prudence is a little how shall we say, *sensitive* right now?'

'Prudence is sensitive as you say but if only it were as simple as an off the cuff remark or a sharp retort!' Tobias scowled. 'My wife found a letter on the doormat yesterday, it was addressed to her so obviously intended for her eyes only, and when she opened it she read this!'

Tobias pushed the folded letter across the desk towards James. Taking it from him, James opened it up and read it, then shook his head. 'But what evidence do you have that my wife had anything to do with this?'

'There has been a rumour circulating now for some time that Charlotte has been gossiping in the village particularly about myself and Cassandra...'

James threw back his head and laughed nervously.

'This is no laughing matter!' Harry stared at James, he'd known him a long time and wanted him to realise the seriousness of the situation they were dealing with. 'That sheet of paper is tantamount to a poison pen letter!'

James's smile vanished, then he cleared his throat to speak. 'In any case, it's just not true as you don't have any other children, do you Tobias?'

Tobias glanced down at the desk and then he lifted his head to look James in the eyes. 'Yes, I do actually. It was me who fathered Rose and Clyde's baby, I'm Sophia's father! It wasn't a well-known fact as Rose wanted it kept quiet, but now everyone will soon know about it thanks to your wife!'

James's face reddened and he ran a couple of fingers beneath the starched collar of his shirt as if somehow it had tightened around his neck. 'B...but if that's the case, didn't you wife already know about the child?'

'No, she ruddy well didn't!' Tobias fisted his hand and slammed it down violently on the desk causing the cups to rattle in their saucers. 'I was waiting to tell her in my own good time and now Charlotte has gone and done it for me!' He gritted his teeth.

'Unfortunately,' said Harry, 'that's not all...'

'Go on,' urged James.

Tobias relaxed a little. 'The letter upset my wife so much that she collapsed in the hallway and it was just a bit of good fortune that Cassandra happened to be calling to our house that particular time of day. She received no answer when she knocked on the door, and so, she peeped through the letter box and saw my wife there lying in a heap on the floor. Goodness knows what would have happened otherwise, she might have gone away and Prudence may have been out for the count for hours. And what if she'd miscarried our child? Our precious child because Pru may never have another, the doctors have said that as it was hard for her to conceive with this one, what then?'

Finally, what Tobias and Harry had been saying got through to James as now the colour drained from his face. Without a word, Harry stood and walked towards a wooden cabinet at the far end of the office where the files and ledgers were kept. He opened the top drawer and brought out a bottle of brandy. James needed a tot in his coffee after hearing that news and come to that so did he and Tobias.

***

Charlotte snipped away at the stems of some white roses in the garden to put in the wicker basket she had looped over her arm, they were for an afternoon tea party she was hosting at Marshfield Manor. She was dreadfully excited as her mind raced back and forth between what she should wear: maybe her best floral day dress or the blue striped one? And how should the tables be laid out for the twenty four women who would be arriving including herself? Four tables to seat six at each? Or six tables to seat four?

Cook had been busy baking a selection of cakes especially for the event: two Victoria sponges, trays of almond and jam slices and iced biscuits. French fancies and chocolate eclairs filled with fresh cream had been brought in too from a speciality bakery shop in Hocklea. Instructions had been given for cream cheese and cucumber sandwiches, savoury puff pastries and such other delights. Martha had been instructed to give the parlour a good going over so the oriental rugs were laid over the washing line and beaten soundly with a wicker slapper to remove any dust and debris. The windows and sills were washed down, the room aired, the grate cleaned out and the ornaments, cutlery and glassware polished until they shone as sparkly as a fallen dew drop. Nothing was to be missed or overlooked.

She hummed softly to herself as James's carriage showed up outside the house. Turning, she frowned. This was most odd as he only left for Marshfield Coal Pit a couple of hours ago, surely he must be returning as he'd forgotten something? She hadn't banked on him being home at this time of day and she hoped he wouldn't ruin her plans for that afternoon as she didn't want him mooching around the place when she had so many ladies to impress.

As he alighted from the carriage, she noticed the glum expression on his face and couldn't quite ascertain whether he was sad or angry, whichever it was, he wasn't happy by any means.

She noticed the determined footsteps as he approached, and then he grabbed her roughly by the arm, so that she was knocked off balance and the basket of roses toppled to the ground.

'What's going on? I hope you haven't ruined my blooms!' She said angrily as she stooped to retrieve them, but he pulled her up to face him.

'Forget about those!' he snarled, 'you're coming back in the house with me!' Then he began to drag her towards the mansion and up the steps so that she had little choice other than to go with him.

Once inside, he pushed her towards the drawing room and firmly shut the door behind them.

'Are you going to tell me what this is all about?' She yelled. 'I have an afternoon tea party to prepare for!'

'You don't any longer—it's cancelled forthwith! Those are a thing of the past!' She opened her mouth to say something and closed it again. 'From now on you are forbidden from having any of your conceited cronies coming to this house spreading malicious gossip around the area! And furthermore, I'm cutting off that generous allowance you've been getting from me. There'll be no more expensive gowns from London and Paris, no more new furnishings, no more fancy parties! Harry Hewitt was right about you years ago! He told me then I ought to curb your expensive habits and I failed to listen, but I'm listening now! At least his wife has been doing something worthwhile with her life not sitting on her posterior like the ruddy Queen of Sheba!'

Charlotte fought to understand why her husband was being like this. 'Has Harry said anything to you this morning about me? Or has his wife caused trouble for me?'

'You silly woman!' He took her by the shoulders and shook her until her teeth chattered. This shocked her as in all her days with James he had never, ever, laid a finger on her, he'd been a mild man. What on earth was causing him to act like this? He was like a man possessed. 'It's not Harry's wife who has been causing trouble but my own!'

'B...but how? What have I done?'

'*What have I done?* She asks innocently. What you have done, my dear, is to write a poison pen letter to Prudence which caused her to collapse but thankfully, Cassandra found her when she did. What if you'd caused a miscarriage with your hurtful words?'

Charlotte's hands flew to her face. 'Oh...' She hadn't forgotten about the letter but she hadn't intended that to happen. 'I didn't want to hurt Prudence, I just felt she needed to know the truth.'

'But it wasn't your truth to tell, was it? It was Tobias's. He was trying to find the right time to tell his wife. In any case, Doctor Bryant had to be sent for.'

Charlotte blinked. 'Is she all right?'

'She is physically, but no thanks to you, my dear. Emotionally, is another story. You could have caused trouble for that couple's marriage and for Rose and Clyde too and as for your vicious tongue...'

'I'm sorry.' Charlotte's shoulders shuddered as the enormity of her actions overtook her and she sobbed profusely.

'Save your tears, you're going to need them for yourself shortly.'

'I...I don't know what you mean?' She sobbed.

'I'm sending you away from here for a few weeks, I can't deal with all of this. I just hope now that as a backer for the coal pit, Tobias won't pull out nor Harry. Both are extremely angry about what you have done.'

'B...but where are you sending me to?'

'To stay with my aunt in Scotland.'

'Aunt Agnes?'

'Yes. And there you shan't be treated like the queen you have been here. Oh no—she won't put up with your nonsense! I've written explaining all to her this morning, you can leave in a few days when I've received a reply. She has a modest home, with only one live-in maid who doubles as a cook for her. You can help out there until you prove yourself, then and only then, if I decide you've learned your lesson, can you return home here.'

Charlotte lifted her chin. 'And what if I refuse to go? You can't make me?'

'Then if you refuse, then I refuse to house you here any longer, my dear. You'll be on your own and I shall seek to divorce you...'

Her husband's words cut through her like a knife sliced through butter and she realised he meant every word he said.

***

'I can't believe James Wilkinson has sent that wife of his away to such a remote area of Scotland!' Polly said caustically as she was stood behind the counter at the tea room as Cassie stood the other side. It was early morning and their regular custom hadn't drifted in as yet except for one elderly lady sat huddled in the corner whose morning routine it was to arrive as soon as Polly turned the key in the lock. It was well known the lady was partially deaf, so Cassie didn't mind discussing it as she knew she wouldn't hear what was being said and she was seated at the farthest end of the room.

'I know,' said Cassie drawing nearer in a conspiratorial manner. 'It's some sort of island in the outer Hebrides I believe. Not a big house like Marshfield Manor, more of a an old stone cottage, according to Harry.'

'I have to say though,' Polly lifted her chin, 'she deserves everything that's coming her way!'

Cassie let out a long breath. 'I don't know

though…'

'Don't tell me you're feeling sorry for her, gal? After all she's done to you! She might have wrecked your marriage with all her inferences about you and Tobias.'

'But she didn't though, Harry knows me well enough by now and I told him all that happened before Tobias left for America and he's obviously forgiven both of us for it.'

'Yes, but you didn't actually do anything, Cassie. It was Tobias who was at fault there really for asking you to leave with him.'

'In a way, I suppose it was, but there was an attraction there nevertheless because Harry didn't seem to have much time for me back then.'

'But he's learned his lesson now?'

'He has indeed and I'm a very lucky woman!'

'Unlike poor Charlotte Wilkinson I suppose!' Polly shook her head in disbelief.

***

It had taken days of travelling before Charlotte arrived at Aunt Agnes's stone cottage on the Isle of Brae. And even before that there had been a boat trip to contend with across a choppy sea. She was completely exhausted by the end of it. But what choice did she have if she didn't want her husband to abandon her completely? It was the only way to get back in his good books and "to learn her lesson" before returning to her old lifestyle of lavish parties and expensive gowns. But my goodness! What if people discovered she

LYNETTE REES

was abandoned here by him in such a bleak hell hole? James had promised before she'd left that the only people he would tell would be his business partners and of course as a result, both Prudence and Cassandra would also know. After what she'd done to the pair of those though she wondered if they'd spread the news of her banishment around the community, she guessed she would if she were in their shoes.

As she stepped off the boat with several other islanders who spoke some language called Gaelic, she felt a complete outsider. They were dressed in very casual clothes. The men in oatmeal coloured thick knitted sweaters and corduroy trousers. One was smoking a pipe, his white whiskered face making him appear rugged and weather-worn. He looked like a fisherman sort to her. The women were dressed in thick calico blouses and dark heavy looking skirts with woollen shawls draped around their shoulders, hugging wicker baskets full to the brim with provisions to take back to the island. They'd obviously been on some sort of shopping trip to the mainland.

Sitting in the boat in one of her most functional day dresses and jackets, Charlotte felt she stuck out like a sore thumb amongst the folk. James had warned her to dress down but she obviously hadn't dressed down quite enough, but she hoped that maybe there were some wealthier islanders she might associate with and who knew, maybe Aunt Agnes herself who James had stayed with as a child, might be more upper crust than this lot. She thanked her lucky stars that sons Dominic and Gerald were away at boarding school and hopefully, she'd be back before they returned home for the break in the school term before Christmas. She'd be forever mortified if they discovered their Mama was banished from the house and now treated like some sort of outcast too.

Chapter Twenty Three

Wakeford December 1916

Cassandra gazed out of the French windows when she noticed someone emerging through the garden gate and headed for the house. She squinted her eyes to see who it might be. *Alice!*

Rushing outside to meet with her she watched as breathlessly, Alice headed towards her. Was there something wrong here? But no, her granddaughter's cheeks were flushed pink and there was a sparkle in her eyes and she was smiling!

'How lovely to see you, my darling!' Cassandra hugged Alice to her chest and then held her at arms' length to inspect her. 'But how are you back from Netley so soon?'

'I'm home on leave as Jonathan has popped the question!' She said with a big smile on her face.

Cassandra's mouth fell open, this she had not been expecting. 'But when? How?' she asked excitedly. 'Wait, where are my manners? Come inside and I'll send the maid to fetch us a pot of tea and some hot buttered crumpets! You must be perished if you walked here all the way from the village?'

'Thank you, Grandma, that would be lovely. Yes, I've walked all the way here, I just couldn't wait to tell you!' Alice enthused.

Once inside the warm living room with its cosy fireplace, Alice removed her coat and handed it to the maid who had just taken Grandma's order. Alice rubbed her hands together and then splayed her fingers in front of the orange flames of the fire to thaw out a little, and then, when quite satisfied she'd warmed up enough, she took one of the armchairs by the hearth as Grandma took the other opposite.

'Now, tell me all about it?' Grandma peered at her over her gold-rimmed spectacles.

'Well, I wasn't expecting it myself, but Grandma, Jonathan is so much better than he was…'

'How so?' Grandma angled her head to one side as she waited to hear the answer.

'His leg has now completely healed and he no longer walks with a limp, also his shell shock seems to have subsided since he's been seeing a psychiatrist at the hospital.'

'Netley?'

'Yes, he returned for a month of therapy and for examination of his leg but before he left to return home, he got down on one knee and asked me to marry him. He'd never have managed that with his wounded leg a few months ago.' Suddenly Alice's burst of joy seemed to dissipate as her eyes clouded over and she shook her head.

291

'But what's the matter, Alice? Don't you want to marry Jonathan?' Grandma questioned softly.

'I do, yes.' Alice bit her bottom lip.

'Then, what is the problem here?'

'It's just that I was hoping Jonathan could have asked for my father's permission to marry me and that he'd be able to walk me down the aisle.'

Grandma sighed audibly. 'In a perfect world maybe, but we've had no word from your father, where he is or even…'

'Even if he's still alive?' said Alice with a catch to her voice.

Grandma nodded slowly with tears in her eyes. 'In this life there are no guarantees, you should go ahead with your wedding, it's what your father would want for you…'

'Do you really think so?' Blinked Alice, her eyes shining once again.

'Believe me, I know so, and if you're seeking approval to marry, remember me and your grandfather are behind you all the way, Alice. Your grandfather will be thrilled to hear the news.'

Alice's eyes began to shine. 'I've just had an idea! Do you think as my father isn't around that Grandpa would walk me down the aisle instead?'

'Oh beautiful, Alice. Do you think you even need to ask? You've been your grandfather's two eyes since the day you were born.'

Alice smiled through her tears. 'That's settled then.'

'When do you plan to wed?'

'Hopefully in the Spring. You never know maybe Father will be home by then.'

'I suppose we never know anything these days...' sighed Grandma wistfully.

***

December 1916
Northern France

Gilbert's head ached so much and the light coming in through the shuttered window hurt his eyes. Where on earth was he? This wasn't in the trenches and this wasn't his bed back home. A sea of white uniforms circled his bed and then he heard a voice say,

'Yes, Doctor, this casualty came to us last night, he has a head injury. He can remember his name though he seems to think he's only just arrived overseas. It's almost as though he seems to have wiped a year or two from his memory...'

Gilbert's eyes came into focus and he noticed the familiar red cross on the nurse's white apron. This woman seemed to have an air of authority about her, so he guessed she was either the ward sister or matron, though he couldn't remember being brought in here last night or any conversation with the woman or anyone else for that matter and that troubled him.

'Ah, Private Hewitt,' the doctor said smiling as he came towards him with a clipboard in hand which Gilbert assumed were his medical notes.

'Yes, Doctor?' Gilbert said, trying to sit himself

up.

'Lie where you are for now, please,' said the nurse. Then Gilbert noticed there were two other nurses behind her and two men in white coats who might have been either junior doctors or medical orderlies. There appeared to be some sort of a ward round in progress.

'I'm Doctor Tyler,' the doctor smiled. He had a pencil-slim moustache and a clipped English accent. Gilbert guessed that maybe he'd gone to Eton or Harrow or maybe Oxford or Cambridge University. 'Now then, do you remember anything at all?'

Gilbert fought to think. 'All I remember is something about being in the trench and the men were singing Christmas Carols to keep our spirits up...' He shook his head. 'Can't remember much afterwards.'

The doctor frowned. 'What year is this?'

Gilbert smiled. 'That's easy, it's 1914 of course!'

The doctor exchanged glances with the nurse. 'I think you're correct about the memory loss, Sister Mason.'

Memory loss! He didn't have any memory loss. 'No, I'm right,' protested Gilbert.

'Private Hewitt,' said Sister, 'it appears that you have somehow wiped out two years of your memory. You weren't in the trenches when this happened. On this particular occasion, you were crossing a bridge with other soldiers which was under enemy fire when you were wounded in the neck…'

Gilbert's hand flew to his neck and he felt some sort of dressing there on the right hand side. 'But that can't be correct,' he protested. 'I don't remember that at all. It's not even hurting me.'

Sister Mason smiled. 'That's because the bullet was removed last night, I assisted Doctor Tyler and you were given an injection of morphine sulphate to kill the pain. In another hour or so, you'll feel it and we can give you more.'

'Oh?' Gilbert shook his head.

'When you're up on your feet again,' said Doctor Tyler, 'you'll see the hospital psychiatrist who will be able to help you to recover your memory. Meanwhile, this is fairly common for soldiers in your position, but your memory should return again at some point.' He turned to the nurse. 'Get him started on light meals for now and up his fluid intake. I'll write a prescription for more morphine today, but tomorrow, he can have something less strong to take in tablet form.'

Sister Mason nodded and taking the clipboard from Doctor Tyler, she scribbled something on the chart and replaced it at the foot of Gilbert's bed. Crikey! How had he lost a year of his memory? He hoped that Marissa wasn't missing him too much and that he'd be allowed home on leave soon. And Ernest, what about him? Was he still fighting in the trenches? He made a mental note to ask someone about his brother.

***

A few days later, Gilbert, who had already been assessed by the hospital psychiatrist, Doctor William Niven, was seated in amongst a group of soldiers. He didn't know any of them as they were from various regiments but they were a likeable bunch of men. Their chairs had been arranged in a semi-circle with Doctor Niven seated opposite them. He listened to various stories of their injuries and progress made so far, some gave harrowing accounts of life in the trenches and many had lost friends and colleagues in battle and had what Doctor Niven described as a sort of guilt for being the ones who lived as they watched others die which was perfectly understandable in the process.

It was Gilbert's turn to speak now and Doctor Niven turned his head to him as the other men looked on. 'So, Private Hewitt, I know you have some memory loss at the moment, but what do you remember most recently?'

Gilbert cleared his throat to speak. 'I remember travelling with my twin brother, being on the train and then the ship crossing to Le Havre. I have a memory of them loading the horses on and off and then...' he smiled at the memory. 'And then I remember we saw some men in civilian clothing and assuming they were French, I spoke to them in what I thought was their native language...'

'And then?' urged the doctor.

'Both men chuckled and one called out to us, "What's the matter, you pair of buggers? We're English like you are!"'

'Ernest and I burst out laughing because we'd both assumed that the men were French...' It was then he began to get upset. 'But I don't know what happened to my twin brother after that...'

'We're going to make every attempt we can to locate him for you,' the doctor said kindly. 'Meanwhile, do you have any memory of your escape?'

'Escape?' Gilbert furrowed his brow and shook his head. 'No, sorry.'

The other men were looking at him now full of admiration.

'Yes, it says in your notes that you and a young private called, Davy Johnson, were hiding out in a barn in extremely dangerous territory on the French/Belgian border and that you made it back to England by the help of a French organisation. You don't remember any of it?'

Gilbert shook his head sadly. 'I'm afraid I don't, no?'

The psychiatrist continued. 'Try not to worry too much about it, I think your memory will return given enough time. When you were wounded crossing that bridge it says in your notes from information given by other soldiers that you rebounded backwards and hit your head on the stone bridge before dropping to the ground.'

'I'm sorry,' said Gilbert, 'all of this means nothing to me, it feels like you've got me mixed up with someone else.'

The psychiatrist nodded at him and then, addressing the group, he said, 'I think it's time we took a tea break anyhow. We'll resume again in twenty minutes.'

As Gilbert waited in the queue at a table that had been set up by two male medical orderlies, he was approached by one of the other soldiers who had been in on the session. 'I don't suppose you remember me?' he asked in quite a refined accent.

Gilbert squinted for a moment. 'There's definitely something familiar about you...' he smiled.

'I'm Gerald Wilkinson. I met you and your twin brother on the ship on the way over,' he extended his hand to shake Gilbert's.

'Of course, I remember now, you're James Wilkinson's son, our fathers work together. I'm sorry, I haven't forgotten who you are it's just my memory is hazy at the moment and you were out of context for me seeing you in the circle like that in a dressing gown.'

Gerald chuckled. 'I suppose I was. I spoke mainly to your brother on the way over.'

'Have you heard anything about Ernest?'

'I'm afraid I haven't, old chap. You see I was

missing in action like yourself for some time and the last I'd heard your brother was at this very same hospital but that was quite some time ago. I don't know if he returned to active duty or if he was despatched back home. I'll see what I can find out for you.' He patted Gilbert on the shoulder with great affection and then whispered in his ear. 'Steer clear of the tea it's like gnat's piss, old boy. Have the coffee instead!'

Gilbert nodded appreciatively, feeling so much better that now there was a link from back home here at the hospital and that was a comforting thought indeed.

***

As a commanding officer, Gerald Wilkinson was able to make some inquiries about Ernest only to discover that he'd been mortally wounded some time previously whilst driving a field ambulance. A German aircraft had dropped a bomb killing or wounding twenty men. Apparently, he'd died a hero whilst leaving his vehicle to attend to a wounded soldier and it was then he was killed.

Gerald toyed with the idea of relating this news to Gilbert, but then decided to speak to Doctor Tyler about it instead, who informed him that it was best to keep the news at bay for now until Gilbert recovered his memory. Too many shocks weren't good for any future progress.

There was nothing that could be done now anyhow, Gilbert's twin who had shared his

mother's womb with him was already dead and
buried.

Chapter Twenty Four

Scotland December 1878

Charlotte had found it tedious living on the remote island with her husband's Aunt. Aunt Agnes was a formidable character who didn't treat her with the same respect she was afforded by her friends and acquaintances in Wakeford. Instead, the woman handled her much the same way she handled her servant girl, Morag.

The first morning under the same roof as Aunt Agnes, Charlotte had got the shock of her life to discover she was expected to rise at first light and go out to gather sticks and bring in a bucket of coal for the fire. She wondered what Morag was paid for until she discovered the poor girl had to cook breakfast for the three of them and then rush off to catch the boat to the mainland every morning to get to the market place for the freshest catch of fish of the day and the best fruit and vegetables. 'Ye cannae lie in bed all day, ye'll not be getting the good stuff at all!' said Aunt Agnes wagging her finger in Charlotte's face. 'Have ye not heard the saying, "The early bird catches the worm?"' While ye are under my roof you won't have time to lie in bed all morning like ye did back at Mansefield Manor House!'

Charlotte had laughed inwardly at that as Aunt Agnes had a habit of mispronouncing words and her Scottish accent was strong indeed. Most of the time when she conversed with Morag she spoke in Gaelic to the girl. Though as time went on Charlotte hated to admit it but she was growing fond of the elderly woman and Morag too. Life was so simple here on the isle, there was no one to impress. In fact, it was useless wearing a beautiful gown here as there was nowhere to go except to the small church where the islanders congregated three times on a Sunday and there were various social groups during the week. Aunt Agnes had put Charlotte's name down to help with the women's group there. At the time, she'd hated it and felt she stuck out like a sore thumb but as time went along the women accepted her and asked her about what it was like back home and living in a grand house. One lady, Katy McNamara, even taught her how to knit and another, Jean McBride, showed her basic baking skills like how to make a loaf of bread and how to bake a sponge cake. Here, her wealthy high living counted not a jot as the women were content with their families and lifestyle. They worked hard but also enjoyed their lives.

***

One day, Charlotte received a letter which had been delivered to the post office on the mainland

and brought over by the boat to the island. The handwriting belonged to her husband and nervously, under Aunt Agnes's watchful gaze, she opened it. What if James no longer wanted her and was asking for a divorce? She couldn't bear that thought, with tears in her eyes, she handed the letter to Agnes. 'Would you read it, please?'

Aunt Agnes nodded sombrely and laying out the letter on the old wooden pine table in the kitchen she read:

My Dearest Charlotte,

I hope all is well with you? Dominic and Gerald are home for Christmas on Friday the 20th of December and I shall make provisions to bring you back home before then so we can all spend the season together. Use the money I gave you to catch the train back home the week before to suit yourself and I can arrange passage from the railway station in Wakeford.

Yours James

'Well,' said Aunt Agnes, 'he's not giving much away about whether he wants you back for good, is he?'

Quite unexpectedly, and suddenly, Charlotte began to cry as her shoulders shuddered and Aunt Agnes took her in her arms. It was the first time the elderly woman had ever shown her any tender physical affection in all the time she'd been on the isle although Charlotte had sensed that the woman was feeling less frosty towards her for some weeks now.

'I don't know what's going to happen to me, Aunt Agnes...' she sniffed.

Agnes handed her a cotton handkerchief for her to dab at her eyes. 'Look,' she said, 'if it's meant to be it's meant to be and the boys need know nothing about the reason for ye stay up here. Hopefully, ye can go back to being a happy family once ag'in before Christmas.'

Charlotte nodded. What the woman said was perfectly true. She'd been keeping up correspondence with her sons since residing at the cottage and could make out she'd just gone there for a holiday but the shame now in front of her old friends when she returned to Wakeford seemed unbearable.

***

Charlotte sent her husband a letter setting out the arrival time for the train she intended catching. After an extremely arduous journey she felt tired out and was sorely disappointed when she reached the family coach to discover her husband wasn't inside, but instead Cassandra was!

Cassandra emerged from the coach to greet her. 'Hello, Charlotte,' she said stiffly.

'Where's James?' Charlotte looked around herself but there was no sign of him and what was *she* doing here?

'James is busy at the pit, there's a big inspection going on there today so he asked me to fetch you.'

Charlotte frowned. Was this some kind of a trick? Would the coach take her back home? She wondered. The driver was new to her, she hadn't even seen him before.

'It's all right,' Cassandra smiled as if reading her mind. 'You are going home, honestly. I wanted to see you anyhow.'

'You do?'

'Yes, I have a proposition to put to you.'

***

Once they were both seated inside the coach and the driver had loaded up Charlotte's luggage and strapped it on the back, the coach jolted as the horses pulled away from the pavement side. Cassandra studied Charlotte for a moment, this was not the woman who had left Wakeford in a haughty fashion after meddling in the affairs of others. This was a woman who appeared weary worn. Her clothing now looked like something Cassandra might wear if she were just out for a walk not like some of the fancy gowns and ensembles Charlotte had previously worn and she wondered for a moment if Charlotte Wilkinson had been denied her best clothing by her husband as punishment.

Charlotte closed her eyes for a moment as if she dreaded what Cassandra might have to say to her and was momentarily blocking her out.

'I came to the railway station to meet with you today not only because James asked me to in his absence but because I have something I'd like to ask you...'

Charlotte's eyes opened wide as she made contact with her. 'Oh? I haven't been up to anything else if that's what you're wondering,' she said in a haughty fashion.

Cassandra smiled knowingly. 'I didn't think for one minute you had. After all, you've been stuck on some sort of remote isle in Scotland for three months. What harm could you possibly do there?' She shrugged her shoulders and then gazed out of the window.

'I'm so sorry...'

Cassandra turned back to make eye contact with the woman. 'Look, I'm sure you are and that you've well and truly learned your lesson but I'm not out to cause any trouble for you. Quite the opposite in fact. I'd like to help you.'

For the first time, Charlotte smiled. 'Thank you,' she said swallowing hard. 'I'm going to need all the friends I can get at this present time as I doubt the likes of the Wakeford Wife Elite will be bothered with me anymore!'

Cassandra nodded. 'That's certainly possible but then again, do you really wish to associate yourself with women who look down in scorn at everything and everybody who is not of their social standing? I understand that...' She hesitated from saying, you were taken down a peg or two at Aunt Agnes's abode, instead she said, 'it must have been a complete new way of life for you living at Aunt Agnes's humble abode, James told me all about it.'

Charlotte smiled ruefully. 'It was difficult at first to say the least and most of the islanders spoke their native language, Gaelic, around me too. I stuck out like a sore thumb there but I worked hard and quite soon they accepted me and I have to say, and I didn't think I'd be telling you this, but I was quite sad to leave them all, especially Aunt Agnes who is full of wit and wisdom!'

Cassandra nodded. 'Now then,' she said, 'I'd like to help you to raise your social standing in the community once again but in an altogether different way if you'd allow me to?'

'Please go on,' Charlotte urged, 'I'd very much like to hear what you have to say.'

'I've started a fundraising group for the village. Harry's father used to donate generously to the church and the widows and orphans of the parish, however, the funds are running low and so, to keep it going in his memory I've formed a group called, The Wakeford Fund Raisers.'

'How marvellous!' Charlotte said as she held the palms of her hands together almost as if in prayer. 'But how can I help?'

'I was thinking with your contacts we might be able to broach some of the wealthier people to donate from Wakeford and the surrounding areas. Also, I'd need practical help at the church hall. We need helpers to teach the children and to cook for them, a knitting and sewing group so we can sell our goods at craft fairs: items like, jams, marmalades, cakes and what we can bake to sell.'

'That sounds a really clever idea and such a worthy cause, Cassandra. I learnt to knit on the island, all sorts of stitches like cable and Aran work.'

'That's marvellous, that sort of thing should fetch in a lot of interest. I know of only one lady who lives in Wakeford called Shelagh Dunbride, she's from Fife and she can knit like that. Can you spare some more time when you get home for us to discuss this properly?'

'Yes. I'll ask the maid to bring us some coffee and refreshments. I'm really excited about this project of yours.'

***

The coach pulled up outside Marshfield Manor and when Charlotte descended from it with the aid of the driver, she looked up at it in all its imposing splendour with a lump in her throat.

'Take your time,' whispered Cassandra behind her. 'You thought you might lose this place for ever?'

With tears in her eyes, Charlotte nodded and turned to face Cassandra. 'I am so sorry,' she said as she let out huge, gulping sobs. 'You really did know what it was like to lose this place after Lord Bellingham's death. Not only that, but you had to begin again and people like me haven't helped at all. It's only being away from this place that's made me appreciate it more...'

Through misted eyes, Cassandra nodded in agreement. 'Maybe that trip to Scotland was good for you then?'

'You know what, I really think it was but I don't know how long I'll be here for as divorce was mentioned before I left here.'

'Oh, you don't need to worry about that, James missed you all right. Just ensure you don't get back into the habit of meddling and tittle-tattling ever again. It's human nature to want to share gossip but there are certain things that reach a different level.'

Charlotte arched an eyebrow. 'The letter I sent Prudence you mean?'

'Precisely.'

'Once I'm settled back here I need to pay her a visit to apologise and to Tobias as well. Do you think that's a good idea?'

'As long as you're not just paying lip service to it. I think it would be a lovely gesture if you offered to do something positive for them both.'

'But how?'

'Maybe offer to spend time with Pru when Tobias is at work to keep her company, perhaps help her with a few chores from time to time.'

'That I can do, I had to do a lot for Aunt Agnes.' She lifted her arm and extended it. 'I built up quite a bit of muscle from chopping sticks and carrying buckets of coal, I can tell you.'

'Where would you like these, Madam?' The

driver looked at Charlotte as he pointed at her luggage.

'Could you please leave the trunk and carpet bags in the hallway, one of my staff shall see to them.'

'Very well then, Madam.' He lowered his head as a sign of respect and carried the luggage with the aid of a young footman who had just appeared, up the stone flight of steps.

'Look, whatever happens,' said Cassandra brightly, 'you've been on a journey and not just a literal one at that. James will see a tremendous change in you when he returns home this evening. Now did you mention coffee and cake?'

Charlotte chuckled and both women quite naturally linked arms and walked up the steps together.

Chapter Twenty Five

April 16th 1917 Military Hospital France

Gilbert couldn't believe his ears, he'd just been told after meeting with the hospital psychiatrist and top consultant that he was fit and well enough to return home. He was overjoyed. His memory had returned to him in dribs and drabs this past few months. He'd been able to write to his parents to discover that his beautiful daughter was to be wed and they had the idea for him to return home as a surprise to give Alice away. Nothing was said to her about his whereabouts so it would be a complete surprise when he showed up at the church. He'd also made contact with Marissa who told him some unexpected news about herself and the doctor she'd been seeing. Strangely enough, he felt nothing at the moment, he was just numb about it all, but he bore the couple no malice and would in time grant her the divorce she so desperately needed. She'd agreed to keep the surprise of his return a secret from Alice for time being.

So all he had to do now was to pack up his belongings and later that afternoon an army truck would be sent to pick him and other soldiers up along the way to transport them to Le Havre so they could make the sailing back to Britain. Things were finally in motion.

***

Wakeford April 21st 1917

Alice awoke early as a shaft of light shone in through a chink in her bedroom curtains. She was staying back at her old family home. The wedding dress Polly had made for her, which was an ivory silk with elbow length sleeves and a silk lace trimmed neckline and dusky pink silk bandeau with matching flower on its bodice, hung on the wardrobe door. Today she was going to be a bride because she was marrying Jonathan the man she loved with all her heart.

The only cloud on the horizon was the fact her father wouldn't be here for her wedding day but at least there was another man she really adored who would be giving her away and that was her grandfather, Harry. He'd been thrilled when she asked and had said it would be an honour to do so.

She was about to wonder if she should lie in bed a little longer with her thoughts before beginning the day when she heard mumbled, muffled voices from downstairs.

Slipping out from beneath the bedcovers she padded across the bedroom floor and onto the landing. Her mother was speaking with someone, a man? But who? That definitely wasn't a voice she recognised. As she glanced down through the banister railings, a door creaked and her mother emerged from the kitchen, with a man walking behind her. A well-dressed one at that. And then she turned to face him and she was in his arms, sobbing.

'I can't do it today of all days...' she whispered.

He nodded. 'Yes, I do understand, Marissa. It has to be in your own time.'

She placed a finger to his lips as if to warn him to keep quiet but it was too late as Alice had heard every word and it pierced her heart. She couldn't breathe as she gulped for air and not caring whether they heard or not, she ran back to the bedroom and bolted the door behind her. Then she flung herself down on the bed as she heard the front door slam shut. Approaching footsteps. Her mother was on her way upstairs and urgently rapping on her bedroom door.

'Alice, please open this door!'

For a while, Alice carried on sobbing into her pillow as she fought to block out her mother's cries, but finally, she relented and got up off the bed to unbolt the door.

Her mother stood there looking unsure and uncertain. 'A...Alice,' she began, 'it's really not what it looks like!'

'Then tell me what it is like, Mother!' Alice folded her arms and gritted her teeth, her upset now transforming into anger.

'Look,' her mother said nervously, 'may I come in?'

Alice nodded and then moved out of the way as her mother entered the room and sat on the bed as Alice stood looming over her. 'Come on then, I'm waiting for an explanation, Mother!'

Marissa let out a long breath and closed her eyes as if summoning up the courage to speak. 'Your father and I drifted apart and so I began to draw close to a doctor from the hospital where I worked. Your father was overseas and I didn't know if we'd ever see one another again and you were working at Netley. I was lonely...'

'Lonely? For one thing you say you drifted apart but that's not strictly true, is it? You were forced apart through circumstances. As for me being away, I was doing my duty for my country. So you're in love with *that* man?'

'Yes, Ralph and I are in love with one another.'

Alice shook her head incredulously. 'And does he have a wife?'

Marissa bit her bottom lip. 'I mean no, but he did. She passed away a couple of years ago that's how we grew close. We were working together and sometimes I'd listen to him over a cuppa at the hospital canteen or we'd drive out to the countryside for a drink or go to lunch. At first, I didn't think too much of it but eventually, I realised I had strong feelings for him and he for me...'

'But that time Father came home on leave, what happened then?'

'It was very awkward to be honest with you,

we both put on a front when you visited that time not to upset you, but if I'm being truthful we both realised it was over before he left here.'

'So, he went back to The Front realising there was no one waiting for his return?'

Marissa nodded. 'Yes.'

'Well forgive me, but I think you've been very selfish, Mother!'

Her mother lowered her head, crest fallen. 'I know,' she whispered, all the while looking at her own feet. 'I tried to fight it, honestly I did and so did Ralph but our feelings got the better of us.'

'It's not too late though,' Alice said suddenly, thinking maybe all might be resolved.

Her mother looked up and made eye contact with her. 'How do you mean?'

'If you gave up Ralph now and Father does return home then you might make a go of it once again...'

Marissa chewed on her bottom lip and tears began to form in her eyes. 'You just don't understand, Alice. It's already *too late!*' Her mother patted her stomach as realisation dawned for Alice.

Alice gulped. 'You mean you're...?'

'Pregnant? Yes.'

'How far gone are you?'

'About four months or so that's what we were discussing just now. Ralph wants me to move to London with him where no one knows who we are, he can get a job at a hospital there and...'

'You'll play the part of the doting wife with your new baby?'

'If you want to put it like that, then yes.' The emotional distress her mother obviously felt was etched on her face.

There was a gnawing pain in Alice's gut, not only was her father being replaced, so was she. Now there'd be a new husband and child for her mother to take care of. She released a long, slow breath. 'I think in view of what's happened, once the wedding is out of the way, I'll return to collect all my belongings and you shall never have to set eyes on me ever again.'

'Oh, Alice,' her mother said stepping towards her. 'It's not like that at all. I want you in my life.'

But it was too late as far as Alice was concerned, her mother was dead to her and was ruining what ought to be the best day of her life.

***

Alice stared at herself in the full length mirror, the beautiful ivory wedding gown dazzled in the early afternoon sun that shone in through the window. She wore a long Belgian lace veil and in her hands she carried a bouquet made up of pink and white peonies, ferns and trailing ivy.

Grandpa had arrived in a hired bridal car to escort her to the church, everything was now going smoothly except she had yet to make it up with her mother. Seeing her there looking so delicate and crumpled in the armchair, she looked at her and whispered so that Grandpa should not hear, 'Mother, I do forgive you and I do want you at my wedding!'

Marissa raised her head and smiled and then said, 'That's all I was waiting to hear, I'll go upstairs and get changed.'

'Yes, you do that. There's a car outside waiting for you with my bridesmaids Eliza and Bronwen inside...'

Alice had spent so much time with Bronwen at the hospital that they were practically like sisters and she felt that way about Jonathan's sister too. Taking one last look around in what had been her childhood home, she let out a long shuddering breath and took her grandfather's arm as he guided her towards the awaiting car which was decorated with white silk ribbon which fluttered in the breeze.

Grandpa helped her into the car and he sat in the back seat beside her as the chauffeur motored the car along leafy country lanes and past luscious green fields until finally they arrived at the church. Grandma was stood outside as they arrived and she fussed around Alice rearranging her dress for her, puffing it out and shaking out any wrinkles and creases that had transpired during the car journey. Then with tears in her eyes, she pecked her granddaughter on the cheek and handed her something.

'What's this?' whispered Alice.

'It's something my Aunt Bertha gave me when I married your grandfather years ago, it's a blue brooch for luck. Here, let me fasten it to the bodice of your dress as I feel you are going to have some great fortune soon!' Without Alice seeing, Cassandra winked at Harry.

Then once the brooch was secured, they walked beneath a stone archway to enter the church grounds and as she moved forward, Alice felt beautiful and serene as she heard music in the distance. Everyone would be inside now waiting, she watched as Grandma entered the church but what was this? Someone was passing in the opposite direction to come out through the church door and there he was…her own dear father in military uniform looking so tall and smart. Dropping her bouquet of flowers she ran towards him and was in his arms sobbing with joy, she'd always been his special little girl.

'But how? When?' She pulled away to look at her father's face whose eyes appeared to water.

'I was given the all clear to return a few days ago, my dear Alice!' He embraced her warmly again. 'I'm home to stay at least for time being. Now please don't say another word, this has all been arranged. Your grandfather was to bring you to me so that I can walk you down the aisle today and it will be my pleasure to give you away to Jonathan as I've heard he's a very fine young man.'

Alice nodded through her tears. 'Oh he is, he really is…'

Then her grandfather was handing her the

bouquet he'd retrieved after she'd discarded it in a rush to get to her father. Choking with emotion, Grandpa pecked her on the cheek. 'Now go on you two, poor Jonathan will think he's been jilted. I'll just nip in and take my seat beside my wife while you two ready yourselves.' Then Grandpa entered the church through the open door.

Father and daughter smiled at one another and then Gilbert took Alice's hand to walk her down the aisle as pleasant piped organ music drifted towards them. Although her father was giving her away today, he was now back in her life and he hoped he'd be there for good from now on.

The Wakeford Chronicles

A saga story spanning three generations of the same family who live in the Village of Wakeford.

The Widow Of Wakeford

It's the approach to Christmas in the village of Wakeford and what should be the happiest time of the year is marred by the death of Lady Cassandra Bellingham's husband, Oliver. The fate of her beloved family home, Marshfield Manor, is tossed to the wind as she discovers upon his death that he has frittered all the family fortune away. She must now summon up the strength to hold everything together; after all, she has a young daughter and an aged aunt to care for. The only thing that is now legally hers is the little cottage in Wakeford where she and the Lord once conducted a passionate affair whilst his first wife lay sick on her death bed. As a consequence, some of the villagers have never forgiven her and nor have most of the staff at the manor house. Cassandra's appearance in Wakeford will have a far reaching effect on certain people living in the village as she encroaches on their lives, even those who despise her.

Outcast and unwelcome in Wakeford, Cassandra fights for survival and before the chiming of Christmas bells, she realises she has a very important decision to make...

A Distant Dream

Following a change of circumstance, Cassandra and her new husband are forced to live a meagre existance in Jem and Clyde's old cottage until Harry comes into good fortune quite by chance. Now the pair should have the chance to better themselves, but it doesn't quite work out that way. Heavily pregnant and alone, Cassie goes into labour at the cottage and it's touch and go whether the twins will survive. A new man appears on the scene who is described as a "rabble rouser" by Polly. But Cassie finds that her head turns towards the handsome, wilful young man, who acts as a voice for the people.

Act Of Remembrance

One woman's grit and determination to keep her family together at all costs as the trials and tribulations they face seem ever mounting and perilous.

A tale that spans the generations...

Wakeford 1877

The rabble rouser, otherwise known as Tobias Beckett has left Wakeford for America. Meanwhile, Cassandra is taking care of his mother, Cynthia, who is in poor health and she fears that something serious might happen to the woman while her son is so far away. It had been a year since Tobias Beckett left Wakeford and there are some that miss him and some that most definitely, do not. Rose has since given birth to a baby girl called, Sophia, so Tobias's return could spell disaster for her and Clyde if he were ever to return and claim his child. There's someone in Wakeford who has it in for Cassandra and plans on making her life a living hell. Can she cope with being the subject of gossip once again?

Wakeford 1914

There have been rumours in Wakeford since the previous Christmas time that Britain is heading towards a war with Germany, but following the assassination of Franz Ferdinand of Austria at the end of June, things begin to surge forward at an alarming pace as the war progresses and folk in the village begin to fret about it. The women in the area in particular worry, realising that soon they might lose their sons, fathers, brothers and husbands to some senseless war that will be fought in a distant land far from home. Cassandra's twin sons, Gilbert and Ernest, sign up to fight for their King and country and she's immensely proud of her granddaughter, Alice, who becomes a nurse. It's an uncertain future ahead for all in the village of Wakeford.

Copyright

The characters in this book are fictitious and have no existence outside the author's imagination. They have no relation to anyone bearing the same name or names and are pure invention. All rights reserved. The text of this publication or any part thereof may not be reprinted by any means without permission of the Author. The illustration on the cover of this book features model/s and bears no relation to the characters described within.

Books by Lynette Rees

<u>Historical</u>

The Seasons of Change Series

Black Diamonds

White Roses

Blue Skies

Red Poppies

Winds of Change Series

The Workhouse Waif

The Matchgirl

A Daughter's Promise

The Cobbler's Wife

Rags to Riches Series

The Ragged Urchin

The Christmas Locket

The Lily and the Flame

The Wakeford Chronicles

The Widow of Wakeford

A Distant Dream

Act of Remembrance

Printed in Great Britain
by Amazon

47631236R10185